Praise for Griffith Review

'*Griffith Review* is the sound of Australian democracy and culture thinking out loud.' Geordie Williamson, *The Australian*

'Where the news cycle tends to feed cynicism, *Griffith Review* is the necessary counterpoint: a place of ideas and possibility. It's a relief to find the quality writing, reflection and observation nurtured in its pages.'
Billy Griffiths, historian and writer

'[*Griffith Review*] traverses genre and form, culture and continent…in what is a vibrant and impressive cross-section of modern Australian writing.'
Good Reading

'A literary degustation… The richness of these stories is amplified by the resonance between them. It's hard to think of so much fascinating story being contained within 270-odd pages.' Ed Wright, *The Saturday Australian*

'…informative, thought-provoking and well-crafted.' *The Saturday Paper*

'[An] outstanding collection of essays, reportage, memoir, poetry and fiction.'
Mark McKenna, *Honest History*

'The *Review* doesn't shirk from the nuanced and doesn't seek refuge in simplistic notions or slogans. It remains Australia's primary literary review.'
Professor Ken Smith, Dean and CEO ANZSOG

'This is commentary of a high order. The prose is unfailingly polished; the knowledge and expertise of the writers impressive.'
Roy Williams, *Sydney Morning Herald*

'For intelligent, well-written quarterly commentary…*Griffith Review* remains the gold standard.' *Honest History*

'*Griffith Review* is Australia's most prestigious literary journal.' *stuff.co.nz*

'*Griffith Review* is a must-read for anyone with even a passing interest in current affairs, politics, literature and journalism. The timely, engaging writing lavishly justifies the Brisbane-based publication's reputation as Australia's best example of its genre.' *The West Australian*

'This quarterly magazine is a reminder of the breadth and talent of Australian writers. Verdict: literary treat.' *Herald Sun*

SIR SAMUEL GRIFFITH was one of Australia's notable early achievers. He occupied positions of authority during some of the most momentous events in the history of Queensland: the frontier wars, the 'blackbirding' trade of people from Melanesia, the shearers' strike and Federation. At times he challenged power, at others he used it – he was a complex yet pragmatic man of words, a man of his times. Not all his decisions have stood the test of time. Sir Samuel was twice the premier of Queensland, its chief justice and author of its criminal code, remembered most for his pivotal role in drafting the Constitution adopted at Federation, and as the new nation's first chief justice.

Griffith died in 1920 and is now most likely to be remembered by his namesakes: an electorate, a society, a suburb and a university. In 1971, ninety-six years after he first proposed establishing a university in Brisbane, Griffith University, the city's second, was created. Griffith's commitment to public debate and ideas, his delight in words and art, and his attachment to active citizenship are recognised by this publication that bears his name.

Like Sir Samuel Griffith, *Griffith Review* is iconoclastic and non-partisan, with a sceptical eye and a pragmatically reforming heart. Always ready to debate ideas. Personal, political and unpredictable, it informs and provokes Australia's best conversations.

During Griffith's lifetime, and while he was in positions of power, the First Nations of Queensland resisted invasion. Sir Samuel made it possible for some Aboriginal people to testify in court when charges were brought against settlers. The First Australians survived, but at a terrible cost. In the twenty-first century, the need for a thorough and lasting settlement is urgent, one that respects and honours the rights, history and culture of the descendants of those who were dispossessed.

Griffith Review staff acknowledge and pay particular respect to the traditional custodians of the lands on which their office is located, the Jagera and Turrbal people in South-East Queensland.

GRIFFITH UNIVERSITY

GriffithReview83
Past Perfect

Edited by Carody Culver

GriffithReview83

INTRODUCTION

7 **Time plays tricks**
CARODY CULVER: Remember, recycle, repeat

NON-FICTION

9 **Nostalgia on demand**
RICHARD KING: Streaming memories in the experience machine

29 **James and the Giant BLEEP**
AMBER GWYNNE: Old books, bad words and the alchemical good of reading

55 **The fall of the madmen**
JANE CARO: How advertising ate itself

62 **Nothing ever lasts**
BENJAMIN LAW: A more complete Australian story

69 **Glitter and guts**
SHARLENE ALLSOPP: Interrogating the truth of the past

109 **Which way, Western artist?**
MYLES McGUIRE: Art of the past and future present

121 **Scarlett fever**
MELANIE MYERS: The seven stages of Windie recovery

134 **Anticipating enchantment**
ALICE GRUNDY: The myth of editorial perfection and the legend of the solo author

142 **From anchor to weapon**
MICHAEL L ONDAATJE & MICHAEL G THOMPSON: The politics of nostalgia

162 **Farming futures**
MELINDA HINKSON: Views from the Millewa-Mallee, past and present

173 **The ship, the students, the chief and the children**
DAVID RITTER: Defying the fossil-fuel order

182 **Walking through the mou(r)n(ing of a)tain(ted life)**
BEAU WINDON: Reflections of the lost

IN CONVERSATION

21 **Always was, always will be**
MELISSA LUCASHENKO and CARODY CULVER: Reimagining Australia's past

40 **The sentimentalist**
CAROLINE O'DONOGHUE and CARODY CULVER: Culture without the cringe

76 **Escaping the frame**
WITI IHIMAERA and WINNIE DUNN: Writing the story of the spider

93 **Lines of beauty**
MICHAEL ZAVROS and CARODY CULVER: Animating the amorality of the image

FICTION

47 **The kiss**
MELANIE CHENG

87 **The green gold grassy hills**
FIONA KELLY McGREGOR

154 **Lost decade**
LUCY ROBIN

192 **Apocalypse, then?**
JAKE DEAN

POETRY

46 **In the Dollhouse**
LESH KARAN

68 **Cinema**
KRIS KNEEN

92 **Pentax ME Super**
ALISHA BROWN

120 **The emperor's twin**
GRAHAM KERSHAW

161 **Threshold**
EILEEN CHONG

181 **Mildew on the whiteness of Hölderlin**
JOHN KINSELLA

191 **Things come together**
AUDREY MOLLOY

203 **Exeunt**
MARK O'FLYNN

PICTURE GALLERY

97 **Eternal reflection**
MICHAEL ZAVROS

Cover image:
Moon Patrol, *Ghost Western* 2019
Digital collage
Courtesy of the artist

Griffith Review gratefully acknowledges the support and generosity of our founding patron, the late Margaret Mittelheuser AM and the ongoing support of Dr Cathryn Mittelheuser AM.

GriffithReview83 2024
Griffith Review is published four times a year by Griffith University.

Publisher	Scott Harrison
Editor	Carody Culver
General Manager	Katie Woods
Managing Editor	John Tague
Senior Editor	Margot Lloyd
Business Co-ordinator	Esha Buch
Typesetting	Midland Typesetters
Printing	Ligare Book Printers
Distribution	NewSouth Books/ADS

ISBNs
Book: 978-1-922212-92-4
PDF: 978-1-922212-93-1
Epub: 978-1-922212-94-8

ISSN 1448-2924

GRIFFITH REVIEW
South Bank Campus, Griffith University
PO Box 3370, South Brisbane QLD 4101 Australia
Ph +617 3735 3071 Fax +617 3735 3272
griffithreview@griffith.edu.au griffithreview.com

SUBSCRIPTIONS: See griffithreview.com

COPYRIGHT
The copyright in material published in Griffith Review and on its website remains the property of the author, artist or photographer, and is subject to copyright laws. No part of this publication should be reproduced without first contacting Griffith Review. Opinions published in Griffith Review are not necessarily those of the publisher, editor, Griffith University or NewSouth Books.

FEEDBACK AND COMMENT griffithreview@griffith.edu.au

INTRODUCTION

Time plays tricks

Remember, recycle, repeat

Carody Culver

IT'S HARDLY A new observation to say that everything old is new again. Nostalgia in the twenty-first century is not so much a feeling as a cultural force: TV shows and movies are now frequently set in the '70s, '80s and '90s, offering exaggerated re-creations of the aesthetics that defined those eras (did my parents' 1980s suburban living room look anywhere near as stylised as those that appear in *Stranger Things* or *Physical*?); Instagram accounts churn out memes and anecdotes that epitomise the decades in which their millennial audiences came of age; and, perhaps most confronting of all, my eighteen-year-old niece dresses exactly like the cool kids at my high school did a little more than twenty years ago.

These examples might sound trivial, but I suspect they're just symptoms of a wider malaise. For *New York Times* critic Jason Farago, we're living in 'the least innovative, least transformative, least pioneering century for culture since the invention of the printing press'. He's not saying we're incapable of producing great art, or that creativity is flatlining – if anything, we're generating more content now than ever before. And perhaps that's the problem: when technology can deliver us whatever song or story or sartorial look we desire, time loses its meaning.

Funnily enough, Farago's view isn't new, either: ten years ago, the late, great cultural theorist Mark Fisher (who makes a couple of cameos in this edition) posited that our 'montaging of earlier eras' had reached such fever pitch that we no longer even noticed our submersion in a sea of bygones. And sitting alongside this purported cultural inertia are our increasingly divergent attitudes towards history – the far-right impulse to romanticise the past, the far-left desire to remedy its wrongs – and how they inflect our politics.

If we're truly stuck – caught between competing strategies to achieve progress as we recycle and remix what's come before – what does this mean for our future?

PAST PERFECT HOLDS this complex prism of the past up to the light. Its essays, fiction, conversations and poems refract myriad perspectives, contexts and approaches. In this collection, you'll discover how technology mediates our memories; revisit the heady world of last century's ad industry, with its questionable gender politics and wild parties; reconsider national narratives and the ways in which literature, particularly by First Nations writers, can challenge them; understand the complex relationship between our words and our worldview; take a tour through the decadent creations of leading Australian artist Michael Zavros, whose work resists moral interpretation; examine the joy of loving lowbrow culture; explore the evolving legacy of Scarlett O'Hara, a character who's been revered and reviled for nearly a century; consider how nostalgia can be weaponised in pursuit of flawed political ideals; and much, much more.

I'd like to thank the Copyright Agency Cultural Fund for their ongoing support of our Emerging Voices competition – we're very proud to publish work by the first of our four talented 2023 winners, Beau Windon, in these pages.

It's probably fitting that this edition, with its double vision of past and future, is the first of the year – a year that will, no doubt, yield yet more technological innovation and political polarity alongside a fresh tranche of cultural and artistic reboots and callbacks. I hope this collection can offer you new ways of thinking through them all.

3 January 2024

NON-FICTION

Nostalgia on demand
Streaming memories in the experience machine
Richard King

Man is in love and loves what vanishes,
What more is there to say?
— WB Yeats, 'Nineteen Hundred and Nineteen'

The Chicken McNuggets Tetris console is nostalgia at its tastiest!
— Tom's Guide

THE BOY LOOKS left. Looks up. Looks out. Almost as if he's taking the measure of his new, or newly strange, situation. Not that he appears unhappy or alarmed. If anything, he seems supremely peaceful, his eyes possessed of an angelic tranquillity, quite out of keeping with his goofy smile (a family trait, like the anxiety it conceals). He looks to the right, and out again, and my love and anger and sadness and grief coalesce into an unsettling ambivalence: I don't know what to think, or how to feel, about this. He is familiar to me, but also *a familiar* – uncannily unlike himself, but enough like himself to trigger again the sharp realisation that he is no longer here, a living, breathing presence in the world that ultimately proved too much for him, and now weighs so heavily on those he left behind. Whatever this is, it doesn't seem right. His smile widens and the sequence ends.

Employing deep-learning algorithms to animate faces in old photographs (or any photographs for that matter), Deep Nostalgia™ is an application on MyHeritage.com, an online genealogy platform founded in 2003. It invites users to upload their pictures and transforms them into short videos that can be easily shared on social networks. For now, its reanimations are subtle. Derived from blueprint or 'driver' recordings of (mostly) MyHeritage.com employees, the range of added movements is small: a blink, a smile, a rotation of the head. But its effect is profoundly disconcerting and, for some, disconcertingly profound. The British novelist Arthur C Clarke suggested that all advanced technologies are ultimately indistinguishable from magic, and Deep Nostalgia seems almost gleefully aware of its supernatural undertones. As new photos are uploaded to its algorithm, a little glittering wand appears on the screen, casting a cloud of amber dust over the soon-to-be-enlivened subject. That the final product resembles nothing so much as the animated newspaper photographs in the Harry Potter movie franchise only adds to the sensation of eeriness.

Is this sensation one of nostalgia, though? My own encounter with the application left me feeling depressed and angry, which no doubt had a lot to do with the beliefs and emotions I brought to the experience: my profound suspicion of algorithmic technologies, the recency and depth of my grief. No doubt it also has to do with my age, and my habituation to other technological media: the photograph in its chintzy album, stored alongside the jigsaw puzzles and Ordnance Survey maps in the family bureau.

But that is not the whole of it. In her collection of essays *On Photography* (1977), Susan Sontag explores the way in which photographs 'actively promote nostalgia'. All photographs, she wrote, are memento mori: 'To take a photograph is to participate in another person's (or thing's) mortality, vulnerability, mutability. Precisely by slicing out this moment and freezing it, all photographs testify to time's relentless melt.' But here the photograph has been *unfrozen* in a way that cuts against that feeling. Nor does the family camcorder footage that became ubiquitous in the two decades following Sontag's masterful analysis offer much of an analogy. For those films, too, were 'slices' of time, and over the years began to take on the patina of faded innocence. Deep Nostalgia is something else altogether. At best it is an impertinence; at worst, it is a form of violence against the past.

Of course, it takes time for our subjectivities to catch up with new technologies. We will grow used to Deep Nostalgia and its more sophisticated equivalents, and then we will grow bored of them and move on to other varieties of magic. But how do we feel about this prospect, about this seeming inevitability? All nostalgia is a species of fiction, but at least it is, or was, *our* fiction – substantially so, at any rate: a set of memories, or sense impressions, written down over many years, for no one's delectation but our own and subject to continuous and largely unconscious editing as our psychic circumstances change. How then do we approach a circumstance in which it is possible to *consciously* curate those memories and sense impressions, such that they become mere features of our 'profile'? Or one where third parties, having gleaned enough data to know us better than we know ourselves, can supply those memories and impressions for us? How, in short, do we feel about a world in which we can have nostalgia on demand?

TO LOITER FOR a while at the intersection of algorithmic technology, capitalism and human psychology is to witness a staggering efflorescence of nostalgia-related phenomena. On social media, for example, applications such as Instagram Throwbacks and Snapchat Memories invite their users to reminisce about days gone by, while Instagram's '1977' filter recasts users' photos as old-style polaroids, applying square white borders and softening the colours in a way that mimics sun exposure. In marketing, too, there is enormous interest in the craze for nostalgia-adjacent content, with crude, self-help-style psychology pressed into service in order to exploit the trend, and an army of media influencers eager to get in on the act. (On TikTok, in particular, the 1980s and 1990s are trending, with vintage clothing, retro accessories and period backgrounds all the rage.) Weirdly, it appears that much of this 'nostalgia' is for a time that preceded the target audience – a phenomenon that has led some commentators to invent the category of 'pseudo-nostalgia'. The Netflix series *Stranger Things* appears to tap into this phenomenon, as does the so-called 'technostalgia' for vinyl records, audio cassettes and their associated paraphernalia. Indeed, it seems that all forms of nostalgia are especially prevalent among the young, with 82 per cent of zoomers using YouTube to watch nostalgic content, according to the website's own research. Where once we would have felt nostalgic for a period in our lives when we were at our most vigorous and excitable, it now appears as if nostalgia is taking on a life of its own, spreading its amber dust as it goes.

By general consent, it was the Covid pandemic that, if it didn't start this trend, almost certainly helped catalyse it. Psychologically, the association makes sense. The link between nostalgia and crisis has long been a feature of the literature on the former, with experts suggesting that nostalgic memory can act as an emotional crutch in the face of jarring or stressful experiences, combining feelings of sadness and happiness into a constructive and protective narrative that allows us to 'move on' from distress. There is even a suggestion that nostalgic memory operates in a similar way to the transitional objects that help young children establish independence from their parents. Like the stuffed toys and security blankets that comfort those children in times of stress, websites such as the Nostalgia Machine, which offers songs from 'your favourite year', or the Museum of Endangered Sounds, which replays noises from the past (the grating riff of a Nokia phone, the *blip blip blip* of Space Invaders), function as emotional pacifiers. It's important not to overdo this comparison: nostalgia is a complex phenomenon that cannot be reduced to Pandy the Panda, or that mouldering expanse of sky-blue flannel that you can't quite bring yourself to chuck out. Nevertheless, the sudden penchant for rewatching memorable sporting events or reconnecting with abandoned hobbies such as knitting, bread baking or community singing does suggest that a variety of regression is fundamental to the phenomenon. Why sit through another Covid presser when you can snuggle up with an ice-cream sandwich and Nintendo's *Lara Croft Collection*?

The observed correlation between the Covid pandemic and what we might call the nostalgia boom is in one respect no mystery. The Covid years were a time of stress, and people responded to that stress with behaviours that immersed them in broadly pleasant feelings. But Covid didn't occur in a vacuum, and the stresses associated with it were not reducible to the fear of getting sick. Indeed, for many, the stress of Covid derived not from the virus itself but from the lockdowns aimed at arresting its spread. It was, above all, the feelings of isolation and disconnection that concerned them most, and this fact, important in itself, is of the utmost importance in understanding the role that nostalgia played in the crisis, and plays in contemporary culture more broadly (a culture, I would argue, that is itself in crisis). Why would a period of enforced atomisation be conducive to nostalgic reminiscence? The answer, it turns out, has to do with the fact that nostalgia is a *social* emotion.

The concept of nostalgia combines the Greek words *nostos* (return) and *algos* (suffering) and describes a longing for people and situations far away in space and/or time. Originally denoting a yearning for home, it is now used to mean any longing for an absent (and, by implication, past) state of affairs, and is often accompanied by, or taken to imply, an idealisation of that situation. It is thus a variety of sentimentality that arouses certain reservations when encountered in the political sphere or even the culture more generally – for it is, one might argue, implicitly reactionary to attach oneself to a situation that can be longed for with impunity partly because it no longer exists. Nevertheless, it appears to be a universal phenomenon, experienced as keenly by Homer (in the *Odyssey*) as by contemporary populists. According to an article in the American Psychological Association's journal *Emotion*, lay conceptions and experiences of nostalgia display a remarkable consistency over time, suggesting that, whatever the content of the nostalgic experience, it performs some function that cannot be simply dismissed or eradicated on the grounds that it is ideologically 'problematic'. Semi-serious cracks to the effect that nostalgia isn't what it used to be turn out to be only half right at best: my guess is that there's a cave wall somewhere on which some neolithic grouch has carved the petroglyph equivalent of 'Life was so much simpler in the old days.'

Though the experience of nostalgia is commonplace, cultural attitudes towards it have changed markedly over time. The word 'nostalgia' was coined in the seventeenth century by the Swiss physician Johannes Hofer, who regarded it as a neurological disease with symptoms such as despondency, weeping, irregular heartbeat and smothering sensations. This attitude persisted until the late nineteenth century, from which point nostalgia began to be regarded as a psychiatric or psychosomatic disorder characterised by anxiety, sadness, insomnia, fever and loss of appetite. By the mid-twentieth century, the diagnosis was more likely to dwell on the subconscious desire to return to an early stage of life; nostalgia was seen as a form of depression rooted in an inability to cope with the challenges of adulthood.

It was not until the late 1970s that a more positive account of nostalgia began to emerge, thanks largely to the work of the sociologist Fred Davis, who studied the way individuals discriminate between 'warm' recollections of childhood and the negative associations of, say, homesickness. Moreover, Davis stressed the way in which nostalgia was a social emotion – one that, for all its personal expressions, serves to 'ground' human beings in a narrative that connects them to a community, a way of life, a set of beliefs: one has nostalgia not for oneself, but for the world of which one was once a part. More recent social-psychological inquiry on the content of nostalgic experiences, as well as their triggers and psychological functions, appears to confirm this emphasis. Nostalgia, it seems, is in some sense essential to humans' psychosocial health – to their individual and collective flourishing.

It is this relatively new understanding of nostalgia as at once a personal and a social phenomenon that connects it to the feelings of loneliness catalysed by the Covid lockdowns. Studies suggest that loneliness is positively correlated with nostalgia, especially among 'high-resilience' individuals, which is to say people who are more likely to cope emotionally with social isolation. Experiments in which some participants are instructed to write about a nostalgic experience while others are instructed to write about a non-nostalgic experience show significant increases in positive affect and self-esteem in the former group. Moreover, nostalgic individuals show higher levels of secure attachment, feelings of being supported socially and interpersonal competence. Such findings raise the possibility that high-resilience individuals may actively *recruit* nostalgia to counteract the effects of loneliness. Time spent looking at old family photographs or assembling a plastic model of a Spitfire is time spent burnishing a sense of ourselves as situated in a particular era or locale.

As healthy as this sounds, however, the fact remains that feelings of nostalgia, while psychologically and socially necessary, are often ideologically ambiguous. As a psychosocial mechanism that will tend to involve a poetic confusion of the real and the unreal, the genuine and the imagined, nostalgia is always apt to compensate us for feelings and circumstances unconducive to our flourishing. I wonder, indeed, if there isn't a connection between the broader atomisation that has occurred as a result of neoliberalism and a quarter of a century of 'high' globalisation, and the current enthusiasm for nostalgic content. In recent months, we have heard many reports of a 'loneliness epidemic' among the young – a phenomenon linked to the very technologies through which nostalgic content is now offered. Could it be that technoscientific capitalism is selling back the very thing it has taken from us? And, if it is, is the thing it is selling us a genuine antidote to the malady? Or is it, like the sociality engendered by social media, an essentially morbid phenomenon, as likely – *more* likely – to deepen the crisis to which it poses as the solution?

NOTWITHSTANDING THE MANY recent attempts to make capitalism *itself* the subject of nostalgia – through tedious movies about Nike shoes or re-instigated product lines (Adidas Gazelles, Furbies, Atari, Polaroid

Originals) – the relationship between neoliberalism and nostalgic longing seems self-contradictory. Neoliberalism, after all, is a system predicated on change and churn, not steadiness and stability. Under neoliberalism, the creation of selves goes from being a given to a task. The 'ascribed' identities of yesteryear become the 'attained' identities of the meritocracy – that fantasy land conceived in the spirit not of recommendation but political satire by the sociologist Michael Young. Where once we might have derived a sense of identity from a town, a local industry, a class, a gender, a church, a football team – and from the social solidarity and parochialism that emerged from such – today we are encouraged (implicitly or explicitly) to get out there and distinguish ourselves, to live our best lives, whatever that means. That this dispensation was ushered in by conservative administrations (Australia is an outlier in this regard) may in this sense look like an irony. But such a radical transformation – not merely the liberation of markets but the injection of economic principles into every area of human existence – could only come from a political tradition superficially wedded to 'traditional' values. The prospectus sold by Thatcher and Reagan was a nuclear-reactor model of society in which the most reactionary elements of national identity served as a sort of protective carapace atop the toxic core of the market, which quickly set about atomising the communities from which genuine conservative values once emerged, while also fraying the unsteady alliance between liberalism and conservatism formed in the face of organised labour.

The role nostalgia plays in the market can be understood in similar terms. In an essay published in 1993, as neoliberalism was beginning to take on its more 'progressive' Clintonite aspect, the political theorist Paul James noted how advertising's veneration of the new coexisted with a wistful regard for the 'remnant places' of an older dispensation, in a way that flattened out the contradictions between movement and stability, cosmopolitanism and parochialism, the global and the local (while always, of course, surreptitiously resolving in favour of the former quantity in those pairings). In this way, the low levels of social solidarity that attend neoliberal capitalism can be compensated for (albeit only briefly) by products that give off an aura of the past: a jar of pasta sauce, for example, concocted in gigantic steel vats on some charmless industrial park in Dublin can be sold on the premise that its recipe derives from a village in rural Tuscany. The so-called nostalgia marketing that exploded over the Covid years was simply this dynamic on steroids: the vending of bland and sugary commodities to a populace suddenly and anxiously in the market for a dose of saccharine fantasy.

There is, then, a sort of self-medication at work in capitalism's embrace of nostalgia – one that was of enormous interest to the late Polish philosopher and sociologist Zygmunt Bauman. In *Retrotopia* (2017), Bauman argued that the way nostalgia is experienced in the twenty-first century is part of the malaise of 'liquid' modernity – a consumer sociality in which people have become (in Foucault's phrase) 'entrepreneurs of the self' and in which the constraining impact of the past has been weakened. Nostalgia (in its various forms) thus becomes a way to cope with a dizzying and dysfunctional present, as sentimental visions of the past are pressed into service as models for the future by populists and demagogues, in a way that brings together narcissistic individualism and fantasies of ethnic communalism. For Bauman, indeed, there is a deep relationship between the 'liberated' subject of neoliberal fame, called upon to construct an identity out of the cultural ephemera of consumer capitalism, and the recent rise in nationalism, as manifested in the depredations of Donald Trump and his analogues. (Remember that the populist wave was constructed on the back of a crisis at the financialised heart of neoliberalism.) Nor is it only political reaction that benefits from this dialectical relationship; mainstream politics, ideology and culture are similarly steeped in it. The ninetieth-anniversary celebrations of the ABC, the death and funeral of Queen Elizabeth II and the recent *Barbie* movie/moment were all the occasion, it seems to me, for a nostalgised cultural commentary that not only downplayed the uglier aspects of these cultural phenomena but also recast them into a broadly progressive and positive discourse of social inclusion. The performative nature of such enthusiasms suggests a deep need for sentimentalised connection, even among those who would ordinarily consider themselves too culturally and ideologically savvy to fall for such (quasi-orchestrated) happenings.

In one sense, these observations fit with the 'slow cancellation of the future' thesis derived from Fredric Jameson and Slavoj Žižek and most thrillingly articulated by the late Mark Fisher in *Capitalist Realism* (2009) and *Ghosts of My Life* (2014). For Fisher, as for his intellectual confrères, late capitalism was now so dominant, so marbled into every aspect of life, that any radical alternative was unthinkable. This situation manifested itself in a fixation on a kind of retro-futurism – a nostalgia for the future, so to speak, which invites us to look back to a time in our lives when we could still look forward with optimism, and in which *technological* innovation held out the prospect of *political* innovation – of a world beyond late capitalism. But while Fisher's analysis can explain certain trends, it is, I think, largely blind to the ways in which technology itself is now 'playing with our heads' and shaping our experience of the past.

IN HIS CLEVER and heartrending memoir *Childhood*, Shannon Burns suggests that one of the reasons he came so late to his own background as a writer was that he wasn't sufficiently good at forgetting. The statement is ostensibly perverse: how can a memoir, of all things, be founded on the events that we've deleted from the past, either out of psychological necessity or simply because of advancing age? But Burns is correct to insist on the relationship between memory and oblivion, in the sense that forgetting appears to play an important role in identity creation, and indeed in the formation of memories themselves. Freud wrote that childhood reminiscences have more in common with 'the legends and myths of nations' than with the memories of one's later years, the brain having discarded or 'edited' much that would be harmful to one's sense of self. In a similar vein, Walter Benjamin wrote:

> Memory is not an instrument for surveying the past but its theatre. It is the medium of past experience, just as the earth is the medium in which dead cities lie buried. He who seeks to approach his own buried past must conduct himself like a man digging.

Such 'excavational' understandings of memory suggest that forgetting is one of the ways we come to assert control over a time in our lives when we had little agency. Memory is necessarily tendentious.

Burns grew up in the 1980s, well before social media, and reading his book I found myself wondering whether someone growing up in the 2010s could even conceive of such an enterprise. For the fact is that most young people today stand in a radically different relationship to their pasts than those of us who reached full maturity before Myspace and Facebook began duking it out for market share in the early noughties. In *The End of Forgetting* (2019), Kate Eichhorn digs down into the likely consequences of this new situation in which pretty much everything we do and say is recorded, either actively or by default. Her thesis, which follows Freud's observations on the importance to healthy selfhood of forgetting, is that social media turns its users into saboteurs of their own development. Contra the usual moral panics that accompany new forms of media, she argues that the danger of digital technology is not that it destroys childhood 'innocence' by throwing open the developing brain to the seedy and chaotic world of adults, but that it makes our childhoods 'perpetually present'. 'The real crisis of the digital age is not the disappearance of childhood,' she writes, 'but the spectre of a childhood that can never be forgotten.'

If Eichhorn is right to characterise memory as a matter of both retention and deletion, and right too to suggest that digital technologies militate against the latter process, the explosion of social media technologies purporting to archive and re-mediate memory begins to look like something more serious than may be obvious at first blush. Indeed, it begins to look like a remedy for a condition it helped create, and goes on creating as it remedies it – a dynamic familiar to all drug addicts, and one that has obvious parallels with the place of 'nostalgic consumption' within capitalism. Nor are the parallels incidental. In their studies of online memory tools such as Timehop and Facebook Memories, sociologists Benjamin Jacobsen and David Beer explore the enmeshing of memory and the market in the digital economy, showing how experiences are quantified and taxonomised according to certain 'memory themes' and then played back to social media users in a variety of different ways. For them, such 'automation' of memory has a profound effect on the memories themselves and on personhood more generally. Our memories become part of our avatars – an element in the micro-celebrity so central to the experience of social media, and as such a source of competition and anxiety. Drawing us further into the reputational economy of 'likes', 'views' and 're-posts' (and further away from the deep recognition human beings need in order to flourish), such applications should perhaps be seen as the vendors of an ersatz nostalgia, appealing enough to prove addictive but devoid of psychological nutrition.

Nor should we be in any doubt that this is just the beginning of the process. As 3D-camera-mapping technologies become ever more sophisticated, and virtual reality continues to evolve towards a fully immersive technology, we will surely be invited *in* to our memories, urged to re-create, and even to relive, our meaningful past experiences, to visit again with our dead or with old lovers. At the same time, researchers in biomedicine will learn more about the way the brain stores memories, in a way that raises the possibility of mnemonic augmentation in the future. Already neuroscientists at the University of Southern California have developed techniques aimed at enhancing the retention of long-term memories in rhesus monkeys. Who's to say that some tech bro with a flair for synthesis and an unquenchable obsession with his own longevity won't eventually find some cool new way to bring these different technologies together?

And at that point? Well, it's anyone's guess. But if I'm right that the nostalgia boom is linked to the rise of loneliness, and that loneliness is a predictable feature of a system built on individual striving and a technologised sociality, then the prospect of an 'algorithmic nostalgia' driving the conditions of its own reception is surely a possibility. Indeed, do we not find something like this at work in social media already: a social or *connecting* technology that engenders forms of *disconnection* in its users, creating the desire for yet more connection, and so on and so on, ad infinitum? As digital technologies become more and more sophisticated, and notwithstanding the possibility of a generalised, politicised rejection of these processes on the back of some AI calamity (we live in fear, but also in hope), this kind of dynamic is apt to become an inescapable feature of contemporary life, and life itself an 'experience machine' from which escape is *literally* unthinkable.

ON DEEP NOSTALGIA, the experience machine has ceased, momentarily, to work its magic. The most recent photograph I've uploaded to the app – of me, aged three or thereabouts, dressed as a medieval knight – seems weirdly incompatible with it. Perhaps it's the fact that only two thirds of my face is visible beneath the plastic visor, or something in my dynamic stance, but the algorithm isn't able to 'read' my features in the normal way. As my head rotates, my features contort. I look like something from a Cronenberg movie, or Elmer Fudd in the middle of a seizure.

It's a measure of how much I hate this app, and the broader trend of which it is an example, that this feels like a kind of victory. But I'm also aware that the app will get better, and will do so very quickly indeed – in less time, certainly, than we need to think through the implications of its development. That's the way it goes with tech, which now takes on a life of its own – a life that can seem dangerously at odds with the lives it should be designed to serve. I still have no idea how this ends. But that armour is looking flimsier by the day.

Richard King in an author and critic based in Fremantle. His latest book is *Here Be Monsters: Is Technology Reducing Our Humanity?* (Monash University Publishing, 2023). His website is bloodycrossroads.com

IN CONVERSATION

Always was, always will be

Reimagining Australia's past

Melissa Lucashenko and Carody Culver

Since she began writing in the 1990s, multi-award-winning Goorie author Melissa Lucashenko has been flipping the script. With grit, defiance and killer one-liners, her novels relate the untold stories of Aboriginal Australians living ordinary lives. In the process, her work dismantles lazy stereotypes and exposes the realities of Australia's colonial legacy.

Her latest novel, Edenglassie, *moves between mid-nineteenth-century and contemporary Brisbane to interrogate the myths of the past and explore how they've shaped our present. In this conversation with* Griffith Review *Editor Carody Culver – which has been lightly edited and condensed for clarity – Melissa reflects on the challenges and possibilities of historical fiction and the writer's role in helping us understand who we are.*

CARODY CULVER: Your work explores class, colonialism, structural injustice and racism: themes that anyone who's paying attention should recognise as part of the fabric of everyday life in Australia. What role do you think fiction plays in making people engage with and understand those realities?

MELISSA LUCASHENKO: I think fiction can be incredibly powerful for certain individuals. On a social level the literary novel is a niche market, but what's happened – encouragingly for literary novelists – is that our work is now sometimes [turned into] audiobooks, film and television. I can get a bit despondent about the state of the world – you know, what's the point of writing books? – and then I pick up something like Barbara Kingsolver's

Demon Copperhead and I just think, wow. There's such power in the right book at the right time, and that gives me a prod to keep going. And the feedback I get from my own work is encouraging, too. I guess everyone has to do a bit, and taken altogether the [power] of literary fiction to improve lives and to bring joy and to shed light on unseen worlds is, I think, extraordinary.

CC: In an interview you did about ten years ago, after your 2013 novel *Mullumbimby* came out, you said: 'Poverty is not the historic norm for Aboriginal people. We have been here for 60,000 years, and for 200 of those we have been marginalised and poor, but it is not our normal condition. One day we will be managing our own affairs and we will be living the good life and that is what I wanted to point to in [*Mullumbimby*].' Do you still feel that way?

ML: Yep, I do. It's a simple fact that we've only been marginalised since some time into the British occupation, and the fact that that didn't happen immediately is what I was trying to get at in *Edenglassie*. Colonisation is an ongoing process, but that doesn't mean it has to last forever, and I think one day we'll have treaty. I don't know how long it will take, but we'll have reparations and we'll be recognised for the knowledge and the skill that we have in living in this place, and that will be to everyone's benefit.

CC: There's a powerful sense of what-if in both *Edenglassie* storylines: before we first meet your historical protagonist, Mulanyin, one of the other characters in that nineteenth-century timeline is predicting that the English will leave soon and things will go back to the way they should be; when we first meet one of your contemporary protagonists, Winona, in 2024, she's fantasising about a better life for herself in a more just and fair Australia. It's a tying together of past, present and future, as though you're drawing a line from the injustices of history to an eventual time when those injustices aren't forgotten, but when life is good again.

ML: What I was driving at in *Edenglassie* was what happened one generation after invasion: what life was like, what Brisbane was like, who was doing what. I've been fascinated by that for decades, and I think all Aboriginal people walk around and drive around and get around with a constant lens of pre-invasion as well as what's here now. When we look at a landscape, we're very often thinking, *Well, take away the buildings, take away the roads, take away this kind of civilisation — so called — and what would have been here in our great-grandparents' and great-great-grandparents' time?* So that was the key question I wanted to explore for my own curiosity as well as for the sake of a narrative. I wasn't looking very far past what it was like in colonial Brisbane when colonists were just about to outnumber Aboriginal people for the first time. And then that seam of: we're still here — what are our lives like now? How are they influenced by history? I wasn't looking very far into the future; I think that was a bit beyond the scope of the book. But certainly there's love and there's joy and there's laughter as well as all the hard stuff going forward from the 2024 narrative.

CC: Do you think there are differences in how contemporary fiction and historical fiction can make us reconsider or reframe the past and the present?

ML: I probably wouldn't have written a historical novel if I didn't think so. We live in a world of instants — what's the latest post on social media? What's the latest sound grab? 'The continuous now', I think someone called it, and not in the good sense. As an Indigenous person, it's a quest to understand where you live. In traditional society, as I point to in the book, you're taken around your country, you're shown particular things, and you don't leave your country except briefly for ceremonial [reasons] or perhaps to marry. And so you understand that country more intimately than almost any modern person can understand where they live. I think that's what ultimately drove me to write historical fiction. I was born in Brisbane. I've lived most of my life here apart from a decade down on Bundjalung country, which I return to just about every weekend. But Brisbane calls to me, and the story of Brisbane called to me, and so it felt like a real quest to understand the place better. [I had] this intense curiosity about the process of colonisation, especially on the south side, and what that looked like and how people would have experienced that, and I found enough stories to fill three or four historical novels. The untold stories are manifold — there's thousands.

CC: Did you always intend to have a contemporary storyline alongside the historical?

ML: No. I had planned to write a historical novel of colonial Brisbane for a good twenty years and almost started it in the mid-'90s; I'm really glad I didn't because I've written a far superior novel to what it would have been back then, when I was younger and even more ignorant than I am now. *Edenglassie* was going to be a straight historical novel, and then I realised the constant thorn in my side as a First Nations writer: the spectre of the dying-race trope was not going to go away in my lifetime nor in this novel's lifetime. And so there had to be a through-line to show Aboriginal continuity, Aboriginal life and love in the present, simply because that trope of the dying race and the vanishing of culture is so strong. It would have been too easy to write a historical novel and have mainstream readers misinterpret it as an elegy for an Aboriginal world view that's no more. I've never set out to do that, but people interpret my work in that way sometimes because that's the yarn that's been around for most of the past 200-odd years now.

CC: Why is it such a persistent trope?

ML: Because it's convenient. There's an element of truth: many, many thousands of people died. The numbers of people who died on the Queensland frontier are just mind-boggling to the point where I'm sure huge numbers of people won't believe the figures I refer to in the back of the book. But that's the job of historians, not the job of novelists, to prove and disprove those figures. If Aboriginal people are all dead, you don't have to negotiate a treaty with us and you certainly don't have to go around feeling guilty about stolen land and stolen wages and stolen children; the subjects of that injustice don't exist anymore if you choose to believe that we're dead or all assimilated, which isn't the case. It's a very practical kind of assimilation strategy.

CC: Were there other tropes or ideas that you wanted to push against or that you felt historical fiction would be a good means of addressing?

ML: No, I think it was a big enough job just to push back against the wonderful British civilisation arriving in darkest Jagera land, but I tried to flip things a lot. I like to surprise my reader, I like to play with duality, and that's a cultural motif from classical Aboriginal culture that I've tried to implement in the book – sometimes consciously and sometimes unconsciously. You don't always know what you're doing with a novel – you can sit and talk into a microphone and make out like you always know why the character did such and such in the first chapter and then did the reverse in the final chapter. You might have one explanation for that and then six months later you'll sit up in bed at night and go, 'Oh, that's what that was actually about.' So you try to be as strategic as you can while you're stumbling through the lives of these characters you've invented but don't necessarily fully understand.

The contemporary storyline was easier to write because it's easier to imagine Blakfellas getting around South Brisbane in 2024 than it is in 1855, and also my main character in the colonial era is a teenage young man, not an elderly Aboriginal woman and her granddaughter. I had that twin challenge of drawing on lots of research, oral and written, imagining myself into the 1850s, and also trying to invent a character who's a young man with very limited exposure to white society, almost no exposure to Christianity, who's thinking and living and acting in a tribal way. That was hard, but I worked my guts out for four years and just about exhausted myself... When I handed in the final manuscript, I just went, 'I really don't know how the hell I wrote that book.'

CC: Well, I'm glad you did! But it must have been a very different writing experience – as you say, you had all that research, those untold stories, to weave into the narrative.

ML: And [I was] trying to make decisions all the time about the right way to portray Mulanyin and the right way to portray [his wife] Nita. I was always conscious of the way mainstream readers were going to approach these characters and trying to second-guess that and head things off at the pass. I have to do that in all my writing, but I had to do it to a different degree in this historical book [because of] the twists and turns of history and what actually happened here.

There are fascinating snippets I found early on in my research. The novel centres on the interaction of a pioneer white family, the Petries, and the Jagera people who live at what I've called Kurilpa Village at South Brisbane – almost exactly where we're sitting right now [the *Griffith Review* office in South Bank]. In the literature, I came across the fact that [Tom] Petrie's Aboriginal workmen at Murrumba Downs had 'P' branded into their arms to identify them as his workmen. I reflected on that, and then I was talking to Gaja Kerry Charlton [about it] and she pointed to her forearm and said, 'Yes, our family had "P" on us.'... That was actually something that the men requested, and that kind of flips the story on its head – rather than being branded semi-slaves, these men wanted to be identified with Petrie. And then you take that a step further, and as a novelist you ask, is it about a kind of tribal affiliation, that they be known as Petrie's men? Is it because they're proud to work for Petrie, or is it a safety thing, so that when they're walking around or getting around the countryside – which was contested country until the 1860s and, in some areas, the 1870s – they could say, 'Look, I belong to the Petrie property, and therefore if you harm me, if you shoot me or do anything to me, you'll have the Petries to answer to'? I don't know the answer, but that's the kind of process I had to go through hundreds and hundreds of times with all these historical facts and situations.

CC: You said that you're always having to think about how mainstream readers might receive your work, and I wondered if you could talk more about that. In *Edenglassie*'s historical storyline, there's terrible violence and a constant sense of uncertainty and threat, but your characters are also just living their lives, and that's the case in all your books – you don't shy away from the tough stuff, but you also want to show joy and laughter.

ML: On a simple writing level, if a book doesn't have love and humour and lightness in it, it's probably going to fail as a novel. As Bruce Pascoe said – no one asked Faulkner if he could include more humour. But we're not William Faulkner and it's not 1860 or whenever the hell he was writing. So there's the simple craft of writing a book that people are going to want to read and get some enjoyment from. It's not all about telling historical truths, or if it is it's about showing the whole historical truth.

On a second level, it's a political act to write Aboriginal people or any marginalised people as fully human, and that's probably [how] I'd sum up the second half of my writing career… The first half was, 'We exist, we're still here. Aboriginal people have not died out or mysteriously gone away, conveniently, for white powerbrokers.' There's some understanding of that now, especially since native title has people frothing at the mouth about living Aboriginal people everywhere. So we're fully human, we fall in love, we fall out of love. We observe white society at least as often and as keenly as white society observes us.

CC: You mentioned duality earlier, and one of the other things I love about the book is how you weave opposing viewpoints into the narrative. There's a great chapter in the contemporary storyline where a character reveals that he's not white – he's recently discovered that he has an Aboriginal ancestor. But when he tells Winona this, she says, 'Hang on, buddy. This doesn't mean that you get to call yourself Black.' This is interesting in terms of how people understand their identity – if you make this kind of discovery about your heritage, you might be tempted to lay claim to a past that you perhaps don't fully understand.

ML: As I wrote in *The Monthly* recently, that's a serious problem – Aboriginal culture is vulnerable to damage by people who unilaterally decide that they want to identify [as Aboriginal] but don't know what that means and don't know how that affects the core Aboriginal culture. There aren't any easy answers, and I wanted to show both sides of that. So [there's a scene with] a white didge player who's fraudulently pretending to be Aboriginal and is quite uninterested in Winona's opinion of him – he couldn't give a rat's arse that this Aboriginal woman thinks he's a fraud, and so she picks the didge up and tries to belt him with it. And again, that's my little flipping of the thing that women can't touch a didgeridoo – I'm playing with that because culturally it's not 100 per cent accurate. And I wanted to show that there are different ways of being Aboriginal and there are ways to become Aboriginal, but it's not as simple as just declaring that you are – that's not the way to go.

CC: You describe the novel's title, *Edenglassie*, as 'a nod to paths not taken'. Could you talk about that idea?

ML: I'm writing about a place. I'm writing about the story and stories that belong to this particular place, around about where we're sitting now, in South Brisbane. And I really love the word – it's got the word 'Eden' in it, which I particularly liked because I think this place would have been an Eden before Oxley sailed up the river and commenced to wreck it all, and it's got 'lassie' in it. As a feminist writer I like the fact that it's got 'Eden' and 'lassie'.

In terms of paths not taken, I couldn't call my book Magandjin or Meanjin, which was my initial thought, because firstly I hadn't sought permission at that stage and I didn't know if I would get it, and second, I wasn't writing about the place as it was before colonisation. I think that's a task that's beyond most people and certainly beyond me. I couldn't call it Brisbane because it's not about Brisbane – it's about a place that wasn't Magandjin, Meanjin, it wasn't Brisbane, it was an in-between kind of place. Again, it's at that tipping point – it's something else. So when I discovered that an early colonial name for Brisbane was Edenglassie, but the name didn't stick, I thought, aha! That's perfect because it just instantly says to the reader,

Brisbane didn't have to be Brisbane, it could have been this other place. It could have been Edenglassie, and what would that have looked like? What would it have looked like if every colonist had done what Petrie did and sought permission to settle where they did? Of course, we'll never know. So it was a glimpse into a future that could have been but never was, and that's why I used the name.

CC: When your novel *Too Much Lip* came out in 2018, Karen Wyld wrote a review in the *Sydney Review of Books* that references a keynote speech you gave at the FNAWN Conference that year in which you (in Wyld's words) 'challenged participants to unpack sovereignty and reconstruct it in our way. [You] encouraged First Nations writers and storytellers to reshape and share who we were before invasion, are now, and will be.' Could you talk about that in the context of *Edenglassie* – was this part of your thinking as you were researching and writing the book?

ML: The book is very much about how I understand classical Goorie culture in Jagera lands, and sovereignty is just automatically part of that. As the Old Man says in the opening pages, we'll have our lives back when these last few British convicts leave; we'll have a sane world where people don't go around calling each other 'master'. And he almost spits when he has to say the word 'master' because it's such a foreign and abhorrent term to him.

Sovereignty is problematic – I think people use it as a shorthand for power, but the legal definition would be different, and then the cultural definition is different again. I think as much as I'm writing about sovereignty I'm writing about what Wiradjuri people call yindyamarra and what Yolngu people call magaya, which is a state of civilisation where people behave lawfully, slowly, politely, respectfully. Where a state of peace exists and there's little dissent or trouble and people are free to lead good lives in a world that's worth living in. That's the world I wanted to portray as being lost, or almost lost, in 1855, alongside a vision of a future that [my contemporary characters] can strive towards in 2024.

Melissa Lucashenko is an award-winning Goorie author of Bundjalung and European heritage. Her first novel, *Steam Pigs*, was published in 1997. Her sixth novel, *Too Much Lip*, won the 2019 Miles Franklin Literary Award and the Queensland Premier's Award for a Work of State Significance. Her latest work of fiction, *Edenglassie*, is published by UQP.

NON-FICTION

James and the Giant BLEEP
Old books, bad words and the alchemical good of reading

Amber Gwynne

I USED TO read to Jack in the library.

'Let's go,' I'd whisper. And we'd walk the cracked concrete path from the multipurpose room with its short-pile orange carpet to the school library at the back of the grounds, where a librarian sat wordlessly at the borrowing desk, eyeing us with suspicion.

I was supposed to be teaching Jack to read and write in English. Originally from China, he was eleven years old at the time, keeping in step with his other educational milestones but still unable to decipher or write more than a few basic words. We would hunch over a desk together, trying to speak over the intermittent blasting of two dozen plastic recorders, and work through exercises designed to develop, like a muscle, his automatic decoding skills.

But Jack loved stories. He could tell them. He was enthralled by them. Even now, more than a decade later, I still think of him when I see an image of the Tasmanian tiger, whose relentless hunting and eventual extermination – even in my clumsy rendering – seemed to prompt as much dismay for him as the plight of the dinosaurs. 'What do you think *extinct* means?' I asked him once. 'I don't know,' he replied. 'Did they smell very bad?'

On the mornings that dragged, when I sensed Jack's enthusiasm beginning to fade, when we'd traversed the short path and the library door had wheezed shut behind us, I'd fold back the pale-blue cover of my childhood copy of *Charlie and the Chocolate Factory* and read to him aloud. Jack, pulling at the sleeves of his school jumper, would laugh as I tried to do the voices. We'd run our fingers over the spiky, gestural illustrations, fold down the corner of a yellowed page for next time.

Even the thin-lipped librarian would smile.

'PUFFIN BOOKS AND the Dahl estate should be ashamed,' Salman Rushdie tweeted on 19 February 2023, days after news broke that the publisher had consulted with sensitivity readers to release a range of revised classics. According to multiple outlets, seventeen of the author's beloved books, including *Matilda*, *The Twits* and *James and the Giant Peach*, had been redacted or retrofitted, in places, to bring the language into line with 'contemporary sensibilities'.

Riffle through the front pages of a brand-new copy, and there on the copyright page, in a delicate serif font, you'll now find a publisher's note: 'This book was written many years ago,' it gently explains, 'and so we regularly review the language to ensure that it can continue to be enjoyed by all today.'

This was not, by any stretch, the first time an enduring classic had been tweaked to reflect changing cultural mores or a particular concern for young and impressionable readers. The original Nancy Drew books were revised as early as 1959, when the publisher, Grosset & Dunlap, attempted to modernise the series by shortening the books and purging them of racist stereotypes. Agatha Christie's whodunnits, Enid Blyton's middle readers and Ian Fleming's James Bond novels have been periodically edited to remove dated and offensive references. Ray Bradbury, author of *Fahrenheit 451*, reluctantly acquiesced when he discovered US publishers had stripped the book of 'damn', 'hell' and other alleged vulgarities to help appease 'classroom anxieties' in the lucrative education market (a similar fate to befall RL Stine, who claims Scholastic went behind his back to bowdlerise dozens of books in the *Goosebumps* series). *The Adventures of Huckleberry Finn* by Mark Twain was famously republished in 2011 to replace more than 200 instances of the N-word. And Theodor Seuss Geisel – aka Dr Seuss – made headlines in 2021, exactly thirty years after he'd died, when Dr Seuss Enterprises 'discontinued' six of his picture books to cleanse the catalogue of strong racial overtones. The list goes on.

But as Rushdie's tweet has come to epitomise (he famously condemned the revisions as 'absurd censorship'), the so-called rewriting of Dahl's novels ignited a controversy of such unprecedented intensity that it not only dominated headlines for months but also laid bare, particularly on social media, a deepening rift over questions of artistic freedom, cultural preservation and the relentless commoditisation of intellectual and creative output. The 'desecration of Dahl', in the words of conservative commentator Frank Haviland, amounted to 'sterilising works of art and meddling with genius'; British comedian David Mitchell described the new editions as a 'tin-eared and dreadful' attempt to wring Dahl's legacy of every last dollar.

Though a spokesperson from Roald Dahl Story Company insisted the changes were largely trivial 'in terms of the overall percentage of text' that had been removed or updated, British newspaper *The Telegraph* – which described the 'overhaul' as an 'example of a growing trend in children's publishing for content that nobody can find offensive' – went as far as to circulate an exhaustive list of the changes, tabulating the original text side by side with text from Puffin's reimagined editions.

Many of these changes are quite natural and seamless. Gendered terms, for example, have either been left out or replaced with neutral alternatives. (In the 2022 editions, 'chambermaids' are 'cleaners'. Families 'with a husband, a wife and several children' are now simply 'families'.) Derogatory or questionable language relating to appearance, class and identity has been diluted – or deleted altogether. Double chins and flabby necks are gone. Freaks, hags and ugly old cows have been recast as more sympathetic substitutes. People don't laugh like *mad*; they laugh *wildly*. Faces turn *pale* instead of *white*. Grandmas who are fond of gin are no longer *allowed* to have a small nip every evening; they merely *like* to. Matilda reads Austen, not Kipling.

I feel disloyal for thinking it, as a writer myself, but it's hard to imagine most readers noticing, especially first-time readers inured to what some have called 'the hair-trigger sensitivities of children's publishing'. At the same time, it's difficult to defend some changes as fitting or otherwise effectual. A discerning reader – an adult, presumably, more familiar with the original text – will detect occasional inelegancies and anachronisms where the Puffin rewrites dampen Dahl's original turn of phrase, distort his intended meaning, or simply fail to defuse the original slight. 'Let's not ask,' the novelist and essayist Francine Prose points out, 'if "enormous" is really less hurtful than "fat".'

Debating their literary or even moral merit, however, seems largely beside the point. We know that Dahl was fussy with words, a tireless tinkerer who claimed that by the time he was 'nearing the end of a story, the first part will have been re-read and altered and corrected at least one hundred and fifty times'. We know that he was openly resistant to editorial interference, arguing that a writer's 'only compensation is absolute freedom', which left him frequently at loggerheads with his publishers. And we know that he took reading for pleasure seriously, invariably favouring the imaginative and the immersive over the instructive. We can safely assume, then, that no matter how well intentioned, the impulse to purify his books of their most harmful stereotypes and objectionable language would not have been met with cheerful compliance.

But the curious thing about this impulse is not the way it polarises.

It's what it takes for granted.

I'm not the first to observe that our desire to keep literature safe, in both senses of the term, reconciles the rubrics of conservative and progressive politics alike, defying even our best attempts to position it 'neatly and conveniently' at only one end of the ideological spectrum. As Trisha Tucker points out in *The Conversation*, what harmonises these efforts is 'a professed desire to protect young readers from dangerous content', which seems sensible enough on the surface. Look a little deeper, though, and another consensus starts to materialise, one that elaborates the effects or results that 'dangerous content' only implies. 'In all times and places', writes Jonathan Zimmerman, a historian of education, the 'deepest fear of the censor' is that readers will 'get the wrong idea' – and this is true, experts have noted since at least the 1980s, 'whether the call for censorship comes from the right or from the left'.

It seems that whichever way we lean, the ascendant value of reading coagulates around some kind of connection between what we read and how we think, a collective vision that amplifies literature as cultural intervention. Our line of reasoning goes something like this: change the things people say or write, and you'll change the way we think about the world, and so the world ends up changing, too. By this logic, books – cultural artefacts often threaded with the social values of their time – represent a particularly gnarly thorn in our sides, capable of perpetuating a world view at odds with contemporary norms and aspirations.

Yet if censorship controversies are anything to go by, it's an intervention, funnily enough, that usually takes place at the level of *vocabulary*. Words matter, the new Puffin editions remind us. But how do they matter? And *how much*?

THE TRUE ALCHEMISTS, according to William H Gass, don't change lead into gold. They change the world into words. In the twenty-first century, that magic is thought to move in both directions. Don't words also render the world?

Philosophers have long underscored a connection between language and perception, but a plausible theory didn't catch on until the mid 1900s, when anthropologist Edward Sapir and his student Benjamin Lee Whorf stumbled across an intriguing phenomenon. Whorf discovered that the Native American Hopi have no way to express time, suggesting that their sense of life and the world is fundamentally at odds with that of ours, as speakers of English. The duo had originally set out to show that cultures traditionally dismissed as 'primitive' (usually those that hadn't developed a written system) were just as sophisticated as those celebrated for their cosmopolitanism. But the Sapir-Whorf hypothesis – that language somehow determines or at least influences thought – rapidly flourished into something more, something that's assumed an almost canonical status, owing, I suppose, to its deeply romantic conviction that we are what we speak.

Let me explain. Early Sapir-Whorf adherents proposed that human beings are 'very much at the mercy' of whatever linguistic habits they've come to share. Together, the vocabulary and grammar of a given language form a 'loosely laced straightjacket' for thinking, in which we're bound to construct realities so different that we're not merely occupying 'the same world with different labels attached'.

Laboratory research seems to support this proposal, though not nearly to the extent Sapir and Whorf originally imagined. So pervasive is the so-called 'weak' strain of the hypothesis, however, that even if you've never heard of linguistic relativity, you're probably familiar with some of the neo-Whorfian science that's filtered its way to a receptive public. I'm not talking about the reasonable observation that we name culturally important things by inventing new words or repurposing old ones (*microplastic, zoom-bombing, covexit*). I'm talking about the idea that language reliably bears or bounces back a certain attunement to the world, so if we don't have an obvious way to express something, we foreclose the opportunity to notice it.

Take colour, for starters.

It might seem an arbitrary choice, but using colour terms such as *black* or *yellow* is one of the most characteristic but variable ways we habitually describe – and apparently perceive – the world. Russian is one of the most frequently cited examples. For Russians, something is never just blue. It's either *siniy* (dark blue) or *golubój* (light blue), just as we differentiate between red and pink in English. And native Russian speakers perform faster on tests distinguishing different shades of blue than speakers whose languages don't make the same obligatory distinction.

In another classic experiment, speakers of languages that verbalise a difference between green and blue (like German, Korean and Icelandic) are compared with speakers of languages that don't (like Tarahumara, a Uto-Aztecan language spoken in Mexico, and the Himba dialects from Namibia). When two groups are shown an array of colours, including various shades of bluish greens or greenish blues, something predictable happens: speakers who 'colexify' variants of blue and green using one catch-all term (what some linguists call *grue*) find it *slightly more* difficult to distinguish between those colours, whereas speakers who have separate words are quick to recognise shades that lean blue.

Recorded to the millisecond, these findings suggest that our perception hinges not only on what we actually see – determined by the sensitivity of the typical human eye to around one million different colours – but also on the relatively few colour terms available in whatever language we happen to use.

Other experiments reveal that if you're a monolingual Mandarin speaker, you may think about time as moving up and down, rather than from left to right, marking a distinct conceptual difference in attitudes towards ageing. Or if you speak a language without a distinct future tense, such as Finnish, you may care *more* about what's to come, including frightening realities such as climate change. Researchers have been able to isolate all sorts of subtle perceptual idiosyncrasies stemming from the way we habitually express things, leading us to surmise that how our language works makes us see the world through word-shaped glasses.

Simple enough, right? Sensible. *Seductive*.

But as the linguist John McWhorter points out in his book *The Language Hoax*, the quirky but infinitesimal differences we observe in the lab are often distorted as 'preludes to something much grander': a pervasive and predictable world view. And if the words we have at our disposal do afford us some unique epistemological insight – if the power to name is indeed the power to see – we're left with an uncomfortable dilemma. Linguistic relativity is an enjoyable idea when it implies something special about the way we speak and think; it's rather less flattering when it implies some kind of deficiency.

Not only that. If we suppose that language functions as a kind of cognitive colander, it follows that 'gobblefunking' around with words (as the BFG might put it) carries serious consequences for the speakers at its so-called mercy.

This deference for the constitutive or destructive capacity of language lies at the heart of George Orwell's fictive but prophetic Newspeak, an artificial derivative of English that's been so simplified, regularised and robbed of etymological richness that it demonstrates a 'geometric uniformity' capable of crushing independent thought entirely. 'All dystopian languages technically belong to Whorf', literary scholars have pointed out, highlighting the recurring alignment of language control with thought control in the bleak science fiction that proliferated in the second half of the twentieth century.

As you may remember, in *Nineteen Eighty-Four* the powers that be – Ingsoc – are destroying words, 'scores of them, hundreds of them, every day', cutting language 'down to the bone'. The minor character Syme, a philologist working at the Ministry of Truth on a new edition of the Newspeak dictionary, is thrilled by the long-term implications of this work. 'Every year fewer and fewer words,' he gushes to our long-suffering Winston, 'and the range of consciousness always a little smaller. Don't you see the beauty of that?'

It's a cautionary tale, to be sure. Orwell was convinced that if thought corrupts language, language also corrupts thought – whether by the presence of bad words or the absence of good. In the novel's totalitarian Oceania, once Newspeak has matured, once society achieves total dominion over the universe of discourse, the conflation of language with reality will be complete. The thing that most excites Syme is the very same thing that horrifies the reader: erase the word, erase the concept, erase the phenomenon.

THE TROUBLE IS – for better or for worse – words don't work this way. Concepts may find expression in a given language. Or they may not. Sometimes a reason is obvious. With alarming regularity, though, that reason is chance.

Common sense alone tells us that what we're capable of thinking and what we're capable of saying are not the same thing. When we struggle to find the right words, when a word lingers on the tip of our tongue, when words just won't do something justice, we understand intuitively that thinking takes place independently of expression. It's in this way that supposedly untranslatable words, for which our language has no exact or close synonym, are often so deeply pleasurable: not because those words reveal something about a worldview that's unfamiliar or foreign to us but precisely the opposite. *Schadenfreude* has penetrated the English lexicon because there's a certain universality to the experience of delighting – usually opportunistically – in the misfortune of others. Who among us has not *tartled*, a Scottish verb meaning to hesitate before introducing someone because their name has slipped your mind? Or felt a sense of *gigil*, a Tagalog term that captures the overwhelming urge to pinch or squeeze something irresistibly cute, such as a baby's chubby thighs or a kitten's whiskered cheeks?

The idea that expression and thought are neatly symmetrical really only works when our noses are touching the data. The further afield we search, the higher the bird's-eye view, the more we see that languages all manage to accomplish much the same thing, the same meanings, even without certain words, bits of words or ways of arranging them. As McWhorter puts it, 'rather than each revealing a different take on thinking, languages – beyond having names for cultural tokens – are variations on the same take on thinking: the human one.'

To hope or to fear that words alone can channel or trammel thought in any profound or inevitable way is therefore feasible only if we disregard how 'hopelessly motile' their connotations are. And connotations, we find, demonstrate an uncanny knack for attaching to new words as old ones are forcefully decommissioned – a process sometimes called 'the euphemism treadmill'. So, *shellshock* becomes *battle fatigue* becomes *operational exhaustion* becomes *post-traumatic stress disorder*, as the late George Carlin observes in a well-known comedy routine. In this case, forms may change while meanings or associations stay the same. Or forms stay the same as meanings move on, picking up odours and flavours from the environment around them like butter left open in the refrigerator. The real magic of language is that we manage to make any sense at all.

It's not that words don't matter. Of course they do. We bend them this way and that, to express love, to convey disgust, to reveal or obfuscate, to pledge, deny, comfort, wound. We venerate their beauty and recoil from their hidden barbs. Words *sound*. They look, taste, feel and smell. You can no doubt think of a word you instinctively hate – *moist*, anyone? – or a series of words you love, words one after the other that you can recite off by heart. (Here are some of mine: 'Words can be like X-rays if you use them properly,' Aldous Huxley writes in *Brave New World*, 'they'll go through anything.' Or these, from David Foster Wallace's *The Pale King*: 'How odd I can have all this inside me and to you it's just words.')

But tell me what *ugly* means, tell me about *home*, about the particular way, when you were a child, the sky was *dark*. Tell me whether *liberal* is good and *bossy* is bad, if *limerence* and *defenestration* are absolutely necessary or *irregardless* definitely wrong, and we may find we can never agree.

In a sense, words matter because they *are* matter: pliant, impure and almost wilful in their powerlessness to either control or be controlled. Thinking of language as 'a list of words with set meanings', McWhorter reminds us in his *New York Times* column, 'is like thinking of the position of the clouds right now as somehow fundamental rather than as a passing moment'.

Better to think of words not as containers that shape the meanings inside them but as vessels into which we pour our own meanings, in different moments and places, according to whatever whims and exigencies make the most sense at the time. Words, we find, are always in motion. We might, from time to time, catch them in the pages of a book, or in a film or song, like an insect pinned to styrofoam. But they never stay still for long.

'A word is dead when it is said, some say,' goes a little poem by Emily Dickinson. 'I say it just begins to live that day.'

JACK AND I never finished *Charlie and the Chocolate Factory*. Fourth term ended. Jack finished primary school. I moved to another city to start my PhD.

In my mind's eye, though, we're still sitting at that desk in the multi-purpose room with its burnt-orange carpet. A textbook is open in front of us, and Jack traces his finger along a line of words, saying each one out loud. *Stream. Ray. Fry. Sky. Spy. Squeal. Spy. Stray. Sky. Slay. Ray. Stream.* The point is not to make sense but to get faster and faster.

Of course, this isn't reading as we'd usually think of it. Recognising words effortlessly and instantaneously is a foundational skill that underlies comprehension, but reading is about much more than individual words. As the inimitable Stanley Fish tells us in *How to Write a Sentence: And How to Read*

One, words are just discrete items 'pointing everywhere and nowhere'. Only once they're tied by 'ligatures of relationships' to one another do they congeal into something we can 'contemplate, admire, reject, or refine'. Put another way, words get us halfway there. Reading is about doing the rest.

In the early 1970s, Dahl became embroiled in a war of words with one of his most vocal critics, fellow author Eleanor Cameron. In a letter addressed directly to Cameron, he rejects the assertion that his books are somehow harmful to young readers, emphasising a prickly opposition to 'patronising' children with didactic literature and a disdain for the idea that nasty stories mean nasty authors – or make nasty kids.

I'm inclined to agree, not in defence of Dahl himself, whose smiling face on the inside cover of my brand-new Puffin editions almost certainly exaggerates his benign appeal. Nor do I mean to say there's nothing squeamish to discover in his stories, characters or turns of phrase. Rather, I agree because I can't help but concede to the capricious quality of words and the ultimately incalculable ways that readers layer texts with their own meanings, the way – if I can pilfer an adage from reader-theorist Louise Rosenblatt – people also 'happen to books'.

Wolfgang Iser, another reader-theorist, likens the words of a book to a constellation in which we see our own patterns: 'Two people gazing at the night sky may both be looking at the same collection of stars, but one will see the image of a plough, and the other will make out a dipper. The "stars" in a text are fixed; the lines that join them are variable.'

So, what troubles me about the way we sometimes talk about books (be it *George's Marvellous Medicine* or *The Satanic Verses*) is its aggressive narrowing. A book becomes language. Language becomes individual words. Words become determinate meanings – some acceptable (in a given time and place) and others objectionable. But when we reduce a book to words like this – when we cleave them from the materiality of the book itself, from the contexts in which we read, from the narratives in which they're embedded, from the recalcitrant nature of words – we abrogate the possibility of those words meaning something else or something more. So convinced are we that preserving the language of a given book is to perpetuate a fixed meaning or view that we deny the reader an opportunity to draw the lines their own way.

Turning the pages of a Dahl novel now, furtively on the train to my inner-city office, I'm a different reader from the one who read aloud to Jack in the library more than a decade ago, and a different reader, it almost goes without saying, from the one who devoured *The Witches* and *The BFG* tucked up in my childhood bed.

And so the book is different, too.

Isn't this the value of 'good' literature? To endure, even as the language and stories date, even as some good words become bad (or bad words become okay), because we're able to make them new, to cast them in a different light? Isn't part of the sorcery of story the chance to contemplate how things have changed and to find in words the residue of a reality we might no longer welcome, tolerate or reject? Rather than indulging in some kind of selective linguistic amnesia, couldn't we instead marvel at the ways we're able to happen to books, over and over?

How whoopsey-splunkers, I say. How absolutely squiffling.

I'm grateful to Waleed Aly, Scott Stephens and John Safran for participating in the Brisbane Writers Festival panel 'War of the Words' that sparked the idea for this essay.

Amber Gwynne is a researcher, writer and editor based in Meanjin (Brisbane). She is a communications advisor in the public service, managing editor of the *Journal of Australian Studies* and a lecturer in writing at the University of Queensland.

IN CONVERSATION

The sentimentalist

Culture without the cringe

Caroline O'Donoghue and Carody Culver

Since 2018, Irish writer Caroline O'Donoghue has been putting lowbrow in the limelight. Her popular podcast Sentimental Garbage *– which has a particularly dedicated Australian fan base – began life as a defence of chick lit and romance fiction. These days, it offers witty and sincere takes on all kinds of cultural touchstones that are often framed as guilty pleasures, from the generation-defining music of Avril Lavigne to the high drama of* Sex and the City *to the incredible versatility of the word 'like'. In this conversation, which has been lightly edited and condensed for clarity, Caroline talks to Griffith Review Editor Carody Culver about rediscovering our pop-culture obsessions without the cringe factor.*

CARODY CULVER: When did you first become aware that women – so often it's women – are made to feel ashamed for enjoying certain forms of pop culture?

CAROLINE O'DONOGHUE: Selfishly, I think it was when I was promoting my first novel, *Promising Young Women*. I had very consciously modelled that book on *Bridget Jones's Diary* and Marian Keyes and all these books I had grown up with and hadn't questioned the validity of. But the whole point of the novel was that it began in this [particular] way – 'I'm a millennial woman enjoying an office job in the big city and just broke up with my boyfriend' – it's a very familiar narrative, but I wanted to subvert it by taking it in a kind of Angela Carter [direction] and making it feel like a classic gothic novel. What I love about gothic literature is that it's drawn from a period where women spent the bulk of their time in their homes, and how a building itself can kind of turn on you, history and ancestry can turn on you, and then you have corridors going on forever and wallpaper patterns repeating. Now people spend the most time at work, and I was fascinated by the modern office as a gothic landscape. So it was this purposeful thing of starting one way and then veering another. But when I read the reviews and gave interviews, the framing of the questions, rightly or wrongly (even from very respectful interviewers), was like, 'You start with a wink towards shitty literature.'

I felt like the stuff [I enjoyed] was being derided and I knew I wasn't alone in feeling like it was worth defending. So the podcast was born out of that, and from there I just kept on expanding, and then I didn't really care about covering commercial women's fiction anymore because it kind of felt like that battle had been won – Emily Henry and all of these emerging romance novelists are scooping thick deals and getting reviewed in big places. So I keep extending what counts as garbage.

CC: There's also a wonderful element of friendship. I love listening to your *Sentimental in the City* miniseries with Dolly Alderton because the two of you obviously have a great relationship. But the whole podcast taps into that special pleasure of finding a person with whom you share a cultural obsession and being able to go really deep with them.

CO: Definitely – that lovely thing of meeting someone you think is cool and then realising you both love Jilly Cooper. It's the most delicious feeling.

CC: There are so many elements of culture we're made to feel a little bit guilty for loving, and at the same time there's a huge appetite for re-examining or celebrating these elements. When you talked to Sloane Crosley for the Enya episode, she had a great observation about 'the laundering of our tastes' and how we can shame ourselves as much as feeling that shame from external sources – you know, 'I love *Spice World*, but it's really daggy.'

CO: I love that word. I love that.

CC: *Spice World*, though – an iconic film! Do you think that idea of laundering our tastes is connected to social media and our urge to consciously curate a version of ourselves for an audience in a way that we didn't maybe twenty years ago?

CO: It's fascinating, isn't it? Now, with the great reclamation of guilty pleasures, there are so many podcasts on cultural figures that are based on this concept. Being the kind of person who listens to an old Britney Spears album has a kind of a weird cachet.

CC: We wear our tastes very publicly now – I suppose we always did in a way, like when you'd have posters all over the walls of your teenage bedroom. But today anyone can have a look at your Instagram feed. Remember early Facebook, with that section of your profile where you could fill out all your likes? The hours I spent thinking which of my favourite bands or books were cool enough to admit to liking publicly…

CO: That was the most curated I've ever been! I remember that so well. I remember, in the novel section, really going hard on F Scott Fitzgerald and Nabokov. And back then I was doing it to impress an invisible boy who didn't exist. But now there's that quite cynical [aspect] of social media where we're curating, we're showing off, we're constantly laundering and showing ourselves to be the kind of person who wants to free Britney. That's a type of person we all know, and we all like that person. I also think that in digging up these slightly older things that were big ten years ago – there's something very hungry for community in that, and I can only really speak to it as a millennial, but I think as a generation we're in a bit of an identity crisis. Particularly now, because most of us are becoming parents and home owners or not home owners or not parents, decisively, and I think there's a loneliness in the generation that [makes us] use pop culture as an olive branch.

CC: *Sentimental Garbage* seems to be particularly resonant for millennial women, and so much of the culture you talk about in the podcast is from the '90s and the 2000s, when we were kids or young women: Alanis Morissette's *Jagged Little Pill*, *Gilmore Girls*, Barbie, noughties fashion. I imagine that for many listeners, certain episodes of *Sentimental Garbage* are very nostalgic – so I was intrigued to hear you say on the show that you don't think of yourself as a nostalgic person.

CO: It's funny, whenever I read reviews of my work and delicious praise, the word 'nostalgia' comes up all the time. I really don't think of myself as nostalgic at all, and I wouldn't think my friends do either. Dolly is incredibly nostalgic – she loves to go through old WhatsApp messages. She likes to go back to the beginning of a WhatsApp thread and read through it like it's a novel, which is so sweet. She'll often quote reply to something one of us said three years ago – one day she was like, 'this private joke was absolutely unhinged' and I wrote back in all caps 'MAKE PRIVATE JOKES WITH ME NOW!' I don't want to talk about how great the summer of '69 was with somebody – it makes me think about death.

CC: The flipside of nostalgia.

CO: Yeah, it's an illness. But then I've positioned myself as somebody who's constantly going through the trash of yesteryear with my raccoon paws and saying, 'Wasn't it grand?' I think it's more that I'm drawn to things I misunderstood rather than things that are just old, and I'm also interested in diagnosing the culture through what we loved, what we made and what we despised. It's becoming much more clear to me the older I get. In [my new novel] *The Rachel Incident* there's quite a lot about abortion and abortion non-access. I started to realise as I was writing it that while abortions have a huge effect on people who need them, they also have a huge effect on people who don't need them. Growing up in Ireland with such limited access [to abortion] completely changed how I felt about my body, how I felt about men, how I felt about sex. And there's only one thing I can trace that to, which is the culture I grew up in. So I use the phrase 'diagnostic nostalgia': why are we this way? It's following the thread back to the jumper rather than just being like, 'Wasn't it better in 2004?'

CC: *Sentimental Garbage* also doesn't critique that culture of the recent past through the lens of today – you're not looking at something from ten or twenty years ago and saying, 'That's very problematic...'

CO: I find that so boring.

CC: It's so boring! Of course we can all look back and say, sure, that movie didn't age very well – but we can still find joy in it and appreciate that it's a product of its time. It seems like that's very much a part of the show's ethos.

CO: I think it's also a reaction to my employment history. We used to have this website in the UK called *The Pool*, which was like *Mamamia* – a feminist lifestyle website, and the whole idea of it was, you know, the internet is such a busy and violent and weird place, what happened to good, fun, friendly zones? But because it was an investor-led business we had to keep proving growth, and the things that would get the most hits would be the most boring stuff, like 'The *Daily Mail* has done this, shame on the *Daily Mail*.' The one where

I felt like I was done was a Kate Middleton story. Pictures of her were taken with a long lens when she was on holiday and she was sunbathing topless. The *Daily Mail* ran the photos, and then we ran the photos and said, 'How dare the *Daily Mail*.' We cropped out her nipples, so I guess that's feminism.

I hated that, but what I also hated was these incredibly banal and pointless articles, like '[the song] "Baby, It's Cold Outside": Problematic or No?' I just found it really unintellectual. Here's what I hate the most about it: it seems to back-pat the writer or the reader simply for being born at the right time. Is your self-esteem so low that you have to congratulate yourself for being born at a time when sexual harassment is slightly more frowned upon than it was then? It's like just identifying that makes you a cultural critic.

Something I've been thinking about a lot lately is how we overemphasise what pop culture can give us, but we haven't thought about what it *can't*. What art can give you is a sense that you're not alone – it can transport you, it can inspire you. What it can't do is tell you how to vote. When people are constantly funnelling political motives into work that was created in the spirit of apoliticality, it almost shows a lack of an outlet.

CC: We're also at this particular moment in time when there's so much content and so many different ways to engage with it. The world isn't in a great place, so perhaps we're putting intense pressure on sources of entertainment to give us this kind of moral or political guidance.

CO: Like, 'Why isn't *Barbie* feminist enough?' It's also increasingly pointless. Particularly because we're living in an incredibly fractured pop-culture landscape – we're not in a world anymore with thirteen channels, where four movies come out a month, where we're basically all seeing the same stuff. I don't know what the number-one movie is right now.

CC: It's probably a Marvel movie.

CO: It's probably a Marvel movie. But we're living in incredibly tailored and very specific pop-culture worlds, which I think is a great thing, by the way. Me and Michelle Andrews were talking about this on the Kylie Minogue episode [of *Sentimental Garbage*] – we perceived there to be way less female-celebrity vitriol today because the celebrity experience is far more tailored. You see as much of Britney as you want to see, and you never feel like she's being pushed on you. That's why I think people hated Kylie Minogue, because they felt she was being pushed on them. So that's the great thing about pop culture now. But the not-so-great thing, or rather the thing we're missing, is that the huge steps forward in diversity – while they're wonderful for the actors and the community involved – I think they give us a false sense of security about how big the domino effect is going to be.

And again, the more we pressure these pieces of culture to have political significance, the more we divorce ourselves from the realities of whatever community is being represented on screen [by an actor in], say, a Marvel movie – we're not actually learning anything about that community or engaging with their struggles.

CC: In the very first episode of *Sentimental in the City*, you point out that 'you don't have to like [*Sex and the City*] to have seen it a billion times'. How do you know when a piece of pop culture has become part of the firmament? I wonder if a single TV show or movie or book can have the palpable effect on the culture that it might have had twenty years ago.

CO: Even the Marvel movies – I don't think they're mass culture anymore. Obviously many, many people saw *Avengers: Endgame*, but I think in general people are taking it or leaving it and it's not watercooler conversation anymore. Taylor Swift is the only monocultural thing I can really think of. Or the Titanic submersible – that felt like the OJ Simpson trial, a moment where everybody on Earth was ripped for the next update.

CC: I think that's part of why *Sentimental Garbage* is so captivating and so popular – we don't have those singular pieces of culture that occupy everyone's attention, so it's lovely to remember some of the things that did have an outsize influence.

CO: Perhaps if I'm nostalgic for anything it's that: a whole populace being captivated by something enough for everyone to have some kind of opinion on it.

Caroline O'Donoghue is a *New York Times* bestselling author and the host of the award-winning podcast *Sentimental Garbage*. She has written three novels for adults: *Promising Young Women*, which was shortlisted for the An Post Irish Book Awards– *Sunday Independent* Newcomer of the Year; *Scenes of a Graphic Nature*, which was longlisted for the Ondaatje Prize; and her latest, *The Rachel Incident*. Her supernatural series for teenagers, *All Our Hidden Gifts*, was also longlisted for the Ondaatje.

Lesh Karan

In the Dollhouse

I don't remember my Barbies,
but Mother once told me I had
twist-popped their limbs
off. I do recall this one doll —
she would wet her nappy
if you fed her. I'd kohl a black
full moon on the open sky of her
forehead, but never feed her.

There's also the time I squeeze-
stuffed kitty into a toy bus:
It needed passengers I must've thought,
and with such a thought
kitty's white fur poked through
the windows — a spiky, plump
cactus that meowed and meowed.
Mother had to crack the plastic —
gently — with a knife and place
an ad on the radio: *free to a good home*
said the host. I was three.

Then there's Big Sis, aka: me.
When I was eight, that felt like driving
a bus bursting with unbuckled kids.
I don't recall mewling, the crack,
though, is still there — a line
of sinewy scar tissue.

Lesh Karan writes poetry and non-fiction prose. Her work has featured in *Australian Multilingual Writing Project, Australian Poetry Journal, Best of Australian Poems 2022, Cordite, Island, Overland, Rabbit, Red Room Poetry* and *Strange Horizons,* among others. In 2023, she won the Liquid Amber Poetry Prize and was shortlisted for the Judith Wright Poetry Prize.

FICTION

The kiss
Melanie Cheng

SHE COULD ONLY find one image of him on the internet, a grainy passport-style photo on page five of her Google search. Who knew there were so many men in the world called Ryan Stewart? It took Gemma a moment to recognise him, sandwiched between a balding, self-published author of middle-grade fiction and a piano teacher from Boston accused of grooming a student. The lips gave him away. Mediterranean thick, even though his family were apparently from some small, cold town in Canada.

Gemma marvelled at how insignificant his digital footprint was. She wondered if he was dead, which made her sad and a little disappointed – in herself but also the world – that this was the most obvious explanation for his lack of social media presence.

And yet death remained a distinct possibility. They were not young. Some would say they were middle-aged. And while Ryan had always been active – in her diary, Gemma had compared his quads to small boulders – he had also always had a penchant for fast food. Maybe with a sedentary job and the time-swallowing tedium of parenting small children, it had all caught up with him – a plaque bursting like hot mozzarella in a coronary artery. Or perhaps (because isn't life surprising sometimes?) the exact opposite had occurred. Perhaps he was living on a retreat somewhere in the tropics, eating nuts and teaching Ayurvedic yoga.

It was this absence of useful information that had led Gemma here, to the airport, waiting for a flight to attend her high-school reunion. That, and the kiss – or at least her recollection of the kiss. Sometimes she wondered if everyone remembered their first pash this way, but then she recalled friends lamenting how awful theirs had been. *Like a washing machine*, one had said. *I stared at the poster of Pamela Anderson on his wall and waited for it to be over*, said another. So Gemma had been lucky. Or maybe she had been the opposite of lucky. Because nobody she had kissed since had quite lived up to the memory. Not even – dare she think it – her husband.

As Gemma nursed her cappuccino (lukewarm and bitter) in the airport café, she felt like one of the less interesting fish in a giant aquarium. She had never been pretty and was quite accustomed to being ignored. Indeed, she felt for women her age who had once been attractive – oh, how they grieved their beauty! And so publicly, their bodies wrapped gladwrap tight in Lululemon lycra (that they could breathe at all was remarkable), their lips injected to look like freshly waxed vulvas. But not Gemma. Gemma was plain. Some might argue her blandness would make a great canvas for collagen and fake eyelashes, but Gemma – plain her whole life – lacked the motivation and the time.

Which was why Ryan's kiss had been so remarkable. He had arrived with a bang halfway through Year 9, when cliques were starting to splinter under the weight of their own boredom. With his North American accent and love of R&B music (which he listened to almost constantly on his lemon-yellow Walkman), he may as well have rocketed in from another galaxy. Gemma, an only child living on a cul-de-sac in a suburb twenty kilometres from the city, had spent much of her childhood waiting for something – anything – to happen. And so when Ryan appeared she convinced herself that, all along, it had been a Canadian boy with generous lips and low-slung pants she had been waiting for. She devoted weeks to working out his timetable, making sure she was optimally placed to brush past him, or at least sneak a look at him, as they moved between classes. But Ryan, unlike other boys Gemma had fancied, took notice. Occasionally, they'd locked eyes. Once or twice, he had smiled.

Gemma heard the boarding call for her flight over the airport speakers. She finished her croissant (dry and burnt at the edges) and looked down at the brown dregs in her mug. Decades ago, while backpacking through Turkey, she had paid a woman to read her fortune in the grains of her coffee cup. Tasseography, it was called, which made it sound like a science. Gemma couldn't remember the details of the reading – it had been vague and open to interpretation — but she did know what the woman with the tobacco-stained teeth *hadn't* predicted. She hadn't predicted that Gemma would marry her book editor because he adored her and because by the time she met him she was nearing forty and yearning for a child. And she hadn't predicted that Gemma would find motherhood excruciating — that it would feel like an outfit she'd forced herself to wear even though it was several sizes too small. And she most definitely hadn't predicted that Gemma's son would be a combination of his mother's sensitivity and his father's people-pleasing — a biological creation of such inconceivable delicacy, he was completely unsuited to the modern world. As it was, Gemma's life had caught her by surprise.

By contrast, Gemma had spent much of high school imagining being married to Ryan. Not the wedding — she was not that type of girl. She didn't enjoy wearing impractical dresses or being the centre of attention. Instead, she had pictured them lying on a couch watching TV together, her stockinged feet resting on his rock-hard thighs. Perhaps there was a baby, *their* baby, sleeping soundly in a nearby room. They were the harmless musings of an adolescent, or so Gemma had thought at the time.

Now she threw her napkin in the bin and hoisted her overnight bag onto her shoulder. She made her way past the brightly lit bookshops and last-minute gift stores towards the gate. Airports had always struck Gemma as melancholic places. The people in business suits appeared especially morose — at the prospect of leaving their lovers or returning to their spouses or leaving their families or all of the above. Gemma joined the throng of people standing and sighing and thumbing their phones at the gate, which, in spite of the boarding call, was not yet open.

She messaged Jasper.

About to board. Hope the test goes well. Love you.

His reply was immediate, as if he had been watching and waiting for her message.

Dad says he's making gnocchi for dinner. Gnocchi makes me constipated.

Gemma closed her phone and dropped it in her handbag. She felt for the hard slim square of her book, an autofictional offering from an up-and-coming British author. She barely read anymore. She was too busy working on her own book or finishing a commission or buying milk and bread from the supermarket or preparing dinner or picking Jasper up from music class or trying to get him to talk about the marks on his arm or counselling Jeff about how to stand up to his boss. When she did manage to squeeze in a few pages before bed or while commuting, she found herself comparing the author's words to her own. She longed for the kind of reading she'd experienced as a teenager – of arriving at a story primed for pleasure and pain, willing the words to tear her apart, daring them to break her heart.

With her hand still on the hardcover of the novel in her bag – as if deriving strength from it, as if it was a touchstone – Gemma felt a pair of eyes on her. She scanned the area and traced them to a man sitting at the gate, his legs spread to make him appear larger than he was. She supposed he was handsome *for his age*. He had a forgettable nose, long-lashed eyes and a good head of hair, greying at the sides. He could be from anywhere in Europe, of mixed heritage, a migrant. Through his tight-fitting jumper, Gemma spied the indentation of a bellybutton, the swell of early man boobs.

THE GATE OPENED, which resulted in a flurry of activity, and when she looked back a few minutes later the man was gone. She walked down the loading bridge to the aircraft. By the time she'd found her seat and squashed her bag, Tetris-style, into a space in the overhead locker, she had forgotten all about him.

Gemma didn't mind domestic flights. They were neat, contained episodes of travel. There was a paradoxical freedom in the confinement of the cabin – she was untethered from her email inbox and other earthly duties. She inserted her earplugs – bright-orange ones she'd found at the back of the drawer in her bedside table – and pulled out her novel. She flattened the pages with her palm. The book had been printed on thick, untameable paper – the kind of paper afforded to only the most famous authors. Gemma's words, by contrast, were published on cheap, friable pages. When she held them up to the light at night, she could see the silhouette of her fingers.

Now she shifted in her seat and tried to find comfort in the narrow space. She was on the aisle and the two seats beside her were occupied by a woman the same age as Gemma and a teenager who was presumably the woman's daughter. The mother and daughter didn't speak to one another but stared into the white voids of their devices. Gemma supposed she and Jasper would have done the same, but it hadn't always been that way. She remembered tram rides to the city when he had delighted fellow passengers with his precociousness. At those times, pride had burned in Gemma's chest like a tiny blue flame.

The plane was filling up. The more experienced travellers were clamping noise-cancelling headphones over their ears and watching the movies they'd downloaded onto their iPads the night before. Others, unaccustomed to early starts, had closed their eyes and were willing themselves to sleep. Only a few, like Gemma, had books open on their laps. Gemma remembered what her publisher had said when she'd asked him what people were reading. *Their phones*, he had said, which had prompted a depressing conversation about the precarious state of literary fiction.

And so Gemma felt ashamed as she tried, and failed, to read her novel now – her eyes repeatedly drifting to the screen of the mother sitting beside her, who was caught in some terrible compulsive loop in which she would look at a photo of herself, zoom in on an area of her face to inspect her wrinkles, zoom out, close her phone and then, a few seconds later, start the process all over again. Gemma only looked away when another passenger slumped noisily into the seat across the aisle. It was the man in the tight-fitting jumper. He smiled.

'Made it.'

Gemma didn't acknowledge him. She flattened the pages of her book once more with the heel of her palm. At the periphery of her vision, she saw the grey flutter of a newspaper being unfolded and the swing of a shiny black shoe as the man crossed his legs.

She was grateful when the aircraft's engine roared to life and her ears filled with its loud, ceaseless hum. She closed her eyes, felt the thrust of the plane as it left the ground. Over the years, Gemma had found it best not to think about the physics of flying: the weight of the aircraft, its cruising altitude, how she and the other dozens of passengers were only alive because of the great speed at which they were hurtling through the air.

With ears plugged and eyes closed, she felt safer. The sensations that did reach her were muted: the melodic ring of the seatbelt light being switched off, the rattle of the dinner trolley, the smell of food being warmed in microwave ovens – a heady aroma reminiscent of canned soup and sausage rolls. But above it all she heard something else. The rumble of a voice – low, male, foreign. *American*.

She opened her eyes, pulled out her earplugs. The voice belonged to the man in the tight-fitting jumper, who was no longer reading his newspaper but chatting to the passenger beside him. *American*. But Gemma wasn't good with accents – it could easily have been Canadian. And now that she thought about it, hadn't there been an ever-so-slight fullness to the man's lips? She needed to get a better look at his face, which was impossible from her current position across the aisle. She slid her book into the seat pocket in front of her, released her seatbelt.

As she walked, she felt his eyes burning holes into her head, her back, her bottom. It was a relief to enter the cramped metallic space of the toilet. Once inside, she studied herself in the mirror, wondering if she, too, had been rendered unrecognisable with age. In her thirties she had begun tinting her hair, and these days it was several shades lighter than the deep brown of her childhood. Her face was thinner too. Elongated. Her mouth drooped at the corners. Perhaps her eyes were the same. *Hauntingly blue*, Ryan had called them once, which now struck Gemma as both clumsy and unexpectedly poetic for a boy in Year 9.

She washed her hands and reapplied her lipstick. Someone knocked, which annoyed her, so she counted to ten, breathing deeply, before she unlocked the door. When she finally emerged, the refreshment service had begun and she found herself stuck behind a trolley of juices and soft drinks and tiny packets of salty snacks that nobody ate except when on planes.

But the obstruction was fortuitous. It gave her more time to examine the man's face. She could see that the greying hair had almost certainly once been light brown, and the lips, full for his age, hinted at a former kissable plumpness. The longer she remained stranded in the aisle, the more certain she became that the man was indeed her old flame.

When the flight attendant wheeled her trolley forward, Gemma was suddenly within inches of him. She looked down at his tray and saw that he had ordered a beer to accompany his snack. A bald patch – a smooth pink coin – capped the top of his otherwise perfect head. Sensing her presence, the man turned and raised his eyes to meet hers.

'Ryan?'

The name, when it came, sounded as if it had been uttered by somebody else. The man's look shifted from one of mild affection to puzzlement. 'Excuse me?'

He was still smiling, but it was a different kind of grin – the type of smile people offer a stranger who begs them for spare change.

It was not him. Now that Gemma had uttered his name out loud, she saw just how preposterous it was to have ever imagined that it was. She felt an unbearable heat in her face, the ache of a fake smile in her cheeks.

'Sorry. My mistake,' she managed to mutter. 'I thought you were somebody else.'

She flopped into her seat, next to the middle-aged woman who had now stopped her compulsive zooming and was sleeping with mouth agape. Gemma reached for her book, reinserted her earplugs. She was seized by a sudden, excruciating thirst, but thanks to her restroom visit she had missed the refreshment service. She contemplated flagging the flight attendant down – she was only a few seats away – but the last thing she wanted was to draw more attention to herself.

SHE SPENT THE remainder of the flight in a disassociated state. She was no longer within her body but hovering at the edges of it. The man in the tight-fitting jumper was nothing but a blur; her family, little more than abstractions.

She didn't know how she made it through the arrival hall to the taxi stand, or from the taxi stand to the taxi, or from the taxi to the generic four-and-a-half-star hotel room. But that was where she found herself when her mind re-entered her body. And when she was reconnected with her feelings, she discovered that her embarrassment had (mercifully) disappeared with the man in the tight-fitting jumper, but that it had been replaced with a weighty, almost malignant fatigue. She collapsed onto the bed.

After several minutes, tears flowed in thin rivulets from the corners of her eyes. She did not sob. Later, when she got up, she would see that her tears had left two perfectly matched oval stains like ovaries on the plum-coloured bedspread.

Ryan Stewart. Why had he loomed so large in her memory? They had *gone out* (in the way that kids in Year 9 *went out*) for less than a week, before he had dumped her on a Monday morning via a note hand-delivered by one of his friends. While Gemma had silently lusted after him for most of the rest of high school, it was still only a tiny proportion of the five decades she'd been alive. And yet she still dreamed of him. And she still dreamed of the kiss. She supposed it had something to do with what the boy symbolised – a foreigner from the other side of the vast Pacific Ocean; living proof that there was a world outside her tired suburb. When she looked back on that time from the vantage point of middle age, she was struck by how ripe it had been, how bursting with possibility.

She knew then, as the tears cooled and dried on the skin of her temples, that she would not attend her high-school reunion that evening. Instead, she would run herself a bath – she couldn't remember the last time she'd had a bath; it must have been years – and she would make herself a drink (perhaps two, three, four!) from the absurdly small liquor bottles in the minibar. And then, when her head was feeling floaty from all the spirits, she would lie down in the painfully hot water and she would soak, like soiled underwear, until her skin was raw and crinkled. And later still, when she had wrapped her wet body in the thick white bath sheet, she would climb into bed with the book by the up-and-coming British author and she would read until she fell asleep – to dream of Ryan, or her family, or if she was lucky, nothing at all.

Melanie Cheng is a writer and general practitioner based in Melbourne. Her short-story collection, *Australia Day*, won the 2018 Victorian Premier's Literary Award for Fiction. Her novel, *Room for a Stranger*, was shortlisted for the 2020 NSW Premier's Multicultural Prize and longlisted for the 2020 Miles Franklin Award. Her work has appeared in *The Saturday Paper*, *The Guardian*, *The Age*, *The Weekend Australian*, *Meanjin* and *Overland*, among many others.

NON-FICTION

The fall of the madmen

How advertising ate itself

Jane Caro

THE MT BUFFALO Chalet was shrouded in mist all weekend. One wag quipped it clearly had a seventy-cigarette-a-day habit. The hotel in the highlands of rural Victoria was crammed to its creaky old rafters with wags and wits that wintery weekend in 1995. It was the venue for the annual Caxton advertising awards. They were run by the newspaper industry to recognise and celebrate the best ads that had appeared in their publications that year.

Back in 1995, change, as well as cigarette smoke, was in the air. Smoking was still permitted in hotels in those days. Even in old weatherboard fire hazards. But it wasn't mist, passive smoke or being trapped inside that so disturbed the conference. In the first time in the eighteen-year history of the Caxtons, there was a sizeable number of female delegates. Nowhere near 50 per cent, you understand, but enough to make their presence felt. They weren't the usual overworked event organisers or the few battle-scarred older female creatives who'd learnt to match quips, drinks and fags with the blokes. They were a new crowd of ambitious younger women who had persuaded their creative directors to cough up the sizeable registration fee and invest in their career. Their presence so unsettled the blokes that there was a running 'joke' about lesbians for the duration of the event.

I was still a copywriter in those days, and one of those female delegates. I spent the weekend rolling my eyes so hard I thought they'd work loose in their sockets. Even so, I had no idea that I was witnessing the beginning of the end.

The men weren't wrong to be rattled. That influx of female delegates was the most obvious indicator of the tsunami of change about to overwhelm the cosy world of advertising and the world in general. Up on that mountain top, we were so busy discussing print, typography, illustration, kerning (who even knows what that is anymore?), photography and so on that we'd hardly noticed the beginnings of digital advertising, the deregulation of Australian content, the radical change in the way agencies were being remunerated or the beginnings of social media. The World Wide Web had launched in 1991 and was bringing a revolution in the way business was conducted and how products were advertised and sold. Over the horizon the likes of Myspace and Facebook were looming. That's the thing about change – you never see it coming, you just get knocked sideways by the tailwind. Every element of that weekend, held so symbolically atop a misty mountain, had had its day. Far from being the all-conquering heroes at the summit of their power and influence, the fall of the madmen had begun.

ANDREW HORNERY, WHO was then the marketing roundsman for *The Sydney Morning Herald* and would go on to become their gossip columnist, remembers how glamorous and larger-than-life advertising creatives were back in 1995. 'They were fully fledged celebrities,' he says, and names Siimon Reynolds, John Singleton and Mo and Jo (Alan Morris and Alan Johnson) as examples. Hornery was reporting on the Mt Buffalo Caxtons for his newspaper, and remembers that – apart from all the women – there was another delegate attending the weekend who turned heads. A young Lachlan Murdoch had been sent along to learn about the industry that fuelled at least a part of his father's empire.

That's how much clout newspaper advertising had at the time.

The Caxtons were anarchic. They were wild and crazy and often obscene. They were sexist and racist and often nasty but, my god, they were fun. I attended regularly from the mid-'80s to the early 2000s, when the sexist bullying finally got me down and I gave them – and the ad industry – away. People drank far too much and took all sorts of illicit substances. The days were taken up with worthy (and unworthy) lectures about the ad industry (and – a nod to our sponsors – print advertising), but the nights were just for fun. Saturday night started with the awards ceremony (a Caxton Award was sought after) and finished with the annual talent quest. You could never get away with that talent quest in these more enlightened times. There'd be headlines, and careers would be ruined. One enterprising pair kidnapped two Japanese tourists (they appeared bemused but quite happy to be shanghaied) and taught them how to swear in Australian. Another group filled wine glasses with cold soup to taste test which advertising luminary's vomit it was – resulting, understandably, in some *actual* vomit. Another group performed a back, crack and sack onstage – take that, puppetry of the penis. It was puerile, naughty and designed to shock, but it was also hilarious. Lifelong feminism notwithstanding, I miss it.

THE CAXTONS ARE no more, but it wasn't the annual bacchanal of bad behaviour that did them in – though, no doubt, it didn't help. They were killed by the huge change in the way we consume media and the terrible price that exacted on the once all-conquering newspaper industry. Even the historic Mt Buffalo Chalet is a relic of the past, unoccupied since 2007. And the advertising industry is a shadow of its former self. In the '90s, ad creatives were exorbitantly overpaid (well, the blokes were, anyway) and had a very high opinion of their skills and importance. No longer, now that budgets have collapsed and digital is king.

Some things have survived and thrived, of course. Not least Lachlan Murdoch. And, as I saw when I attended the 2023 Cannes in Cairns conference, women have all but taken over the advertising industry. Account Director Liz Ainslie, a forty-five-year veteran, has a theory about why so many women are now running ad agencies. In 1995, unless they ran their own show, a woman boss was a rarity. 'When I first started, us chicks were given the shitkicker work as account executives. The group account directors, all blokes when I started, would be schmoozing the clients, having long lunches and all that stuff, and we'd be hunched over a calculator doing budgets and timelines – then considered the grunt work.'

That's another thing no one anticipated – how the way agencies were paid for their work was about to change dramatically.

First, media commissions disappeared. Next, agency retainers also evaporated – no longer were agencies awarded a major account they might keep for years, or even decades. Today, like architects, engineering firms or even lawyers, they mostly tender competitively project by project. And, as Ainslie points out, what are the skills you need to make a profit in a job-by-job world? The ability to manage timelines and budgets. And who had been busily honing and perfecting those exact skills while the blokes were out getting pissed? All those undervalued young women working away at their open-plan desks.

THE DEMISE OF old-style ad agencies has not been all upside, however. As Hornery laments, 'It's sad, because the old ad industry deserved to die, perhaps, but it was creative and fun.' Scott Nowell, founding partner of The Monkeys, looks back with a mixture of nostalgia and scepticism. 'When it felt like creative people were divining messages from God, you could get away with being an eccentric or an alcoholic.' Long-time advertising headhunter Esther Clerehan expresses it as the end of 'the smoke and mirrors – the dark arts of advertising'. Rocky Ranallo, creative director and founder of Western Sydney Ad School, says 'it used to be all about the ideas – now all clients care about is likes and shares'.

Alcoholic? Dark arts? Eccentric or not, the blokes at the Caxtons were right to fear the sudden influx of women. In hindsight, the female infiltration was part of the growing demystification around men and work. Perhaps that is one of the reasons so many men resisted the entry of women into previously male-dominated workplaces. Perhaps they could sense that it heralded much more than just increased competition. It was the beginning of a comprehensive change to the status and prestige previously afforded to the men in the grey flannel suits – or jeans and T-shirts. Forget glass ceilings, it was the sanctity and privilege of secret men's business at the office that was being shattered.

With that demystification went the glamour. Esther Clerehan says 'the craft of advertising [the typography, illustration and kerning I mentioned earlier] has been democratised by the computer'. Rocky Ranallo is blunt. 'The industry changed when Apple made the Apple Mac and it became really easy for the clients to make their own ads.' And this democratisation has spread much further than clients. 'We're all Kardashians now,' says Andrew Hornery, pointing out that anyone with a voice and a presence can build a brand thanks to social media.

No wonder so many were made uneasy by those first signs of change. And it was perhaps understandable (if inexcusable) that the so-called 'career' women in the '80s and '90s bore the brunt of that discomfort, because their arrival was easier to resist than changes in technology, and easier to blame.

Copywriter, now novelist, Kate Hunter had a boss who wanted her to type something for him urgently. When she told him apologetically that she was – as most copywriters are – a one-finger typist (and so not the right person to ask), he took affront. She recalls that he said, 'Come on, don't go all feminist on me. It's only a couple of pages' – as if the ability to type is something all women are born with, and she was being deliberately difficult by refusing to help him out. Marie Mansfield, art director, now award-winning artist, was expected to do the dishes after lunch, in rotation with the other office 'girls'. When she objected, she was told it was 'the dishes, or her job'. Art director, now bush regenerator, Pic Andrews remembers that every woman at her first agency, regardless of seniority, was expected to take a turn answering the phones. Roseanna Donovan, copywriter and creative director, was asked to give a speech for a large packaged-goods company about making their ads more 'female friendly'. When she suggested that having more women in senior roles, creating and approving such ads, might help, the conference descended into uproar. Her speech was cut short, and the company refused to pay her because she had not provided a checklist of 'how to write for women'.

Not all the blokes resisted, of course. Nancy Hartley found out she was paid much less than her male counterparts. She asked her boss about it and he not only upped her salary immediately but sent her off to a prestigious conference in New York. Nancy is one of the few women from the '90s who is still in the industry and has risen to the storied ranks of executive creative director.

However, the excesses of the old-style agency had been noticed – and not in a good way. Not only the sexism, but the lack of care in spending other people's money and the lazy and often unprofessional approach that false glamour and celebrity encouraged among the lucky and the talented. Unsurprisingly, this rankled with both the media and the advertisers who paid the bills. I remember one of the members of a creative department I worked in during the '80s who drove a Maserati (or something – I've never been one for cars, but it was flashy) being asked not to drive it to client meetings. It wasn't a good look, he was told.

Jonathan Kneebone and his partners, David Johnson and Gary Freedman, were of the new breed. They launched The Glue Society in the late '90s. 'I think our rule was to be anything but an agency,' he recalls. They also attracted an early client: Lachlan Murdoch, who perhaps had not been as madly impressed with the alcoholics and eccentrics he encountered on Mt Buffalo as expected. Somewhat ironically, he tasked The Glue Society with encouraging the advertising industry to lift its game creatively. He felt the ads that featured in News Corp's publications were, according to Kneebone, 'letting the quality of the papers down'. Perhaps we were all idealists once.

Kneebone speaks eloquently of the need for humility, not just in advertising but in all communication. He wonders if advertising lost its way when it began to believe that 'the purpose of advertising was to make a great ad, not to sell a client's product'.

Andrew Hornery points a finger at the rise of the mantra of accountability. He thinks the death knell of the glory days began when 'everything you produced could be measured by accountants'. If something went wrong, someone would be held to account. Understandably, everyone became more cautious. Liz Ainslie puts it this way: 'Swagger didn't cut it when marketing people became accountable. The old hustle of mates just stopped working.'

The problem with a fear-based workplace – and indeed world – is that caution and compliance are not compatible with creativity. Creativity searches for the things that have never been done before, on which, by definition, there is as yet no data. Scott Nowell argues that the obsession with data has made us lose faith in our own instincts, so it's not surprising that creativity is not valued the way it once was. And the source of creativity has shifted to the consumers themselves. 'Now that kids on TikTok are churning out stunning short videos, no wonder ad creatives are no longer rock stars,' says Esther Clerehan.

IT WAS A gorgeous day in February, only a few short weeks before Covid sent us all inside. A sizeable group of ageing ad guys had gathered for the annual 'Legends' lunch thrown by the trade magazine *Campaign Brief* at an Italian restaurant on the sparkling waterfront alongside the W Hotel in Sydney's Woolloomooloo. I was one of a handful of women who turned up. Maybe more had been invited but didn't show, or maybe chicks still don't quite qualify as advertising legends, I don't know.

As the much-older-than-I remembered faces (no doubt they thought the same about mine) swam into focus, it was both lovely and poignant to see so many of the old ad 'rock stars' in one place. Most of them, despite their bad habits, had aged rather well. They had mellowed and softened. Indeed a few

I remembered as outrageous misogynists back in the day were now at pains to convince me of their new-found feminism. We reminisced and bantered, but I was no longer in a lather of sweat trying to win the who-can-make-the-wittiest-remark competition that had so characterised lunches like this in the old days. There were no running jokes about lesbians. And, as far as I could tell, although copious bottles of chilled white wine were drunk, no one left the table to do a few lines of coke. A few of them still smoked cigarettes, of course, but now they had to do it not just outside but downwind. They weren't bad boys any longer. They were fathers and grandfathers, grateful for the fun they'd had and that they were still alive, despite their excesses.

We were all just legends in our own lunchtime that day, a bunch of old codgers waxing nostalgic for a world that no longer exists. But perhaps there is still room for the creativity and fun – without all the self-indulgent, sexist crap that went with it. After all, the ABC's smash hit show about advertising, *Gruen*, regularly attracts almost a million viewers nationally per episode. Those are the sorts of ratings that used to get old-style advertising media buyers and planners very excited. I guess you really know how much the world has changed when the only place ads can attract that many eyeballs these days is on the ABC.

Jane Caro AM was an award-winning advertising copywriter for thirty-five years. She also taught advertising at the University of Western Sydney for seven years and was a regular on the ABC's *Gruen*. Now she is a Walkley Award-winning columnist, novelist, non-fiction writer, social commentator and public education activist.

NON-FICTION

Nothing ever lasts

A more complete Australian story

Benjamin Law

IT WAS MORE than a decade ago now, but I still have vivid memories of my first Sydney Writers' Festival. I was in my twenties, and I'd arrived in Sydney as a wide-eyed debut author from the faraway exotic lands of… Queensland. And I was overwhelmed with gratitude, the kind of gratitude every first-time author feels at such an event: I was grateful to be published, grateful to be in the flashy capital of Sydney, and grateful to be programmed out of the hundreds of writers they could have picked instead.

That kind of gratitude is amplified when you're in the minority. I understood that Sydney Writers' Festival was for Important Authors, and if you'd asked me what an Important Author looked like at the time, I would've summoned a Franzen or a Eugenides, a Winton or a Flanagan – all iconic straight white men who I worshipped. But the festival organisers had picked me – some random Asian gay who grew up in the suburbs of the Sunshine Coast. Strolling in the sunshine by the wharves in a synthetic suit jacket, taking in the sun and salt air among all these relaxed white people who cared about books, it felt like I had made it.

As I walked to my first session, a cheery festival volunteer recognised and stopped me (me!).

'Welcome!' she said, beaming. 'How are you enjoying the Sydney Writers' Festival so far?'

'It's my first one!' I said, no cool whatsoever. 'I can't believe I'm here. I'm so happy.'

She clapped her hands together, delighted. 'Well, enjoy it while it lasts–'
'I will!'
'–because nothing ever does.'

I blinked, taken aback. In hindsight, I'm pretty sure she meant it as encouragement – a rousing call to arms to suck the marrow out of life while I was still young, et cetera – but at the time it felt like she was a prophet, possibly a witch, who had single-handedly cursed me to a future of professional doom.

I managed to croak out a *thank you* for her advice ('Any time!' she said) and slunk off to my first session with her words ringing in my ears. They continue to haunt me. Because, honestly, how much longer can this possibly last? When you're an anomaly – an outlier, a caveat – in your chosen industry, you already feel in your bones that it's only a matter of time before it's all over. The volunteer just confirmed it. *Enjoy it while it lasts.*

FAST FORWARD TO the lead-up to this year's Sydney Writers' Festival, and I was asked to give an opening-night keynote address alongside Bernardine Evaristo – the Booker Prize-winning author of *Girl, Woman, Other* – and Alexis Wright, the Miles Franklin-winning and Stella Prize-winning author of *Carpentaria* and *Tracker*. I was honoured; I was thrilled.

I immediately said no.

I know I'm a good writer, but I had no business being on stage alongside those two. I had too much respect for them, and too much self-respect, to say yes and risk shitting myself in front of a live audience.

But then, in a moment of weakness and vanity, I was ~~emotionally manipulated~~ persuaded by Festival Director Ann Mossop, and then I had to go through with it.

I'm not internationally acclaimed or lauded like Evaristo or Wright, but I felt the topic, on how the past affects the present, would be especially poignant with all of us there together, side by side – an Aboriginal woman, a Black British writer and an Asian-Australian writer – where only a mere decade earlier I had felt grateful to even have a single slot. We'd be accompanied with a performance by Madison Godfrey, a trans non-binary poet, and together it felt like we'd be forming some sort of diversity-and-inclusion Voltron on one of the biggest literary stages in the country. (The piece you're reading now is an adaptation of the speech I gave on the night.)

One thing that First Nations people, immigrants and their kids have in common is we think about the past constantly – and not only because we can hold grudges that are passed between generations. The stories of our lives are also defined by what-ifs. The places our ancestors left by choice or by force; the lives they escaped; the lives we could've led and live now instead. It's what makes us good writers, I think, this pondering over our histories and how they've brought us to this moment.

My past felt aggressively ordinary. I grew up in the sleepy suburbs of the Sunshine Coast. The place is synonymous with beautiful beaches, but my family lived next to an arterial road synonymous with car crashes. Instead of the sound of crashing waves, we went to sleep to the *blipping* of the pedestrian-crossing button. Our neighbourhood was also incredibly, disproportionately white. Looking back, I now realise that this closeted little Asian kid immersed in a sea of aggressively white heterosexual suburbia was constantly seeking out stories about people who were different, whether he was conscious of it or not.

When I wasn't glued to the TV watching SBS – for world movies, art-house films and full-frontal male nudity – I loitered at the newsagent reading British counterculture magazine *The Face*, or I was at the library borrowing Amy Tan novels, or I was at Bookworld looking for any book that would take me anywhere else. It's clichéd, but stories were my lifeline, and a reminder that other places and people existed. After a while, though, I didn't want to just read them. I wanted to be a participant. Admittedly, I also wanted attention.

I was a teenager when I had my first byline published. Email had just exploded – a new and novel technology – and I wrote to *Rolling Stone* magazine about the 1999 referendum on Australia becoming a republic. They declared it letter of the month. My prize: a Panasonic stereo. As one of five children who shared most things in our three-bedroom house, this was a huge deal, and I thought to myself, *Wow – writing pays really well*.

At university, I started writing for magazines. I didn't quite clock it then, but I was always the only non-white person in the office, or in the meetings, or in that month's issue. Editors would wonder aloud around me whether they could have Black, brown or Asian models on the cover, before deciding against it because *it felt tokenistic*. Or: 'We tried it once, but the issue just didn't sell.'

'Ah well,' I agreed. 'What a shame.' Servile. Compliant. Just grateful to be there.

By the time I scored myself a book deal, I was fuelled by the two conflicting emotions core to every writer: deep arrogance (keep in mind I was writing a memoir in my twenties) and crippling insecurity. When I submitted the manuscript, I was close to breaking out in hives from anxiety, having long internalised the sense my story didn't belong. Who was I kidding? A story about a gay Asian kid in coastal Queensland whose parents' marriage falls apart to the backdrop of the rise of Pauline Hanson's anti-Asian politics? Didn't exactly scream 'classic Australian story'. No farms. No surfing. No sheep.

What I didn't expect was how many people got the book immediately. Weirdly, you didn't have to be a multi-layered lasagne of minorities to connect with it. You just needed to be an outsider, which everyone – even straight white men – has been at least at one point in their lives. It's a lesson and paradox that I've held on to throughout my writing career: the more specific you get, often the more universal it becomes.

So yes, people did read *The Family Law*. And it was also made into a TV show that was seen across the world – on Comedy Central Asia, Hulu and even SBS. It was also pirated heavily – and inexplicably – in Jamaica, which I didn't know was a personal yardstick of success for me, but is the only yardstick I care about now.

IN CONCLUSION, THINGS have shifted, racism is solved and I have finally made it in this industry. Nowadays, I'm living the life every child from an immigrant background dreams of! And I know what those kids dream about. They go to bed every night thinking, 'One day, I hope to be a diversity-and-inclusion consultant.'

But for the entirety of my writing career, I've also led an unexpected parallel life where I speak in front of crowds, reeling off statistics about the Australian population: how one in five of us speaks a language other than English at home; how half of us have at least one parent born overseas; how more than one in ten of us have significant Asian ancestry, and yet our parliament, TV shows, media and arts don't reflect that – and don't even get me started on the critics who review the arts, et cetera and so on.

When I make these speeches, one of two things happens.

'Ah,' the ones who get it say. 'It is a bit shit, isn't it?'

And I agree.

And then they go away and think about how they might change things…eventually. Somehow.

Or: they get defensive. And I'm asked, 'What are you complaining about? You're doing well.' And any success I have is held up as evidence that it's all fine, even though any success I have is also still a statistical anomaly. And even I'm not immune to certain kinds of experiences – such as the one I had in a TV writers' room, ten years into working in that industry.

I'd recently finished working on *Wellmania* – the Netflix show I co-created, co-executive produced and co-wrote alongside Brigid Delaney and Celeste Barber – and I'd happily buried myself in that project, but I also felt excited to work on someone else's show and help their vision come to life. One of the people leading the room was a legend of Australian TV, known for creating, writing and producing such award-winning shows as [redacted], [redacted] and [redacted] – all I'll say is that if you've watched Australian TV in the past three decades, you've seen one of his productions.

And yes, the core writing team at this point had been uniformly middle-aged to senior, heterosexual, cisgender, able-bodied, middle-to-upper class and white, and nearly all men. It was clear the commissioning network must've insisted on some diversity, which explained the parachuted presence of me, an Aboriginal writer and an Italian-Australian colleague in the room.

It's almost the premise for a joke, really.

But I hate thinking of myself as the diversity hire. As I said, I've worked in the industry for over a decade. 'I belong in this room,' I told myself. I'm not a token – despite being called that so many times in my career that I've lost count. I've earned my place.

'Look,' the head writer said, addressing the newcomers on day one. 'I don't know who any of you are. I don't know your names. And by the end of the week, I still won't.'

We thought he was joking, so we laughed.

He was not joking.

Throughout the week, he talked over us, loudly and constantly. Never asked a single question. One character was Asian, and none of the core team even knew what kind of Asian they were, and ignored any attempt from me to help flesh out the character. And no, he didn't remember any of our names. If I'd led the room the way he did, I would've been fired.

As much as I'm annoyed, I'm not angry. Why should I be? After all, while things stay the same, they also change quickly. Both can be true. I'm now forty. I'm a godparent several times over. I'm an uncle several times over. I've got so many kids in my life who I care about fiercely. So these conversations are no longer simply academic to me. The stakes are personal.

My nephew Coen is three. His book explaining where babies come from doesn't just feature sperm and eggs from one dad and one mum. It also features adoption, surrogacy, cross-generational families, fostering, same-sex parents, disabled kids, disabled parents. He's learning about First Nations history, the history of Chinese people and other migrants. He's getting a more complete Australian story. Things are changing. And it turns out the Sydney Writers' Festival volunteer was right – nothing lasts forever.

Thank god for that.

This essay is adapted from a speech given at the opening night of the 2023 Sydney Writers' Festival.

Benjamin Law is the author of *The Family Law*, *Gaysia* and the *Quarterly Essay: Moral Panic 101*, and editor of *Growing Up Queer in Australia*. He's the co-executive producer, co-creator and co-writer of the Netflix comedy-drama *Wellmania*; creator and co-writer of three seasons of the award-winning TV series *The Family Law*; and author of the play *Torch the Place*. He hosts ABC Radio National's weekly national pop-culture show *Stop Everything*.

Kris Kneen

Cinema

I cry in the cinema
Or not cry
So hard that my head aches with the holding back
Not in the film
When those beside me weep
Manipulated by the stranglehold of act three turning-point catharsis
Or at the midpoint
When the protagonist learns
That he has been pursuing a false solution and must change his quest
Not at the deaths or at the terminally ill
Not I
Instead I cry
Before the opening credits
In the ad for a telephone company
Or an airline
Or a tablet
When the child calls his father
Or runs into his arms
Family the copywriter throws at us
And I, resentfully, shed tears
Reverting to my fatherless self
A child
Who never seemed to mind
Until
This celluloid manipulation
Ambushes me with canned sentiment
And a baby
Held up to a low-angle close-up
Of manufactured paternal love
In advance of the opening credits.

Kris Kneen is the author of ten works of fiction, non-fiction and poetry. Their poetry collection *Eating My Grandmother* (UQP, 2015) won the Thomas Shapcott Award and their latest book is *Fat Girl Dancing* (Text, 2023).

NON-FICTION

Glitter and guts

Interrogating the truth of the past

Sharlene Allsopp

RIGHT NOW, I am obsessed with the past. My debut novel is finished and ready for publication, and I am wrestling with the fear and insecurity that comes with writing a second. To alleviate the anxiety of unknown plot points, unfamiliar characters and structure problems, I've sought refuge in the past, in the familiar. I watch and rewatch beloved time-travel movies. I read and re-read dearly loved books that transport me to a previous version of myself. Sometimes I roll my eyes at the person I was. Sometimes I weep. But always I return to the past to understand my present.

A few years ago I read *Kindred* by Octavia Butler for the first time. Written in 1979, when I was six years old, it tells the story of a Black American woman who travels through time against her will. Its voice is seamless, its form, style and prose the perfect template for any novel writer, but it is the revelation of the plot that stays with me. The truth that there is no time in all of history when it is safe to be a Black woman.

The entanglement of time, race, gender, equity, consent and power has always informed my work, but *Kindred* gave me a clarity that I did not have before, because my skin is not the same colour as my mother's. It took a long time for me to see clearly, because I can hide behind a cloak of whiteness any time I choose. For protagonist Dana, the past informs her present and her future. When she is in the future, the past is always controlling her present. There is no neat division. The past is not a foreign country.

Interstellar is a sci-fi movie that polarised reviewers and critics, but it so bewitched me that I am tempted to use a person's response to it as a judge of their character. Time is relentless. No matter who we are and what we do, time *will* have its way with us. And yet, *Interstellar* beautifully illustrates that time is a messy spiral, not a straight line. In this endless circle/spiral, a bookcase functions as a portal, connecting Murph and her dad, Cooper, across time.

A few years ago when I found a collection of words in a digital online archive, I felt like my great-grandfather had reached through time and connected with me, just like Cooper does with Murph. Soon after that, I found a book that transported me back in time to World War I – the context of my great-grandfather's life. The book masquerades as history, but it's mostly fiction. It opens, 'This Short History of Australia begins with a blank space on the map.' Partway through it states unequivocally, 'The federation of the United States of America was born of revolutionary warfare…but there were no such impulsions in Australia. The country had never known war. It was safe from outside aggression… It had never endured rebellion.' Utter fabrication elevated to the genre of truth because it was written by a professor of history at the University of Melbourne.

This book took me back in time without my consent. I kept snapping the covers closed to shut this professor up, but then I had to continue because I needed to know what other lies he was telling. I needed to know why Australia thinks the way it does. This country's story of its own past is the greatest evidence on Earth that nations can manufacture a fantasy and call it history. This is how the past intrudes upon the present and becomes vulnerable to dangerous re-imaginings.

IN 2013 MY husband and I travelled to France for my first, and only, time. I designed my entire Paris itinerary around another time-travel movie: *Midnight in Paris*. There is something alluring about the lost generation post-World War I – think Hemingway, Fitzgerald, Stein – and its rejection of materialism, and disillusionment with capitalism, that grips me. And the hypocrisy of the indulgence and privilege it takes to do such rejecting grips me equally. Because nostalgia is always selective in its remembering. It memorialises the best and erases the worst – however we seek to define those qualifiers.

I laugh as I type this because that trip was an exercise in nostalgia. I spent my youth constructing a mythology that I called France. When I finally travelled there, I chased a fantasy. I sought to gaze upon Monet's *Waterlilies* painted in every shade. To run through fields of scarlet poppies singing Edith Piaf songs at the top of my lungs. To plunge into shallow Mediterranean waters with 'La Mer' ringing out from some random balcony. That girl, that past version of me, came and she conquered. Like many beauty seekers before her, she kept her France skin-deep and left none the wiser. Her fairytale posture was as distorted as all those reflections strung out like a funhouse mirror in that iconic hall in the Palace of Versailles.

Until I discovered my great-grandfather's war record, I had no idea that a member of our family had travelled to France before me. I had never seen a Black or brown face in any of the Anzac propaganda. I didn't know that he had spilled so much blood in that country. I had sought the romantic past in a foreign land because I thought that place held no grief for me. I could examine France's failures and celebrate her beauty with zero skin in the game. Until the day I discovered I not only had skin in the game, but blood in the soil. Is there any place on Earth where beauty isn't cultivated with blood?

All those years I had been excluded from the Anzac narrative because the Defence Act had outlawed Black enlistment. *Lest we forget* morphs into satire when you uncover the depths of collective amnesia surrounding Black service in World War I and Black resistance since colonisation. The more accurate catchphrase would be *Best we forget*. How can we be 'one' when we are not allowed to remember equally? Nostalgia is selective about remembrance.

Yet, even now, knowing what I know, I ache to return to *her*, to the *me* that I was in Paris. I want to see France with those eyes again, just for a short time. I want to remind myself of who I was and who I can still be if I tell that version of myself new stories and imagine alternative futures. I want to say to her, *You will survive what's coming and you might even learn to thrive.*

BACK IN 2013, on our first crisp Paris morning, the first icon I recognised was an imposing gothic spire, rising up out of the rooflines ahead of us as we walked towards the Seine. I grabbed Rick's arm and told him what we were looking at – the very tallest tip of Notre-Dame, 800 years old. In 2019, six years later, that glorious spire with its jagged, prickly beauty and that roof with its arched timber beams burned to the ground. At first, I was devastated.

She had stood through great storms of history and hosted millions of people, all with their own agendas and stories and proclamations and heraldry. She had soaked up innumerable prayers and groans. She had seen all manner of hypocrisy and evil. But as I watched billions of dollars of donations pour in to restore a stone and wood cathedral, the veil of nostalgia was ripped violently from my eyes.

As Notre-Dame burned, I spent the day with an extraordinary fourteen-year-old boy named M——. He is from Iran and he is bright and confident and opinionated. He *loves* soccer. He is handsome. And he has been imprisoned by our country for a third of his life. Upon leaving Nauru after five years, he had a curfew every night and his family was not allowed to work. When they were eventually given a bridging visa, they were kicked out of their accommodation, with no rental or work history, and had to reapply for that visa every six months or be deported back to Iran. He has suffered loss that I cannot imagine and yet his heart is open and his face full of light.

Can you imagine choosing to spend billions on restoring a cathedral and not on living, breathing humans? It is unfathomable that an 800-year-old building is more valuable than a beautiful fourteen-year-old boy. No one is raising their hand to restore his present and future. *It's complicated*. It wouldn't be complicated if he was yours. The past is not a foreign country; it is alive, right here, right now.

I have two beautiful boys of my own. I would die for them. It's much harder to live for them. To die for them requires a split second of instinctive protection. To live for them requires a daily/yearly mundane choice to love, provide, teach, disagree, pay, protect, cry, connect, drive, listen – you get the picture.

In the time-travel movie *About Time,* Tim Lake has a magical power. He can get into a dark wardrobe, clench his fists and time travel to any point in his past. This movie is my favourite because of where Tim chooses to travel. He always revisits the everyday, mundane moments spent with the people he loves. Tim knows that it is not the extraordinary moments that matter the most in life. Notre-Dame v his sister? His sister wins.

This is what frightens me about where we are right now in Australia's history: the lies of the past still have too much power in our present. The ideology of colonisation insists that Western cathedrals matter more than living, breathing humans. And some humans matter more than others.

As I write this, we are weeks away from the 2023 referendum – a question posed to a nation asking us to change the constitution. I ache for the Blakfullas who want to vote No because they contest the very authority of that document. I ache for those who want to vote No because they refuse to cede their sovereignty to a document that props up a system designed to dispossess and destroy them. I agree with those who want to vote No because they believe that change of this magnitude will never come from political parties. But there is no part of me that can vote No and admit even a glimmer of agreement with the liars who have done what all colonisers do – gaslight a nation into believing that the truth-tellers are the liars.

The lies that have been told in the lead-up to the referendum make me want to flee to a foreign country where my heart isn't squeezed so tight that I think I might die. Where my intellect isn't so insulted that I think my brain might explode from the depth of casual cruelty that I see in public forums. No, I am obfuscating now. What I really want to flee from is the terrifying possibility that these liars know the truth and continue to actively cultivate a false version of the past.

How did we get here? Only the past can tell us that. How can we change this place that we are in? Only through action in the present.

AND HERE IS where my problematic relationship with nostalgia collides with the current moment: whales. Stay with me.

I just returned from a week in Cavanbah – Byron Bay – celebrating my thirtieth wedding anniversary back on home Country where my hubby and I first met, fell in love, got married. Where I had my first holiday without my parents at seventeen.

What a submersion in memory Rick and I had. Every day I lay on my favourite sand in the world – Wategos Beach. And every day we saw many, many whales. Far away, close-up, flukes, flippers, noses, adults, babies. When I was seventeen these whales were exotic, majestic, all shiny skin and performative aerobatics. They took my breath away with their size and grace. In them, I saw the glossy hull of my own life surging effortlessly forth into a shiny future full of goodness and glory. I expected no blood and no guts.

When Rick and I first stood on a Bundjalung beach together our future stretched out ahead of us brimming with hope and possibility, glistening bright like it was dipped in glitter. Thirty years on, some of that future has become our past, and it has been glitter and guts, both. Now, I see more than shimmering dancing whale skin. I see all the blood and guts hidden below our blubbery surface. I see the cost of our life together. The lie of nostalgia is that it seduces us into remembering the glitter without the guts.

Rick is my greatest anchor to the past and the future. As Dr Amelia Brand reminds us in *Interstellar*, 'Love is the one thing we're capable of perceiving that transcends dimensions of time and space. Maybe we should trust that, even if we can't understand it.' Maybe love insists on rejecting half-truths and embracing full truths. Maybe the best definition of love is that we see the whole whale, not just the pretty parts. That's a present I can embrace. In it, I get to sit there on Wategos, my home Country, and raise my beautiful boys and girls in the belly of the whale. If we don't stink of whale guts – the complete truth of our history – then we have no hope to create a different future.

It's easy to long for simpler times – for ignorance. But in the words of my novel's protagonist, Scarlet Friday, 'the times were never actually simple. We were. The world wasn't shiny and new; we were. I hadn't been inside the whale's belly back then. I was ignorant. When I say they were simpler times, what I am really saying is that I yearn for who I was back then, the way I thought the world was.'

In the movie *Arrival* the protagonist Louise Banks tells us, 'I'm not so sure that I believe in beginnings and ends.' The alien language that she encounters is circular, therefore the way that time is presented in the movie is circular. I do not want to spoil *Arrival* for you, as it is one of the greatest movies of all time, so skip to the next paragraph if you want to keep its magic concealed. It isn't until the end that we realise that the viewer – you/me – is the time traveller in this story. The alien beings can see all of time and so they live outside of it. They can communicate with Louise in such a way that the past and the future are all affecting her in the viewer's now.

This present me looks back to past me. What would my future self say to my present self? What will future Australia say to present Australia? What could we create if we owned the guts *and* the glitter of this country?

Arrival is the movie that best illustrates my worldview: that I am a time traveller. I am formed by those who came before me and those who come after me, my ancestors and my descendants. My present inherits the past, my present gifts to the future. And it is not a neat, linear story. The day I discovered my great-grandfather's online war record, I forged a connection with him through time, like Murph and Cooper in *Interstellar*. And just as that link to my past has shaped my own future, I dream of an Australia informed by the past and enacted in the present – one that owns the truth of us all.

Sharlene Allsopp was born and raised on unceded Bundjalung Country into the Olive mob. She was a 2020–21 fellow in The Wheeler Centre's Next Chapter program. Her work has been published widely, including in *Jacaranda Journal*, *Portside Review* and *Aniko Press*. Her debut novel, *The Great Undoing*, is published by Ultimo Press.

IN CONVERSATION

Escaping the frame

Writing the story of the spider

Witi Ihimaera and Winnie Dunn

When Witi Ihimaera was young, he realised that Māori people and stories were mostly invisible in the books he was reading at his New Zealand high school. In the decades since, he's celebrated his culture and its rich history and literary traditions through his award-winning short stories, novels, memoirs, libretti and more. Today, he's one of New Zealand's most important and accomplished writers, and his work has resonated with audiences across the globe. His best-known book, the 1987 novel The Whale Rider, *was adapted into an Oscar-nominated film in 2002.*

In this intergenerational dialogue – which took place at the Brisbane Writers Festival in May 2023 and has been lightly edited and condensed – Ihimaera talks to Tongan-Australian writer Winnie Dunn about writing as an act of reclamation and recognition.

WINNIE DUNN: I want to share with the audience how humbling, fundamental and special this moment is for me as an emerging Pasifika writer: Witi, tulou. I'm completely honoured to be interviewing you on your life, work and legacy; your literature changed my life as a young Tongan reader/viewer. In a world where Chris Lilley and *Once Were Warriors* were my mainstream, *Whale Rider* showed me the strength and beauty of Indigenous Pacific girls, women and men. My five sisters and I, along with my two brothers – yes, that's eight of us little Islanders – owe you a lot of our laughs and tears when we watched *Whale Rider* while lounging in a bundle of blankets on our living-room floor. What called you to writing?

WITI IHIMAERA: When I was a boy in the 1940s I was brought up by many grandmothers. One of them was Teria, who was waiting for me when the bus dropped me back home in my village of Waituhi after my first day at school. 'So, what great wisdom did the Pākehā teach you today?' she asked. I answered, 'I learnt a nursery rhyme, Gran, about a boy called Jack and a girl named Jill.'

Although I was thrilled with my new knowledge, Teria frowned when I recited the rhyme to her. 'Who are Jack and Jill?' she asked. 'Why aren't they called Māori names, like Iwi and Hera? Why is Jack wearing a crown? It's his own fault if he falls down and breaks it – and where's Jill's crown?' And then she asked a killer question: 'And why are they going up a hill to fetch water? What a stupid place to put a well!'

So, from a very early age, Winnie, Teria taught me that I was going to be walking into a white world where people had different names to ours; they also had bad gender models, and actually it would be a world where they built wells on hills and nothing would make sense.

On my second day back from school, there was Teria again to ask about my new wisdom. 'I learnt about a girl called Little Miss Muffet,' I answered.

Oh no, Teria started to interrogate this rhyme too! 'Who is Miss Muffet? Why can't she be called Miss Matapihi? What's a tuffet? What are curds and whey?' And then Gran asked her usual killer question: 'And why was the little girl frightened of a spider? Why didn't she say "Kia ora!" to it and put it out of harm's way?'

So, again, my gran was telling me not to take anything for granted in the new world waiting for me – to always question everything about it because it had different value systems, which were in fact anathemic and hostile to ours. For instance, if I re-gender the second nursery rhyme, it would read: 'Little Master Muffet sat on his tuffet eating his curds and whey / Along came a spider and sat down beside him and…' What would Little Master Muffet have done, do you think? Yes, squashed it!

Therefore, to answer your question, Winnie, you could say that Teria called me to writing when I was five by showing me that the predominant patriarchal structure of my world would need to be aggressively critiqued for the rest of my life and that the sovereign position of Indigenous people in it had to be protected.

I chose to do this by becoming a writer; others became politicians, educationalists or activists. Every book I write has been an attempt to establish a decolonisation process. To become a humanitarian. To be environmentally conscious. In metaphorical terms, you could say that I have been writing the story of the spider.

WD: What was it like writing, and finding publishers, in early '70s New Zealand when no novels written by Māori people existed?

WI: I always knew I wanted to be a novelist but the novel at the time was mainly a Western European construct. After village school, I went to a number of high schools where I managed to become a good English student but with mainly C passes. And then it took me nine years to get a very bad Bachelor of Arts – again with C-pass averages. My father sent me a telegram when I graduated university that read: *Congratulations stop. About time stop. Even the tortoise didn't take this long stop.*

Nevertheless, by the time I was twenty-seven I had actually written a short-story collection, *Pounamu Pounamu*, and two novels, *Tangi* and *Whānau*. Three publishers rejected my work, the third because 'Māori don't read books.' Ironically I found myself having to create a readership among Pākehā, where the country's bicultural aspirations worked in my favour.

Three years later, however, I realised that I would have to become a literary activist in order to further create the circumstances for the growth of Māori writing. One of the ways I did this was by becoming an anthologist of Māori writing, and sometimes I think creating those sixteen anthologies over the past forty years has been more important than my own writing. I also placed myself strategically in the 1970s at points where Māori arts organisations could possibly be developed. I became the first Māori member of the newly formed Arts Council, and created a Māori Arts Council and added a Pacific component to it, both with their own funding.

All my work as a writer and activist over the last fifty years has comprised various attempts at what I call 'escaping the frame of European colonisation, European story and European ways of telling story'. I've served on organisations like the New Zealand Film Commission and Learning Media, and today, for instance, am president of honour of the New Zealand Society of Authors and patron of the 100 books in the Māori language trust. Latterly I have reframed myself as an international Indigenous writer, walking the talk as well as writing it, this year going to French Polynesia and Australia, and soon to Sweden, Finland and Germany. I will paddle my waka to Canada and the US to meet up with First Nations, Inuit and Coastal Salish artisans to share our stories as Indigenous peoples at risk in a world where we are politically, economically and culturally disempowered.

WD: Your first novel, *Tangi*, is a poetic drama in prose about a young man and his father. It is an account of death but also an affirmation of life – of aroha. Firstly, I love the title because 'tangi' means 'cry' in Tongan. Secondly, what does having a newly revised version fifty years later mean?

WI: You know, Winnie, when I think about the subject of *Tangi*, it is so far away from my very first effort at writing when I was ten, which goes something like this: 'Once upon a time there was a princess locked in a tall tower guarded by a fierce dragon. Every day she would go to the window and see a handsome prince ride past on a white horse and cry out: "Help me! Help me! Save me from this dragon!" But because she was so ugly, the princes on their white horses would take one look at her, go "Yuck!" and keep on riding to rescue a more beautiful princess further down the road. Day after day this would happen until one day, she got so sick and tired of waiting she went out and married the dragon.'

Interesting things are happening in this story. Everything is being subverted. The princess is ugly. The princes may be handsome but they are not chivalrous. The tall tower is representative of Pākehā culture. When the princess marries the dragon, she rejects everything that culture has to offer; in metaphorical terms, she embraces the land of danger.

Clearly there was a lot of imaginative and aesthetic growth required between being ten and being twenty-seven! And much later I realised that my dragon story was really about a taniwha, its Māori equivalent.

Tangi turned out to be another attempt to 'escape the frame' – this time, of the European novel. A twenty-two-year-old young man who has left his rural village and gone to Wellington receives a message that his father has died. He returns to Waituhi for the funeral, and the reader goes with him into a Māori world where there's not a white person in sight. A world informed by what we call kaupapa (purpose), tikanga (the Māori way of doing things), ihi (energy), mana (distinction), wehi (spiritual dread) and, in particular, wero (deep emotional and intellectual engagement).

Writing *Tangi* I came to regard the Western European novel as an alien construct, a horrible syllabic non-singing arsehole of a thing, usually linear, with a beginning, middle and end. And English was such a profane language lacking in sacredness. *Tangi* was my first attempt at destabilising those tendencies. I must admit, I probably substituted the Pākehā alien construct with another one, but where *Tangi* triumphed was that it was a spontaneous text. It's the writing of a young man who doesn't know much of the craft, but his Māori voice hasn't been tampered with by his university training and it isn't trying to mimic anybody else. It's full-throated and innocent just like he once was.

By contrast, the fiftieth-anniversary edition is the work of the mature Ihimaera. Indeed I have a habit of rewriting my work: there are two versions of *Pounamu Pounamu*; the 2023 *Tangi* will be the third edition; there's *Whānau* and *Whānau II*; *The Matriarch* has a redux edition; three of *The Whale Rider*; and so on. I don't believe that literature should be static. Story, as far as Māori literature is concerned, is always fluid. Personally, I am always seeking the perfect sentence.

And Māori politics has changed a lot since the 1970s, so the new *Tangi* is a more political text. It addresses Treaty of Waitangi issues kanohi ki te kanohi in a way the first aesthetic text couldn't within a colonised publisher context. It deploys more Māori language, now that the same industry has become not only bicultural but also bilingual. And of course there are all my ancestors scraping my skull out: 'Work faster, Witi. Go faster. Push, stretch, reach.'

Actually, the famous French writer Marcel Proust said it for my relationships with my ancestors with his words from *The Captive & The Fugitive* (*In Search of Lost Time, Volume V*). 'When we have passed a certain age, the soul of the child we were and the souls of the dead from whom we have sprung come to lavish on us their riches and their spells.'

WD: You're marking your fiftieth anniversary as a writer with your short-story collection, *Pounamu Pounamu*, too. It was your first publication, a year earlier than *Tangi*, and I am interested to know what is different, craft-wise, between a novel and a short-story collection. How did the short story inform your longer works of fiction?

WI: *Pounamu Pounamu* was a fulfilled childhood vow. When I was fifteen, in 1959, our class was given a book of New Zealand literary classics. One about Māori was written by a white author that demonised and misrepresented us as savages, dirty and unsanitary. I had a revelatory moment similar to Black African writer Chinua Achebe, who upon reading a similar English text about his culture realised: 'Although fiction was undoubtedly fictitious, it could also be true or false.' I threw the book out the window and was caned for mistreating the property of the Education Department. I vowed that I would write a book about Māori and that it would enter the education system where every schoolkid would have to read it whether they wanted to or not.

Pounamu Pounamu is still crucial to my process. I call it my greenprint: my origin-stone or runestone, the source for *Tangi*, *Bulibasha*, *Whanau*, *The Rope of Man* and of course *The Whale Rider*. If ever my voice starts to sound too learned, artificial, academic or tricky, I follow *Pounamu Pounamu* back to the original source of my river of words.

As for the novels, they are structured according to what I call the 'Indigenous time frame'. They follow the seasons from summer when everything is happy, through autumn where the story darkens, into winter and a crisis or tragedy. Redemption or resolution comes with the radiance and rebirth of spring.

My works have their basis in what is known as 'urtext' – the ancient mythology that assures the umbilical to the Māori not Pākehā world. And they pay due attention to pre-text, intertext, subtext, context, parallel text – all to create, hopefully, the psychic text that will subvert that horrible alien English form. In the Māori novel, what is unseen is as important as the seen, and the unwritten as important as the written.

WD: Being one of the most important and recognised writers in the Southern Hemisphere, you've also written two memoirs, *Māori Boy* and *Native Son*. The first covers your childhood and the second the writer's life. Why separate the two? Is the journey from childhood to writer distinct in that way?

WI: I still have a third to write, *Indigenous Elder*, so there's a clear progression to it from *Māori Boy* and *Native Son*. I actually think of the three books as providing the excuse for me to, again, write not about myself but about everyone else and everything else. They parallel my work as an anthologist, which is also not about me but about the other Māori writers whom I share 'writing the tribe' with. The memoirs simply use the form to similarly witness our times so that people will know who we were and are – that during the turbulent years of colonialism we fought for and claimed our sovereignty.

I separated the first two memoirs because there were separate scores to settle with myself. The first, in *Native Son*, details the trauma that happened to me when, at twelve, I was raped by a relative. The second, *Māori Boy*, carries on the thread – I actually tried to commit suicide – and adds a surprising, dark dimension to it. The third, *Indigenous Elder*, will detail how I left my marriage and two daughters to live with another man. I shall turn my unflinching eye on the dissolution of a marriage and coming out. I will not be easy on myself; in fact, I harboured a lot of self-hatred. But I owe it to the boy I once was to acknowledge him. He deserves the radiance of resolution.

I have always remembered something Albert Camus said: 'In the midst of a dark winter, I found within myself an indomitable summer.' I have continued to reach down into myself to find that indomitable light.

WD: As an emerging writer, I'm constantly learning new terms, theories and concepts. *The Whale Rider* is described as an antipodean classic. Firstly, what is an antipodean classic? And do you agree with that categorisation?

WI: I guess *The Whale Rider* is an antipodean classic because of its Pacific setting. Its urtext takes us into Pacific history with its story of Kahutia-te-rangi, the original whale rider. The book begins in Tierra del Fuego, Chile, and chapters encompass Easter Island, Hawaii, Australia, Papua New Guinea and Antarctica as well as New Zealand, so its context is certainly antipodean in scope. It has an intertext involving the relationship between humankind and cetaceans and thus a very strong environmental subtext concerning the survival of the natural world.

At heart *The Whale Rider* is a story involving the intertwining genealogies of many times, spaces and species. I like to think that although it is a contemporary story about a young girl living in a Māori village nobody ever heard of, the book has actually transcended its antipodean locations and become universal. It's taught in schools and universities around the world, and it became a set text in the Kenyan education system. Kahu is now a heroine like Heidi.

WD: *The Whale Rider* was adapted into a film that grossed $41 million worldwide and received numerous accolades. It was also the catalyst for Keisha Castle-Hughes, who played the protagonist, to be the youngest person ever nominated for the Academy Award for Best Actress. Why do you think the story of Kahu, deeply set in her culture and home of East Coast New Zealand, was received so earnestly across the globe?

WI: Luck had a lot to do with that! Film critic B Ruby Rich was on the selection committee for films at the Toronto Film Festival in 2002. She took *Whale Rider* from the bottom of her pile and put it on the top. You know, it wasn't produced for that much money, around NZ$5 million, and it was shot on location in Whāngārā, which gave it an authenticity of place. You stepped through the frame right onto the beach.

Keisha Castle-Hughes' performance was so pure and innocent and so was Niki Caro's direction. I think that was one of the reasons why the film connected across the globe and, well, in the process Keisha became Moby Chick. She showed that no matter where you come from, with vision and courage you can do anything. And of course, the film wasn't only about a young girl fighting against patriarchy. It was also the story of Nanny Flowers, of women within patriarchal society. About first sons too. And second sons.

WD: You've also written plays! Namely the 2000 script, *Woman Far Walking*, in which Tiri Mahana is turning 160 years old and waiting for her royal confirmation letter of age from the Queen of England. What can theatre and – an extension of my previous question – film do that the bounded written word can't?

WI: That play was inspired by my mother, Julia. We were watching a woman on television who was receiving a congratulatory telegram from the Queen and my mother said, 'If I received a telegram from the Queen, I would spit on it.' I'm sorry if that offends some people but I am talking about Māori, who at the time had little love for a monarchy that had taken away their land.

In my opinion, theatre is where you get the closest to replicating Māori culture. Not through a book, which is a read experience, or film and television – viewed experiences, or aurally through radio, which is a heard experience. The spontaneity of the stage and its ability for actors to perform in front of you is like being back on the marae.

Last week, I was at the opening of another, different, play about my work but written by Nancy Brunning, called *Witi's Wāhine*. It creates a kaleidoscope of anger, passion, fun, tragedy but always the Māori story – irradiated with hope for a better and inclusive world.

WD: I want to read some passages from your most recent collection on Māori creation myths. My favourites are: 'Some believe that at the beginning there was nothing. Others, when considering our ancient origins, reckon existence began with darkness. Imagine the darkest darkness, and it was darker than that. They saw a daily reminder of the fabulous odyssey of humankind in the way that night gave way to day: a progression from darkness to the incredible moment when the sun brought light and warmth. And then there were those who said that a god created everything.'

And: 'Our ancestors were never afraid to seek taonga (treasure, anything prized) for the benefit of humankind. They would go to the ends of the Earth – even the stars if they had to!'

What drew you back to the old stories? Are they 'myths', in how we understand mythology in a Western sense? Or something else?

WI: Some of my cuzzie bros and whanaunga from across the ditch are here today. They know more about some Māori traditions than I do. For instance, my haka skills are tragic, and when I was a young skinny boy I was always in the back row. When they put their hands up, I put mine up. When they put them down, so did I. When they said 'Hii!' I followed. When they said, 'Haa!' all good. Trouble was that one night, one of the boys was sick so Uncle Pita said, 'Witi, go to the front.' Me? What was he thinking? I totally messed up. When the boys moved to the left, I moved to the right. When they said, 'Hii!' I went, 'Haa!' They moved forward, I moved backward. I brought an entire kapa-haka team crashing to its knees.

The point of this story is that there are some things my cuzzies (and others) do better than I can. At the same time there are things they can't do that I can, so we balance ourselves out. For instance I am able to offer them their past, a long line of ancestors stretching all the way back to the beginning of time with whom we have an implicit contract.

Thus, writing the old stories for a new generation is an important part of my kaupapa or commitment. The stories were first written into English by missionaries or settlers, whose views of Māori were sanitised or malevolent. Often the retellings lacked our original intelligence, wisdom and science. In *Navigating the Stars* I tried to put them back into the original firmament, because they are as amazing and as mind-blowing as any Greek epic. There's a scene in the movie *Clash of the Titans* where Zeus commands a cephalopod monster be let loose on the city of Joppa: 'Release the kraken!' I am saying the same thing in Māori: 'Wetewete te wheke! Release the taniwha of our old knowledge so that we can begin to remake our universe!'

WD: You were awarded the prestigious Chevalier des Arts et des Lettres for services to Indigenous literature. Congratulations! Your other accolades include the Prime Minister's Award for Literary Achievement, an honorary doctorate from the University of Wellington and a Distinguished Companion of the New Zealand Order of Merit for services to literature. You are rightly recognised as one of the world's leading Indigenous writers. What is the importance of Indigenous literature, especially when we consider almost all Indigenous cultures are traditionally oral storytellers?

WI: My particular compulsion to tell the Indigenous story comes, of course, from Gran Teria. In many ways, she is my Sycorax, the Indigenous matriarch William Shakespeare refers to in *The Tempest*.

You're going to have to trust me when I tell you that Indigenous knowledge has the capacity to save the planet. It will do this by providing kaupapa (correct purpose), by training everyone in tikanga (appropriate practice), by applying the concepts of whanaungatanga (family), manaakitanga (collective action) and aroha ki te iwi me te whenua, me te moana, me te rangi (holistic purpose).

WD: Now, we are on the lands of the Yuggera people and the Turrbal people, and I come from the lands of the Durag people, which is known as Western Sydney. Clearly, we have connections to this complicated continent by just sitting here today. Australia, in comparison to New Zealand, is severely lacking in Pasifika literature. Why do you think that is? And what can Australia do in order to catch up?

WI: You remind me, Winnie, that Māori, Pasifika and Aboriginal peoples share the same connections. I join you in acknowledging and paying my respects to the traditional custodians of the land upon which we stand, the Yuggera people and the Turrbal people, to Elders past, present and emerging.

I think Australia knows it has an Aboriginal identity – aren't you having a referendum soon acknowledging this history? – and Pacific roots but still has to create strategic pathways for both that will truly lead to an inclusive antipodean culture.

For my part, Aboriginal – and Pasifika – artists and writers have long been an inspiration to me. I lived in Canberra for three years from 1976 to 1979. I knew the luminous Oodgeroo Noonuccal, taught Ruby Langford Ginibi's work when I was a professor, and met up with Roberta Sykes in Kings Cross. I know Marcia Langton and Anita Heiss, and I included Aboriginal novelist Alexis Wright in one of my Pacific anthologies. Aboriginal writers like Melissa Lucashenko and Ali Cobby Eckermann are revered in Aotearoa.

I have a proud memory of my Māori friend Teremoana Sparks picking me up in Canberra one night and taking me to join Aboriginal activists in 1979 protesting the raising of your parliament buildings on sacred Aboriginal land. Sovereignty was never ceded in New Zealand; nor was it here. This was and always will be Aboriginal land.

Witi Ihimaera is an Aotearoan writer of Māori descent. He celebrates his fiftieth anniversary as a writer with a newly revised version of *Tangi*, the first novel published by a Māori person. His most successful novel, *The Whale Rider*, is the most translated novel in New Zealand. He has many national and international awards, including a Chevalier des Arts et des Lettres for services to Indigenous literature.

Winnie Dunn is a writer of Tongan descent from Mount Druitt, Western Sydney. She is the general manager of Sweatshop Literacy Movement. Her work has been published in *Meanjin*, *The Guardian* and *Sydney Review of Books*. She is also the editor of several critically acclaimed anthologies, most notably *Another Australia* (Affirm Press, 2022). She was the recipient of a 2023 Australia Council for the Arts grant. *Dirt Poor Islanders* (Hachette) is her debut novel.

FICTION

The green gold grassy hills
Fiona Kelly McGregor

I DROVE UP to the house at the end of the day. I had been there once before but barely remembered it. Unusually for a farm, there were no vehicles parked outside: Bernice hadn't been able to drive for years. She emerged onto the porch in her wheelchair, wearing a long red-and-yellow dress.

I greeted her cheerfully and asked how she was.

'Oh you know, a mess.' She squinted at me in the late sun, pulling up her hem. 'See?'

Her calves were thin shanks, her feet swollen and twisted at odd angles; every toe was stubbed. There were bruises and abrasions all the way up her legs. Yet her arms and face were tanned and smooth, her teeth shiny white, her hair still dark. I, two years younger, was completely grey.

I had been warned; I had read the articles, been informed by a mutual friend. Still, I was shocked. We hadn't seen each other in twenty years. The Bernice I had known had been watchful, quiet, confident yet awkward. Now she was sullen, brusque and weary.

'I bang myself all the time,' she announced. 'But I don't feel a thing.'

'I'm so sorry.'

'It doesn't matter. You can't do anything. Come in.'

She could still turn the wheels of her chair with those withered hands, also bruised and grazed. Her beautiful long hands gripping the steering wheel on the coast road, cupping my face, slipping inside me. The wheelchair caught on the runner and Bernice jerked sideways, bashing her left foot into the door. I put down my bag and steered her through.

The house was open plan, built from recycled timber. A miner's couch in one corner, a large table covered in magazines, books, a cardigan, gardening gloves, pliers. Dirty cups, packets of seeds. The kitchen annex was clean. I brought in my groceries and began to prepare the agreed-upon vegetable curry.

Bernice had a carer who came every day to help her wash, get her meals, keep the place clean. She was able to lift herself out of the chair and 'sort of fling myself' onto the bed, or shift across to the toilet commode. One of her sisters and her father visited; an old friend came from town to look after the horses. Nobody else. 'I don't want to see people,' she said. 'I don't really have anything more to say.'

I guessed then that I was lucky to have made it through. I'd missed her fiftieth birthday party the year before due to the usual restrictions of time and money. But as I stood at the window scrubbing vegetables, I wondered what had been so important that I hadn't been able to make an exception for someone to whom a year could be a lifetime. Under-eights soccer game? Kids' sleepover? But my partner could have done that on their own, couldn't they? *Please babe, I just need you to be there*, they'd said when I'd missed one of the kids' concerts. Maybe there'd been nothing more important than standing at my own kitchen window scrubbing vegetables, just like now, but looking out to the wall of the house next door instead of down a long sloping yard and across paddocks to the hills I'd driven through to get here, burnished with late sun. A phrase from a story Bernice had written about us came to me. *The green gold grassy hills, shivering in the wind...* As I watched, a black horse ambled up from the paddock and began to rub its long muscular neck on the fence.

'You nearly killed me on your horse, remember?' I called. 'You put me on the stallion and sent us down the paddock, then as soon as he turned back to the house *BAM*, he bolted! I hung on literally for dear life!'

Bernice didn't answer. *Shit*, I thought. *Too many deaths in that sentence*. But we'd both seen a lot of people die. Maybe she just didn't hear. Maybe death was so familiar to her now that mentions of it were banal. But did the dying know death any better? A lot of the dying people I'd known had gone to their end bewildered, protesting and in denial. What can any living person know about that one thing that lies beyond us?

I cleared a place on the table for dinner but Bernice said she'd be more comfortable in her bedroom. It was a big room with sliding doors that opened onto a verandah. Through the glass I could see the same view of the rolling hills I'd seen from the kitchen.

'Why aren't you writing?' she said with that new asperity, not looking at me. Having 'sort of flung herself' onto the bed, she was shuffling back against the pillows. I placed the tray over her legs and arranged the food. Her hands rested on the edge like claws.

'I write letters to the government,' I said, still attempting humour, like poking a dying fire. 'To the media, companies, banks. I write all our newsletters. Status updates. You know, consciousness-raising.'

Bernice looked nonplussed. She'd never done social media. 'Are you happy in this life of activism and children?' she was now looking directly at me, but the room had become suddenly dark. Nightfall in the subtropics: like a shutter coming down. Her face a black oval. I switched on the floor lamp in the corner. 'I love the kids,' I said. 'It's an incredible gift to find myself parenting unexpectedly.'

'Well, it's a noble cause, Vivienne. The activism.'

'It could well be pointless. They're still clearing,' I said gruffly, taken aback by the use of my full name. How intimate it sounded, instead of the usual Viv, and formal all at once. The felled forests I'd driven through flashed before me like a crime scene. Scarred, I was about to say to Bernice, or worse, still bleeding, like a field of fresh corpses.

She had picked up a spoon and was bent over the tray holding it with wobbling hands. She nibbled then put the spoon down. 'I'm sorry, Vivienne. I don't think I can eat it. You're a wonderful cook, but can you get me some ice cream?'

I found the freezer packed with cartons of locally made gelato. 'I've regressed to my old ways,' Bernice's quavery voice floated out of the bedroom. 'Sugar.' When I returned she was aiming the remote at the television. The screen remained black; the remote dropped from her trembling hand. 'You see? Even my hands are useless. I can't write anymore, so what's the point?'

'Do you use the dictation option?'

'Of course,' she said irritably. 'But it's not the same. I've got the nembutal. I'm just waiting for the right time, in terms of my family. Can you press play? I want to watch that documentary on the clitoris. Would you like that?'

No, I thought, alarmed. 'Yes,' I complied, assuming her question was rhetorical.

It was an old documentary she had taped on VHS. The grainy footage of a diagram of the clitoris and the stuffy English narration pitched me back to the hideous sex-education films I'd been shown at my convent school. I remembered the diagrams of male and female genitalia, the male growing as the narrator intoned, *When a man and woman are married and the man becomes aroused...* They'd invited our mothers to accompany us and I now wondered why. To help explain? As buffers against the presumed trauma of sex? I remembered mine, who had birthed eight children, writhing with discomfort in the seat beside me.

I ate my dinner watching the clitoris documentary with Bernice, thinking I should stop being astonished by how much had been hidden about women. This is how we'd always been, yet the information was so recent and revolutionary that Bernice and I hadn't known it when we were lovers.

'When I think of you, I think of how overpowering our sex was,' she said now. 'Remember that day you gave me about twenty orgasms? Then you skipped down to the river for a swim while I just lay here in a stupor.'

I felt a sort of guilt for not feeling the same. An image came to me of her on all fours on my mattress, squirting down my thighs as I fucked her from behind, how amazed I was, yet at the same time detached. But I'd loved her. Hadn't I? What was love? My heart ached so much for her now that I could barely swallow. I had lied. I wasn't happy. My stepson was a nightmare, my partner so jealous it had taken me almost a year to arrange this visit, tacked on finally to a work trip to the activists unsuccessfully guarding the forest. I sat in the blue flickering gloom, rigid with embarrassment. Our old conundrum: me the kinky city slicker, shaved head shaved cunt; her the shy country girl, far less hung up about sex.

When the documentary was over, Bernice told me where the bedding was and said it was time for her sleeping pill.

IN THE MORNING, out on the porch, I took her hands in mine.

'Good luck,' she said. 'We won't see each other again.'

I drove back through the gold grassy hills, from the dirt road to bitumen, then to the highway. I couldn't get radio reception but left it on anyway and drove to the sound of static. I remembered coming north five years earlier with my partner when we'd first gotten together. Bushfires had driven us from our camp site and we'd driven at a crawl for hours through smoke so thick the road was barely visible.

Today it was clear, clouding over gradually as I got nearer to Sydney. I drove without stopping, swigging from the bottle of water in the hole by the seat, clocking the burnt forest, some recovering, out of the corner of my eye. I wanted to blubber to someone but I knew my partner wouldn't handle it. I wanted to reminisce with Bernice and to comfort her. *It was so weird*, I was saying in my head. *It was so* weird.

I finished the water and kept on driving, till just after dusk I pulled up outside our house. My partner was at the kitchen window, their beautiful face visible beneath the overhead light, and as they looked up frowning, shaking their head, I realised I still had the radio on, untuned, its white noise abrading the quiet suburban night. I ducked my head, smoothed the emotion off my face and got out of the car.

Fiona Kelly McGregor has written for a variety of publications including *The Sydney Morning Herald, HEAT, Sydney Review of Books, Meanjin, The Times Literary Supplement, Art Monthly, The Monthly, The Saturday Paper* and *RealTime*.

Alisha Brown

Pentax ME Super

The first roll I developed,
with its saturated drought-skin
landscapes, spliced
my hometown into a sepia
I could almost swallow.
Five sheep and a fence line –
overexposed spinifex –
Dad's face in a motorbike mirror –
before. I had been starving,
and the ritual stuck.
Roll by roll. Grain by grain.
Sometimes, when I'm tired
of my own eyes,
I slip the lens cap into my pocket,
its hard little circle
pressing into my hip
as I walk this big soft circle earth
incompletely.
I need to shear my experience of everything
but its texture. Cauterise the moment.
The cattle grate –
the kangaroos –
the manic flick of crickets
in the waterless tank.
History is a heavy handful
and a sore neck, but it
is safer than memory.
You don't see their little fried bodies.
Only the jump.

Alisha Brown is a poet and traveller born on Kamilaroi land. She won the 2022 Joyce Parkes Women's Writing Prize and placed second in the Judith Rodriguez Open Section of the 2021 Woorilla Poetry Prize. You can find her work in *Westerly*, the *Australian Poetry Anthology* and *Fine Print Magazine*, among others.

IN CONVERSATION

Lines of beauty

Animating the amorality of the image

Michael Zavros and Carody Culver

Michael Zavros is a familiar face in the art world – literally. For more than two decades, this leading Australian artist has put himself, his family and his fondness for beautiful things, from luxury cars to high fashion, at the centre of his practice. Best known for his hyperrealist paintings and self-portraits, Zavros also applies his aesthete's eye and astonishing technical skill to sculpture, photography, film and performance. His work confronts some viewers as much as it captivates others – is it a critique of consumerism, or a celebration of it? For Zavros, it's both: an exquisite paradox that's all the more enticing for its refusal to moralise.

CARODY CULVER: In 2023, Brisbane's QAGOMA exhibited *The Favourite*, a major retrospective of your work over the last twenty-five years. In putting together the exhibition, did anything surprise you about the evolution of your artistic preoccupations? Did you find yourself viewing particular works in a new light?

MICHAEL ZAVROS: Yes, I did. I guess I've been aware of different ways the work has evolved, but there is something striking about assembling examples of that twenty-five years and showing them together. The work has physically changed a lot. The first works from the late '90s are all painting, and then by about 2005 I was making small bronze sculpture and drawing with charcoal. A few years later I was showing photography and film, even performance works. For this show I made more ambitious large-scale sculpture and a massive temporary wall painting/installation [of the Acropolis]. It's also interesting to consider how the work obviously doesn't change but we change, the world around that work changes. For example, my early paintings of cropped figures from GQ magazine were for me aspirational and celebrated a sartorial dandy fetishisation, but audiences encountering them today would think of straight-white-male privilege. Most artists make work that's autobiographical – their lived experience, observations or views of the world. I think this is very true of my practice. Sometimes writers talk about my work being all self-portraiture.

CC: You studied printmaking at Queensland College of Art, but your primary artistic medium is painting. What prompted this shift, and how has your method of painting changed over the last couple of decades?

MZ: I studied printmaking because in the mid-'90s there wasn't so much exciting painting happening in QCA studios, but also because I really wanted to learn new processes for my undergrad and, like most artists, I'd always painted. Painting had fallen out of fashion, and everyone was making installation, then photography and film – the new digital world reigned supreme for a decade. Now it's all about painting.

My first forays into painting were very much a response to photography or, more specifically, *pictures of things* that I was drawn to in commercial advertising or glossy magazines. I re-authored or appropriated found imagery. Later, as I became more interested in photography or became better at it, I shot my own source imagery, keeping much of that art-directed aesthetic I found in magazines as I turned the camera on myself or my own life. As to the physical painting, I keep changing. I often mine very traditional old-master painting techniques.

CC: There's a real sense of art direction in many of your works, such as your still-life paintings of fantastical floral arrangements and your *A Guy Like Me* photographic series, which features a life-size mannequin Michael in various poses. What appeals to you about the creation and replication of these detailed tableaux?

MZ: I think perhaps *art directing* is what I do best. And it's very gratifying that after twenty-five years this thing I became known for – realism and painting – isn't the best thing I do, that stepping away from the easel has been so successful. At its heart I think it's visualising a thing in great detail and problem-solving, refusing to compromise until that thing materialises. And that goes for anything I make, from painting to sculpture or performance, or a Mercedes convertible filled with water, the design of a garden or our family home or the opening event of a new museum, or some other party. And even in terms of my painting, the art direction or the creative moment is now far more elaborate.

CC: Some critics and viewers have interpreted your work as a form of commentary on capitalistic excess and consumerism; others have criticised it for its lack of criticality; others still have celebrated it for that very reason. What do you make of these opposing responses?

MZ: I like them, and I think such wildly opposing views about what you're making or whether it's any good are essential. The work is both a criticism and a celebration of all that's on show and I cast myself as a protagonist within it. I do find it a little bit art school, even Australian parochial, to assess a practice in terms of the artist's *intentions* and I get this a lot.

I watched *The Andy Warhol Diaries* on Netflix recently and I was amazed at how often critics derided his work over decades, about it not being *about* anything or at least different to what Andy thought it was about. And his frustrated diary entries were at odds with his public persona of not noticing or not caring.

The GOMA pairing of my work alongside [a concurrent exhibition by] eX de Medici is on point. She leaves no room for interpretation. She's didactic. She's clear about what she does and why she does it and what the art is about. She follows a recipe most artists follow – here is my politics or issue, here is a metaphor I'm weaving through this and here is the delivery (watercolour). I say this not to criticise my fellow artist; I'm a fan of her work. But describing this recipe perhaps better suggests what I eschew in my own practice.

For me the other striking difference is one of virtue. She takes on the world's evils as she sees them and finds herself on the right side of history. Virtue now so completely suffocates contemporary practice, and the artist now replaces the art. We assume that where there is a moral good that what flows from this is good art. It seldom does.

CC: In a 2013 interview for *The Art Life*, you said, 'I do think it is interesting that beauty is still a pejorative term in contemporary art.' Do you think this has changed in the past decade?

MZ: No, I don't think this has changed. And I don't want it to. I like that what I'm drawn to is at odds with so many of my contemporaries. Add to this that I often paint flowers or shiny trinkets or horses or other things hobbyists are drawn to.

CC: A number of your works – most famously your 2013 Archibald-finalist painting *Bad Dad* – respond to the myth of Narcissus, and much of your work is self-referential in some way. What interests you about Narcissus, and about the role of narcissism in contemporary culture?

MZ: *Bad Dad* is both a meditation on self and a reflection of self, literally. Historically it looks to Caravaggio's painting of Narcissus. Caravaggio's painting is formally quite structured but perhaps less beautiful than others. It has a *Picture of Dorian Gray* quality to it, a slightly sinister quality. My version is more pop, saccharine like a pop song with a dark lyric.

I look at Greek myths quite frequently, myths that have endured for hundreds of years. Narcissus is a maligned character now, and narcissism has become a kind of catch-all pejorative term for so much in contemporary society. We like to call it out but so much in contemporary culture celebrates narcissism. We are constantly asked to make time for ourselves, to indulge in 'me time' or self-care or to ask what do I want for myself, to put our own needs first. These are all narcissistic tropes, but entire industries are [based] on this. So on one hand we despise narcissists but on the other we are creating a whole new generation of them.

I think all of us have a tendency to lean into that side of ourselves. I am probably just more honest about it. My success as an artist relies on my self-obsession; I need to isolate myself, to make myself an island, cut myself adrift, to make the work I do. Being an artist is inherently selfish. *Bad Dad* is more of a self-deprecating study than a moral position. Do I put art before being a parent? Maybe. But it just makes me a human being.

Michael Zavros works across painting, drawing, sculpture, photography and film. He has exhibited widely within Australia and internationally, and his work is held in the collections of most major museums within Australia. In 2023 QAGOMA staged a solo survey exhibition of Zavros' work. In 2024 Zavros will show at MONA, Hobart, plus solo exhibitions at ART SG, Singapore, and Dunedin Public Art Gallery in New Zealand.

PICTURE GALLERY

Eternal reflection
MICHAEL ZAVROS

ad Dad 2013, oil on canvas, 110 x 150 cm

Top: *Ars Longa Vita Brevis* 2010, oil on canvas, 210 x 167 cm
Bottom: *Self Portrait with Seon O'Pry* 2015, lightjet print, 120 x 90 cm

MICHAEL ZAVROS: Eternal reflection 99

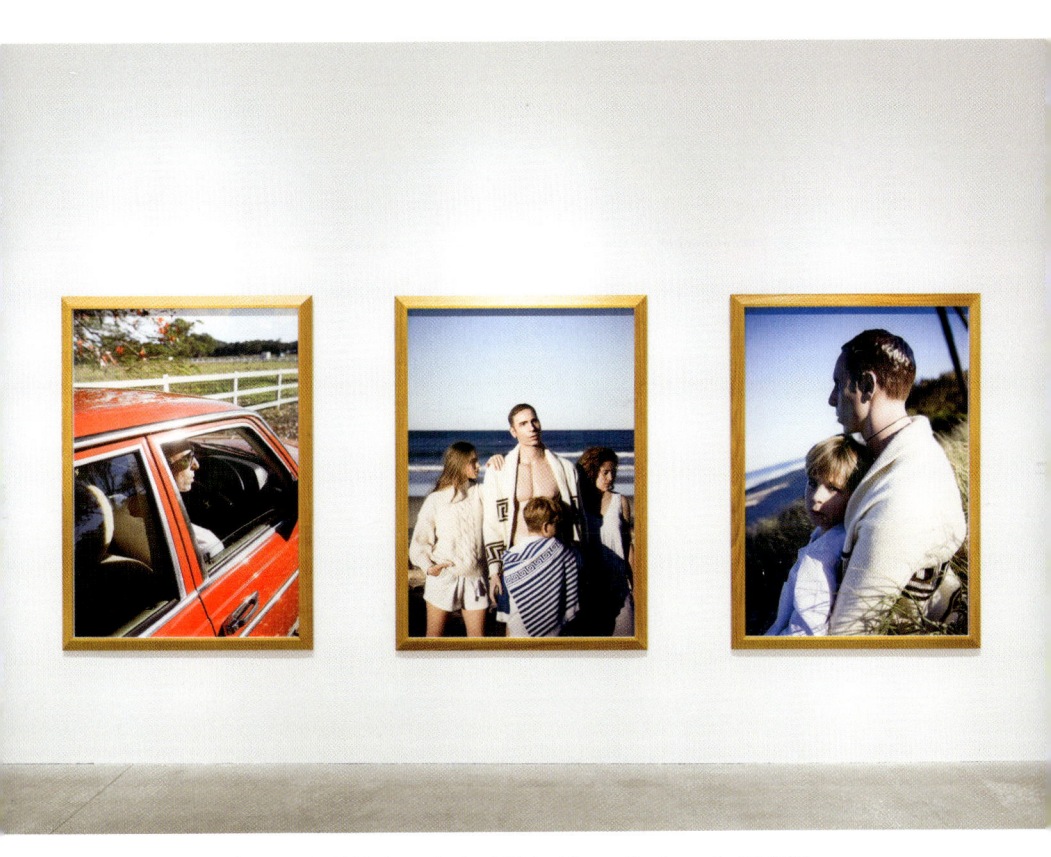

Three pieces from the *A Guy Like Me* series 2020, shown in situ at *Michael Zavros: The Favourite*, QAGOMA.
Photograph by Joe Ruckli

Top: *White Peacock* 2017, oil on canvas, 220 x 200 cm
Bottom: *The Greek* 2014, oil on canvas, 100 x 85 cm

[...]e Poodle 2014, oil on canvas, 135 x 155 cm

Drowned Mercedes 2023, found car, resin, steel, water, 129 x 181 x 450 cm, shown in situ at *Michael Zavros: The Favourite*, QAGOMA. Photograph by Joe Ruckli

MICHAEL ZAVROS: Eternal reflection   103

eft: *Amore* 2018, oil on canvas, 170 x 115 cm, shown in situ at *Michael Zavros: The Favourite*, QAGOMA.
hotograph by Joe Ruckli

Mum's Wedding Dress 2021, oil on canvas, 160 x 205 cm

MICHAEL ZAVROS: Eternal reflection

om Com 2023, lightjet print, 140 x 115 cm

The Lioness 2010, oil on canvas, 210 x 180 cm

MICHAEL ZAVROS: Eternal reflection

eus/Zavros 2018, oil on canvas, 105 x 150 cm

Phoebe Is Dead/McQueen 2010, oil on canvas, 110 x 150 cm

NON-FICTION

Which way, Western artist?
Art of the past and future present

Myles McGuire

INSIDE YOU THERE are two wolves. Their names are Mark Fisher and Camille Paglia. They are the only 'philosophers' you have read and basically understood.

You are at the opening of *The Favourite,* a QAGOMA survey of the artist Michael Zavros. There is a second show, *Beautiful Wickedness* by eX de Medici. Your husband is taking a picture on his phone of a cream puff that has fallen to the floor. He says this is art. You are anticipating the puff's impalement by stiletto.

You have three hours to ingurgitate free champagne or ogle the art. Do you:

a) embark on a jaunt through *Beautiful Wickedness,* a rubbish tip of machine guns, plastic crap and skulls scrummed together like the *Where's Wally?* book from hell. Avarice, exploitation and the (de)valuation of human life by capitalism are the exhibition's baroque subjects; still, you can imagine these works wallpapering a celebrity's walk-in robe in an *Architectural Digest* video. Do you feel:
   i. nothing.
   ii. confronted and/or challenged.
   iii. guilty (constantly).
   iv. as if the anti-capitalist project in art is not only redundant but insincere; there is no possibility of separating art from capitalism. As Mark Fisher writes: 'The power of capitalist realism derives

in part from the way that capitalism subsumes and consumes all of previous history: one effect of its "system of equivalence" which can assign all cultural objects, whether they are religious iconography, pornography or *Das Kapital* a monetary value.' Visual artworks are the perfect expression of this capitalist logic; the creative product is most analogous to commodity. A thing can – in fact, must – be sold and bought, its value derived from its scarcity. An original artwork is, by definition, one of a kind. While other cultural products (television, music, clothing; to mention publishing is to speak ill of the dead) may lubricate the machinery of capitalism, the value they command in saturated markets is negligible.

By endeavouring to critique capitalist realism, eX de Medici's work reproduces its logic, transferring its incoherence and banality to the canvas. Unable to meaningfully subvert the system, critical artworks instead adopt a posture Fisher describes as interpassivity (a term derived from Robert Pfaller). The artwork performs the viewer's anti-capitalism for them, functioning as a pressure valve for material and moral anxieties. Critical artwork is thus an integral part of capitalist cultural production – because there is no revolutionary threat, the consumer-subject can have a little anti-capitalism as a treat.

b) choose *The Favourite*, likewise preoccupied with capitalistic excess but untethered from the moralism next door. Much has been made of Zavros' fetishisation of luxury; virtually every critique of his work references conspicuous consumption, the tone usually finger-wagging (he's not an artist, he's a very naughty boy). The implicit moral doctrine of the superficially left-wing cultural industries dictates that artists should not engage with capitalism except as the site of critique, leading defensive admirers of Zavros' work to interpret satire where it is not present. Designer shoes, suits and scarves are painted lovingly, the reproductions so precise that, looking at them, one can imagine how they feel to lick. It is possible to:

    i. take this at face value. These are beautiful things painted beautifully, as Zavros himself claims (elsewhere, in conversation with Scott Redford in *Eyeline*, he says 'artists should never open our

mouths'). Until somewhat recently beauty was an acceptable justification for art.
  ii. consider this in the context of capitalist realism. This requires a room-temperature IQ. The argument writes itself, and if there's one thing you hate, it's writing.
  iii. behold them and spiral.
c) enter neither of the exhibitions but remain at the reception. Here you do not have to choose between champagne and socialism. On one side of the room Zavros and his assistants have painted the Acropolis; eX de Medici, bullets. The dialectic: we should all be lined up against the cradle of democracy and shot. Drinks cannot be taken into the exhibitions. They can only be guzzled here, in the no-man's-land between opposing forces. And they are opposing; in form and ideation they are irreconcilable, and so this is perhaps the only way in the twenty-first century to have a polite debate – when the disagreement cannot be expressed through words. (Most people choose the champagne.)

YOU CHOOSE OPTION b) iii. *The Favourite* (if choices can only be articulated through the market, there is only an illusion of choice). Inside you are greeted by the first in Zavros' *Dad* photographic series, wherein the artist's plastic golem – a 3D-printed, life-sized or slightly taller mannequin – reclines behind reflective sunglasses. You hear the strains of Lady Gaga's 'Paparazzi', earworm torture of the sort favoured in Guantanamo Bay (in another room, Zavros' daughter lip-syncs to the song in a home video). You pass the miniature paintings of suit cuffs, re-creations of yuppyish *GQ* magazine adverts; an oil painting of cologne bottles, designer shoes and sunglasses, arranged in the shape of a skull. There are 'self-portraits' featuring the model Sean O'Pry – the love interest in the music video for 'Blank Space' by Taylor Swift, itself set in Zavrosian hyperreality – and then you re-encounter dummy Dad, photographed surrounded by his flesh-and-blood brood.

These exhibits characterise the exhibition's themes: family life and the fetishisation of objects. You might interpret this as:
  a) the evolution of the artist through fatherhood. The young man who painted the fine things has mellowed, been normalised. Whatever excited him to paint the superficial subjects of his early work is eclipsed by domestic concerns. In Nietzsche's words, 'The angry and

reverent spirit peculiar to youth appears to allow itself no peace, until it has suitably falsified men and things, to be able to vent its passion upon them.' The younger images are frozen, petrified objects refuting age and decay. The clothes depicted in fashion advertisements are objets d'art, existing in the sterile suspension of a studio photoshoot: immortality as consumer good. But for a parent – someone who keenly feels the passage of time as they observe their growing children – this is a perverse fantasy. The child who is not in a constant, perceptible state of change is dead (see *Phoebe Is Dead/McQueen* from 2010, which depicts Zavros' daughter Phoebe lying corpse-like beneath an Alexander McQueen skull-print scarf).

b) a natural continuation. The object of fetish has transferred from consumer good to the ultimate luxury product: a beautiful life, replete with beautiful family. The works in *The Favourite* depict gorgeous objects, glistening pearls strung on a thread of narcissistic will. Like Medusa's, the artist's stare is petrifying. It turns on his children not because Zavros has succumbed to sentimentality – as the anthropologist Margaret Mead says, fatherhood is a social invention – but because his criteria for object selection have become sophisticated. Fisher's argument is taken to the extreme; the family itself becomes commodified, integrated into a system of equivalence alongside shoes and suits.

THE NEXT CHAMBER is populated with floral still lifes. These are not your grandma's still lifes; Margaret Olley, whomst? The obligatory descriptions emblazoned on the wall, with their insistence on whimsy and play, are insane. You think of the Italian poet Gabriele D'Annunzio, heralded by Mussolini as the John the Baptist of fascism, who rearranged the flowers at his bedside three times a day.

Sculpting the flowers into animal silhouettes – octopus, poodle, lobster – the artist sneers at nature as a purveyor of inferior forms. Zavros acknowledges this: interviewed by Rhana Devenport in 2014, he referred to the paintings as 'baroque folly, nature made better, more pretty'. The designer dog featured in *The Poodle* (2014) is both overbred and cross-pollinated. With its fleecy coat of hydrangeas and shapely Waterford Crystal legs, the neutered hound can only sit and stay (in another painting, *The Greek*, Zavros arranges vase and hydrangeas into a phallus with big, fluffy balls; the stems visible inside the vase are the dorsal veins of a glass penis).

Frigid and ectomorphic, the bouquets are centrepieces – in what? Where? Another white-walled gallery, more exclusive than this venue, where copies are exhibited by the state? With no contextualising environment the florals are fetish objects, arctic and lapidary. Their visual logic is that of a stocking wanked over by someone who has never seen a thigh. Suspended in white space, the flowers are as unnatural as those photographed by Robert Mapplethorpe. Nature as vaginal flower is mummified into hard, glowing object, the traditional tribute of lovers excised of fleshy sentimentality. The blaspheme of Mother Earth is crystallised in the skeleton giving voguish shape to *White Peacock*, the bones stripped of meat as if by nuclear cataclysm. The roses and dahlias remain intact, perfected like diamonds by heat and pressure.

Writing about this exhibition in *The Conversation*, Sasha Grishin claims 'It is difficult to view pieces including *The Poodle* (2014) other than as a critique of a society completely out of control and sacrificing function for the sake of cute design.' Okay, Sasha. Zavros' self-professed motive echoes the philosophy of Camille Paglia of art and civilisation as contest between Apollonian form and Dionysian nature. Paglia defines the Apollonian as the 'hard, cold separatism of western personality and categorical thought… Apollo is obsessiveness, voyeurism, idolatry, fascism – frigidity and aggression of the eye, petrifaction of objects.' For Paglia, the Apollonian is emphatically masculine, a productive manifestation of male sexual anxiety. Feminine nature is generative: no placid, Rousseauian idyll, but a wildly maximalist totality. The Apollonian is its compressed sadomasochistic parody. So do you:

a) concur with Grishin. (Most of) Zavros' work is explicitly capitalistic; not a bad idea. If the contemporary artist wants to make a living from his work, he might as well depict things that will not give his patrons nightmares. A beautiful thing painted beautifully will not disrupt the equilibrium of a living room, a toilet, an *Eyes Wide Shut* orgy, a state-of-the-art storage shed where pieces are stowed for tax purposes. The sacral figures of Western art – the Renaissance masters – understood this; they made sure their work reflected their patrons' contradictory desire for decadence and spiritual piety, while injecting it with hallucinatory avant-garde flair.

b) concur with Zavros' admitted intention, the editorialisation of nature. If the paintings depict a (futile but vigorous) struggle of Apollonian form over Dionysian nature then this predates capitalism by millennia, and so cannot arise from its logic. The capitalist trappings of Zavros' work are era-specific expressions of an ancient, abiding preoccupation with an aristocratic hierarchy of aesthetics: though nature can create more beautiful things than man, only he/she/they can be a connoisseur. This, more than the post-critical attitude to capitalism, is why Zavros infuriates sectors of the art world. To admire beauty is to admonish ugliness, ascribing moral value to aesthetics. (Ironically this attitude, originating in modernism and embraced by the so-called left, is perfectly suited to capitalism, conferring on it the moral right to produce inexpensive, uglier things. The subjects of capitalism participate then not out of desire, even manufactured desire, but out of the moral compulsion of the indoctrinated.)

The primary charge levelled at Zavros, and photorealistic painting generally, is that it is surface level – a charge he has elided by making surfaces his subject. As an artist friend of yours argues, anyone with the time, resources (that is, assistants – a whole other essay about exploitation and labour relations, which – whatever) and technical skill could create a photorealistic painting. Though this has mass appeal you argue that the genius of Zavros' work is in the unity of form and conceptualisation. While it is realistic it is not natural; familiarity is the precondition for the strange. (Familiarity tickles your inner etymologist, as does family: the Latin root describes not cosy, nuclear relations, but servitude to the master of the house.)

THE CENTRAL ROOM of *The Favourite* is devoted to Zavros' family. Because it is a parody of a living room it follows that it is a dying room, equal parts family photo album and fabulous dynastic crypt. At the centre of this holy of holies is his ark of the covenant, the sculpture *Drowned Mercedes*: a flooded Mercedes Benz SL-class drop-top, from which security guards repel admirers. You desperately want to climb in or open the door. The license plate reads AGAPE, which your drunk husband reads as a-gayp. When you tell him that a-gah-pay is the ancient Greek word for love – the perfected, selfless form later endorsed by Christians, including CS Lewis, as superior to horny eros – he responds that a-gayp is funnier. (Your dad does not find it funny when you tell him what this artist has done to this car.)

Drowned Mercedes is the only artwork in the room that gestures explicitly to capitalism. It is adolescently provocative (your friend describes Zavros as an edgelord, a term popularised on 4chan in 2014, when Zavros was forty). The wordplay licence plate links the sculpture to the painting *Amore* (2018), wherein Zavros' glamourised daughter Phoebe supernaturally elides the transition from girl to woman (in Greek myth, goddesses emerge fully formed from the father, in feats of onanistic conceptualisation: brainy Athena by blow to the head and sensual Aphrodite by castration). Rouged, with a voluminous blowout, Phoebe wears a shirt with *AMOUR* embroidered on the collar – not amore, the Italian title of the work, but amour, understood since the sixteenth century to refer to an illicit affair. Nearby, in *Rom Com* (2023), Phoebe beams coquettishly as she pulls at dummy Dad's tie; what at first appears to be a pin on the sleeve of his suit is a fly, drawn to Dad's mephitic carcass. Incest *and* necrophilia, and…look over there! It's the former Governor-General, Dame Quentin Bryce. Agape, agape, amore, amour. The reflective surface is a two-way mirror.

What is the reason for this pivot, from giddy consumerism to ambivalence? Is it that:
- a) the artist, having made his name as a documentarian of the superficial, seeks to establish depth.
- b) things that once seemed beautiful – clothes, horses, nihilistic floral arrangements – pale in comparison to children, beheld in the dewy eye of their doting dad. The parent's irreconcilable project is to protect the flesh of their flesh from harm while guiding them towards the long decline of adulthood: for dust you are, and to dust you shall return (Genesis 3:19).
- c) there is no pivot. The work was never about capitalism. The miniature paintings, nominally indebted to magazines, replicate a mode popular with European royalty of the seventeenth century. The exhibition's title, *The Favourite*, situates it in the system of courtly economics, which even the most ardent Marxist-Leninist would concede is more unjust than capitalism. In this way Zavros' rejection of capitalism is more radical and reactionary than eX de Medici's. It aligns with the vision of alt-right darling Curtis Yarvin, an advocate

for neo-monarchy. By dangling the shiny things of late twentieth-century capitalism, Zavros distracts his critics from an altogether more sinister political vision. Meaning that:

i. the work is highly political, but its politics are inconceivable to the liberal, capitalist subject (and we are all liberal, capitalist subjects) and therefore they are misconstrued as capitalist apologia.

ii. the work is not political. It is an unfortunate reality that the ideals of the aesthete dovetail with those of the fascist, hence the well-documented relationship between classical aesthetics and fascism. Theodor Adorno is often misquoted as saying that there is no poetry after Auschwitz. The actual quote, 'to write poetry after Auschwitz is barbaric', obfuscates that the creation of art has always required a refined sense of barbarism (in the word's modern sense – etymologically it describes one who does not speak Greek).

iii. the artist cannot have politics, by virtue of being an artist, but can only be beholden to politics. Though paintings like *Mum's Wedding Dress* (2021) recall the society portraits of John Singer Sargent and Valentin Serov in composition and in the blend of verisimilitude and smudgy impressionism, the artist's status in society is contingent. Whoever his master is, the favourite is an extravagant pet.

THE MOST STRIKING painting in this room is titled *Zeus/Zavros* (2018). It hangs alongside *Bad Dad* (2013), the uncanny self-portrait in which Zavros depicts himself as inner-suburban Narcissus. Head bowed in aquiline profile, Zavros in *Bad Dad* resembles Christian Bale as Patrick Bateman, whose creator, Bret Easton Ellis, is referenced elsewhere in Zavros' oeuvre. While Ellis' novel *American Psycho* remains banned in Queensland, Zavros commands its state art gallery; *Bad Dad*, his Bateman-esque self-portrait, was a finalist in the Archibald Prize. Comparison between the two men is illuminating – the artist who expresses his ideas verbally is more likely to be subject to censure, due to the literalism assumed of language, even of satire. The visual artist, communicating through the image, maintains plausible deniability – a notable exception being Bill Henson, also referenced by Zavros; one of his photographs is depicted in the painting *The Lioness* (2010).

Zeus/Zavros is one of a suite of paintings that recall the scandal ignited by Henson's photographs of young girls (scandal Zavros courts with *Phoebe Is Dead/McQueen*). The notable difference is that Zavros' subjects are his own children. Should anyone remark that these depictions are eroticised, he is armed with a brilliant rebuttal: why are you eroticising my kids, you pervert? Despite his insistence in the blurb accompanying *Bad Dad*, the artist cannot paint solely for himself; the viewer's implication in the act of seeing is anticipated. Perhaps for this reason there is little published commentary about Zavros' family paintings, though there is plenty of gossip, the low-hanging fruit of capitalistic excess being easier game for the intrepid art critic.

Zeus/Zavros is the darkest painting in *The Favourite*, literally. Tilting her face to the sun Phoebe hangs draped from the neck of an inflatable pool toy, her nude brother prostrated on the back of a blow-up swan. Where the rest of his oeuvre abhors chiaroscuro in favour of blinding exposure, more than half of *Zeus/Zavros* is engulfed by shadow. Shadow for Zavros is cobwebby, a necessary concession to realism, avoided wherever possible. It manifests in surgical lines differentiating the contours of form from the seething morass of nature. Though Zavros indebts the modern Narcissus depicted in *Bad Dad* to Caravaggio, he has no affinity for the old master's tenebrism; Apollonian form must triumph over Dionysian murk, lest all the fine things be swallowed. Still, the objectifying amoralist cannot help but be contaminated by the vision of his daughter as Leda, raped by swan-Zeus; his corruption spills across the canvas, an inky oil slick.

The predominance of shadow in *Zeus/Zavros* reveals more than it obscures. Here Zavros the artist concedes to the neuroticism to which Robert Leonard considers him immune when he describes him as 'a well-heeled, high functioning pervert' (2011). Is the atypical shadow:

a) a confession of moral anxiety – not for having painted *Zeus/Zavros*, but for having conceived of it.

b) a calculated manoeuvre of pre-emptive defensiveness.

c) another self-portrait. *Zeus/Zavros* shares one feature uniting it with the depictions of Zavros showcased in *The Favourite*, including the adjacent and literal *Bad Dad*: when painting himself, Zavros never meets the viewer's eye. His gaze is obstructed, pitched elsewhere, or obscured by sunglasses or medallions of cucumber. The adult recuses himself to the plane of imaginative play, while the children confront reality – that is, the viewer. Perhaps the titular Zeus is the swan, a creation of Apollonian idealism, and Zavros his daimon, the Dionysian shadow – engulfing his scions like Kronos, the cannibalistic child-eater, father of Zeus.

d) hauntological, a spectre; in Fisher's words, 'not so much [of] the past as all the lost futures that the twentieth century taught us to anticipate'. The imaginative violence of antiquity, synthesised into Apollonian form, has no relevance in the twenty-first century. As eX de Medici demonstrates, modern violence is systemically distributed and bereft of glamour. The king of the gods is a plastic pool toy; no Leda was harmed in the making of this image. Pastiche and reiteration do not signal nostalgia (in Greek, the ache of homecoming) but an ironic disavowal of the present.

THOUGH IRONY IS perceived as a modern malady, it too derives from ancient Greek: Socrates pretending ignorance to expose another's. To sincerely evaluate the symbolic content of these paintings is to make oneself a victim of irony, too often confused with satire. The modern iteration of irony, or affected ignorance, drives not at truth but at chic, a phenomenon Susan Sontag described in 'Notes on "Camp"'(1964). It is not a conscious attitude, but a defensive posture adopted against the fact that certain knowledges are lost. In this sense it is certainly not unique to postmodernism.

By the time of Leda's popularity among the Renaissance artists her motif was only that, hence da Vinci's almost obscene prettification of what was to ancient cultists a scene of bestial violence, the prologue to the perfected violence of the Trojan War (Leda birthing Helen from the rape). As Richard Wagner writes in 1880 in *Religion and Art*:

> what could now be borrowed from the ancient world, was no longer that unity of Greek art with Antique religion whereby alone had the former blossomed and attained fruition… Greek art could only teach its sense of form, not lend its ideal content; whilst the Christian ideal had passed out of range of this sense-of-form, to which the actual world alone seemed henceforth visible.

In this way you are led back to capitalist realism. Without belief in the supernatural, or the sublime, or anything, what can art depict but the visible world – the only thing left in which to believe? Can art be anything but ironic, even art as earnest as eX de Medici's? We are too clever to believe the superstitions of the past and too stupid to recognise superstition as an epistemology to which we no longer have access. The only choice, if one can call it that, is to believe the visible world is:

a) an infernal machine, à la eX de Medici.
b) impossibly beautiful, and beneath that beauty, nothing.

In this belief, more than form or historical references, Zavros inherits classical and Renaissance traditions. His paintings are formal expressions of faith, without which they could not be conceived. They are religious artworks – from the religion of modernity, which is not an absence of belief, but a devout belief in nothing. It is a belief in no future, no past; about the present it is agnostic. Adherents of the faith surround you; its hymns reverberate. Padam. It is the goddess, Kylie. Padam. You hear it, and you know:

a) Padam, the show is over.
b) Padam, the bar is closed.
c) Padam, it is true, as Nick Cave says of 'Better the Devil You Know', that 'love relationships are by nature abusive…this abuse, be it physical or psychological, is welcomed and encouraged…the most seemingly harmless of love songs has the potential to hide terrible human truths'.
d) Padam, this is the last prayer, the only plea you may offer to the god/dess/x of nothing; the onomatopoeia of the heartbeat.

Myles McGuire's writing has been nominated for the Peter Carey Short Story Award, the Newcastle Short Story Award, the Monash Writing Prize and the QUT Writing Prize. In 2023 he was nominated for the Queensland Premier's Young Writers and Publishers Award. He teaches creative writing at QUT and is currently at work on his first novel.

Graham Kershaw

The emperor's twin

In the absence of gods, must we choose monsters?
You can never really know the difference, or see under.
These creatures are all skin; hence history's endless
conjectures over The Man Within, as if the emperor
had a smaller, kinder twin we'd never seen publicly.

If we'd known what was coming, we might have settled
for the mute ambassador, the temporary exemption,
all the cooling-off, hot-desk non-testing of means,
those semi-punitive, introductory soft-touch schemes,
that slow, numb selling off of egalitarian dreams,

might have taken that French kiss of the ringmaster's
fist on the chin, as he served us up old sacrifices,
new regimes. If we'd only known what was coming next,
we might have settled for the long evening in
the market bribed us with, and voted twice for Keating.

Graham Kershaw is the author of *The Home Crowd* and *Dovetail Road* (both Fremantle Press), and a collection of poetry, *Undersummer* (Sunline Press). He is also the editor of *Dark Diamonds: Poems from the South Coast of Western Australia* (Hallowell Press) and winner of the 2012 Blake Poetry Prize. His poems have appeared in *Westerly, Southerly, Australian Book Review* and *The Weekend Australian,* among others.

NON-FICTION

Scarlett fever

The seven stages of Windie recovery

Melanie Myers

NOVEMBER 1994. A Saturday. The weather was as you'd expect for Brisbane that time of year: that is, far too warm for 300-plus cosplaying Southern belles and their chaperones to comfortably assemble at Channel 9's Mt Coot-tha studios. But gather we did, in polyester crinolines and oversized hats scavenged from costume-hire places all over town. Young women – blondes, redheads but mostly brunettes – flocked from north and south of the river, from Bayside and the western suburbs for their chance to be anointed 'Queensland's Scarlett'. Auditions started at 10 am, and by nine the coiled inner verge of Sir Samuel Griffith Drive was chockers with the cars of the hopeful.

The search for 'Queensland's Scarlett' was a publicity lark cooked up by Channel 9's *Extra* – a local infotainment program hosted by Rick Burnett that aired 5 pm on weekdays – *The Courier-Mail* and 'classic hits' radio station 4KQ. They were in cahoots to promote the miniseries *Scarlett*, the oncoming trainwreck of a sequel to *Gone with the Wind* (*GWTW*). The judges would choose five finalists. The winning Scarlett, as voted by the public, would take home $5,000. Plenty to pay the taxes on Tara and more besides. At twenty-one, it seemed my moment had finally arrived, though I had no idea I was also partaking in something of an Australian tradition.

I loved Scarlett from the very first time I read about her.
I wished I could be just like her.
– Sarah

JULY 1940. 'THE girl must have a facial resemblance to the screen star, must be of average height, must have a good figure and deportment, and must have good teeth and a cheerful presence.' So reads the 'qualifications' for a 1940 search for a 'Queensland double of Scarlett O'Hara', conducted by Brisbane's *Telegraph* and radio station 4BH in co-operation with Metro-Goldwyn-Mayer (MGM). Every Australian capital city – as well as many smaller cities and towns, including Newcastle, Wollongong, Horsham, Mt Gambier, Rockhampton, Grafton and the Tweed – hosted a quest to find a local Scarlett in the early '40s.

Sydney, predictably, kicked things off in March 1940 with the Sydney *Sun* and 'Younger Set committee of the Lord Mayor's Patriotic and War Fund' setting out to find 'a girl like Scarlett O'Hara' to attend the gala *GWTW* preview at St James Theatre on 30 April 1940, dressed in a prize replica barbeque dress. To enter, all a girl need do was turn up at Norton-Trevaire Studios in the Strand Arcade, where she'd have her picture taken to be sent off to MGM. After an 'intense weeding out' of over 200 entrants, seventeen-year-old Joyce Field was chosen as the winner from seven finalists, who were given screen tests for their trouble. Joyce, meanwhile, was 'rushed from one store to another' to be fitted for her 'Scarlett O'Hara gown' in preparation for the premier of *GWTW*, after which she would be engaged as a 'special hostess' for the film's run at the Liberty Theatre.

Along with a replica Scarlett dress, this was the major prize for all Scarletts chosen from cities and towns across our wide brown land. These hostess engagements lasted anywhere from two weeks to six months, with no indication whether the young women were paid for their services. Presumably so, but perhaps the honour of greeting patrons trussed up as Scarlett O'Hara was considered compensation enough. For Tess Cupitt – who would marry an American serviceman and then move to Montana as a war bride – such was the biographical highlight of being crowned Brisbane's Scarlett it rated a mention, sixty-three years later, in her obituary. She did, after all, greet Sir Leslie Wilson, the Governor of Queensland, at the Brisbane premier of *GWTW*.

These Scarlett lookalike competitions were no doubt inspired by the publicity juggernaut that was *GWTW* producer David O Selznick's legendary quest to find an actress to play Scarlett O'Hara. From unknowns to Hollywood's biggest stars, 1,400 women were auditioned and ninety formally tested for the most sought-after role in cinema history. Dozens of would-be Scarlett mugshots were published in local newspapers, presenting not just the best historical evidence, apart from book sales and box-office receipts, of 'Scarlett fever' among young Australian women, but something unique to *GWTW* fandom that persisted for decades after: a fixation and intense self-identification with anti-heroine Scarlett O'Hara.

The lookalike competition is a particular iteration of this phenomenon. Film theorist Jackie Stacey, in her 1994 book *Star Gazing: Hollywood Cinema and Female Spectatorship*, identifies several 'extra-cinematic identification processes', which include 'pretending, resembling, imitating and copying', that a spectator engages in 'to close the gap between her own image and her ideal image' – in this case Vivien Leigh as Scarlett O'Hara. The lookalike competition allows the spectator/fan to indulge in the practice of 'resembling' by establishing a link based on 'shared physical appearance', while also offering a platform to involve others in formally recognising that similarity. It is also a forum where other, more 'transformative', extra-cinematic identification practices can take place. Replicating Scarlett's behaviour and mannerisms, for example, is 'imitating', while duplicating her hairstyles and dressing as a Southern belle is 'copying' – processes that allow the spectator to transform their own identity into their ideal.

> *My first impression was something like, hey, this sounds a lot like me. I think that's why I like her so much, and always have.*
> – Anonymous

OCTOBER 1985. *GWTW* premiered on Australian television over a Sunday and Monday night on the Seven Network. For Gen X, *GWTW*'s small-screen debut was our initiation into the film our grandmothers and mothers had so adored. *GWTW*'s entree into suburban lounge rooms shored up a new generation of fans and primed them to lap up the hype of the sequel ten years later. Official sponsors Richardson-Vicks paid $75,000 a minute, five times the usual rate, to advertise its Ulan (now 'Olay') Beauty Bar.

Every 'Windie' – the suggestion of flatulence in this group sobriquet has never bothered the fanatical – can tell the story of their first time. I was twelve and couldn't have been more impressionable. I was a goner from the first 'fiddle-dee-dee' as the camera zooms in on Scarlett – a phantasm of primness in that exploded pavlova of a dress – to a close-up of her bewitching face. The day after, I began reading the novel, taking the 1,000-page tome to school with me, enraptured with Margaret Mitchell's confected Old South and her wilful, rule-defying heroine. Watching Vivien Leigh embody the character of Scarlett O'Hara was the most profound experience of my life up to that point and, in want of a juicy female role model, I latched on like a rabid dog.

In *Frankly, My Dear: Gone with the Wind Revisited* (2009) – an examination of *GWTW*'s continuing hold on the American imagination – author and film critic Molly Haskell suggests that for those who fell under *GWTW*'s spell 'the range of emotions attached to the film fluctuate over time'. Drawing on her own lifetime relationship to *GWTW*, she calls these the 'Seven Stages of *GWTW*: Love, Identification, Dependency, Resentment, Embarrassment, Indifference, and then something like Half-Love again'. My relationship to *GWTW* has followed a similar trajectory, with Love and Identification dominating my adolescence and early twenties, when I would read the book at least once a year.

> *I loved her immensely because I saw so much of myself in her. I have been compared to Scarlett O'Hara and Vivien Leigh since I was five…and am proud to be 'Scarlett'.*
> – Amanda

DECEMBER 1989. *GWTW*'S fiftieth anniversary unleashes a flurry of breathless press about the movie's ongoing appeal and a range of new merchandise: namely, a 'special edition' video box set of the remastered film, which includes David Hinton's 1988 documentary *The Making of a Legend*. At this point, *GWTW* was the highest grossing film of all time (with the 'adjusted for inflation' caveat, it still remains in the top spot with worldwide earnings of $4,192,000,000). *Women's Weekly* published a '*GWTW* Turns Fifty' spread in their September 1989 edition, mostly regurgitating fabled 'making of' talking points, including the search for Scarlett, and Vivien Leigh's eventual triumph.

So mythologised was the story by this point it had already been turned into a two-part television series: *The Scarlett O'Hara War* (1980), adapted from Garson Kanin's 1979 novel *Moviola*. Morgan Brittany's sixty-second cameo as Vivien Leigh was the show's promotional set piece. But if Brittany's moonlighting as Leigh highlights one thing, it's the near universal acceptance that only Vivien Leigh could have been Scarlett O'Hara. No matter how well Paulette Goddard – the actress most likely to have landed Scarlett if Leigh hadn't materialised – might have inhabited the role, it is difficult to imagine her inflaming either the desire for identical physical replication, such as performed in a lookalike contest, or the more intense personal identification, the need to *be* Scarlett, attested to by her most ardent acolytes.

Helen Taylor's *Scarlett's Women: Gone with the Wind and its Female Fans*, also published, shrewdly, in 1989, was the first serious study of *GWTW* fandom. Taylor, a British academic, analysed 'hundreds of letters and questionnaires by *GWTW* enthusiasts', mostly British and American women, as part of her methodology to explain *GWTW*'s 'enduring appeal'. On her analysis of Leigh's Scarlett, Taylor notes how few of her respondents, who'd also read the book, noted any 'disjunction' between Leigh and Scarlett as depicted in the novel. 'It is as if,' Taylor says, 'most reader-viewers accept her interpretation of the role as naturally right,' which also 'closes off other readings of Scarlett, and ideas about how she might look, speak, behave'.

While Taylor's conclusions are multifaceted as far as explaining *GWTW*'s persistent popularity with reference to race, class and gender, most salient here are those that concern Scarlett as the work's heroine. 'Again and again,' Taylor says, 'women described to me their identification with and admiration of the strong, resourceful Scarlett, getting what she wants out of life,' with some correspondents 'expressing total identification with Scarlett and all she does'. For many who came to *GWTW* in their teens, Scarlett was 'a prototype of female action or attitudes', and their 'first flawed heroine' – 'ruthless, scheming and selfish' – whose 'rebelliousness' was one of her 'most exciting characteristics'.

Taylor also identified different generational responses to Scarlett. For those who lived through the Depression and World War II, Scarlett's survivalist instincts, her tenacity in overcoming poverty and hardship, offered inspiration and hope for regeneration: 'She was "the New Woman", representing 1940s wartime women workers.' For baby boomers, like Taylor, who encountered *GWTW* in the '50s and '60s – 'women who did not remember the war but were busy reacting against their war-scarred, security-minded parents' – Scarlett's knack for survival was 'seen in more personal, individualist terms'. She appealed to women's libbers as 'an example of gutsy individualism or feminist self-determination'. By the 1980s, Scarlett's 'feminism' had morphed to fit the stylings of the Me generation – a poster girl for post-feminist neoliberalism – with her drive and business acumen representing 'Thatcherite/Reaganite models of career feminism and yuppie success'. For those of us who came of age in the '90s, to some point Scarlett's '80s vibes carried over, but this was also the era of 'Big Scarlett', where she became, more than ever, a beautiful and commodified effigy to be endlessly marketed and consumed. Literally, a Barbie doll.

> *I view Scarlett now as a woman and am still as captivated as ever. A woman who is strong, determined and not bothered by what people think. A woman for the '90s!*
> – Lelia

SEPTEMBER 1991. THE world's most anticipated literary sequel, Alexandra Ripley's *Scarlett*, is published by Warner Books to, if not critical acclaim, then expected commercial success. As *The Sydney Morning Herald* put it, 'the most vicious critics were no match for the hype that preceded the book's publication'. In the US alone, it sold 1.2 million copies in its first six weeks. With the TV rights selling for $9 million, casting speculation was set alight. *Women's Weekly* ran a 'Vivien Leigh lookalike competition' to find a locally sourced Scarlett, who would be awarded a role in the 'long-running hit series' *A Country Practice*. As no winner was ever declared, I can only assume my entry got lost in the mail.

When the cast of the small-screen adaptation was announced, with the brown-eyed (!!) Joanne Whalley-Kilmer as Scarlett and Timothy Dalton as Rhett, the *New Weekly* launched a 'Could you be Scarlett O'Hara?' competition in December 1993, requiring an entry form and photograph. The prize included a 'professional make-over with make-up, hairstyling and a fabulous period costume'. The winner, the first entry drawn out of a barrel, would be photographed in 'a very "Scarlett" pose' and spend two nights with a friend at Sydney's 'sumptuous' Park Lane Hotel. I still have my rejection letter, the returned photograph and a chip on my shoulder: the winner was hardly a Vivien Leigh doppelganger, but that wasn't the point. The point was, even in the '90s, many young women saw themselves as Scarlett O'Hara. Cue the siren call for Queensland's Scarlett.

> *Finally, a movie character that reminds me of myself.*
> – Jennifer

NOVEMBER 1994. AS fate, the high priestess of mockery, would have it, I'm eight-and-a-half months pregnant. Still, like Scarlett, I persist, just without the seventeen-inch waist. I cobble together a costume from a floral maternity frock, the hoop skirt from my wedding dress, hoicked over my beach-ball stomach, and some green fabric tacked to the bottom half of the skirt. It may not have the panache of Scarlett's green velvet dress made from Tara's portières, but doesn't look totally ridiculous.

From the original 300 or so, forty of us are recalled to see how we look on camera. As the day wears on – 'the Southern flowers started to wilt', reported Tony Biancotti – the forty are chiselled down to thirteen. Despite the could-give-birth-at-any-moment impediment, I remain in the mix. The judges, a trio of local casting agents, then put our improvisation skills to the test before choosing their final five. I go all in with a lot of impassioned eyebrow acting, while my rivals fling around *fiddle-dee-dees* like rice at a wedding. The strategy pays off: pregnant Scarlett makes it to the voter play-offs.

The following week, we five finalists – Varena, Renee, Kate, Kylie and me – each have our moment on the telly doing our best Scarlett impersonations, while Rick Burnett urges viewers to vote for their favourite for a chance to win $1,000 every night. I'm dismayed to have landed Thursday evening, which will surely diminish my chances. And thus, late-night shoppers be damned, it was not to be. Kate, who promised her youth group half the prize money to start up a coffee shop (not that I'm suggesting anything), is crowned Queensland's Scarlett. To be fair, her Scarlett is more high spirited and flouncy than mine. Besides, I have a baby to birth, and there's nothing quite like a newborn to vanquish petty outrage and disappointment.

I think Scarlett is the most beautiful woman in the whole world...she's influenced my whole life... I've even developed a similar eyebrow raise.
– Anonymous

APRIL 1999. I head off, unofficially, but nevertheless taking my duties seriously, to represent Australia at a three-day sixtieth anniversary *GWTW* event in Savannah, Georgia. In Haskell's timeline, this pilgrimage to the Deep South – taking in the Road to Tara Museum, the Margaret Mitchell House in Atlanta and other Southern enchantments, including New Orleans – is the pinnacle of my Dependency phase, with the advent of the internet entirely to blame. From the mid-'90s, Windies around the world started connecting through Yahoo!, *GWTW* forums and godawful AOL websites. On the collectables front, Faye's *GWTW* Memories store in Florida was only too happy to post *GWTW* dolls, figurines, ornaments, plates, books and the rest to Australia. I may or may not have bought *GWTW* playing cards, paper dolls, stationery, mugs, magnets, a watch, a jewellery box, T-shirts, a throw rug, the game – basically, if you could put Scarlett's face on it you could, and I did, buy it.

Scarlett, the sequel, had come and fizzled – 'A Powerful Wind Drops to a Breeze' penned Neil Melloy in *TV Week* – but *GWTW*'s popularity remained undiminished. If anything, it was reinvigorated by, first, a 1994 biopic on Margaret Mitchell, *A Burning Passion*, starring Shannen Doherty, then, in June 1998, a theatrical premier of the digitally remastered film.

For the DVD release in October 1998, Time Warner and MGM Home Entertainment launched a US-based nationwide search for a 'Scarlett of the '90s', in which contestants presented their own 'Scarlett's rules for living in the '90s', covering 'romance, style and being a woman of today'. And nothing says '90s Scarlett more than winning $2,500, Chanel cosmetics and a $1,000 shopping spree at Bloomingdale's.

The competition was notable for its shift away from being a Vivien Leigh lookalike contest. The bid to find a woman who, instead, 'most closely' resembled how Scarlett 'would act and speak today' and embodied 'her spirit and sass' opened up the search to any woman with a bit of chutzpah, including, in theory, Black and other women of colour. The framing of the competition did seem to be a nod to changing times and, perhaps, an acknowledgement that the traditional Scarlett lookalike competition was inherently exclusionary and insidiously valorises the whiteness of those eligible to participate. Whether this happened in practice is another thing – there were only white women featured in photographs I've seen of the contest, and the winner, Clarissa Jacobson, an 'aspiring actress' from LA, was one of them.

I certainly wasn't going to let my Australianness, accent included, stop me from being the most Scarletty Scarlett of them all at the final night 'barbeque and ball' in Savannah. To the organisers' chagrin, or so rumour has it, I easily out-Scarletted the official 'lookalike' hired for the event. A limp replica barbecue dress, however – found in a last-minute dash to a costume-hire shop in a less salubrious part of town and held together with a dozen safety pins – was never going to cut it in the 'best costume' (not 'lookalike', it was firmly reiterated) contest. A very blonde woman in her immaculate and expensive reproduction of Scarlett's red velvet dress walked away with that prize. Folks, I did my best.

> *I thought Scarlett was the greatest woman ever… Everything she did I understood even if she was mean, selfish and hard-headed. I wanted to be just like her.*
> – Melly

MARCH 2009. I greet Elizabeth Meryment, a journalist from *The Australian*, at the gates of the Eastern Suburbs private boys' school I'm teaching at in Sydney. She's writing an article on whether people 'still give a damn' about *GWTW* and has come to interview me, as a former damn giver, in my lunch break. By this stage, *GWTW* is a faint hum emanating from my bedroom cupboard. The dolls and plates, once the decorative highlight of whatever rental I was living in, have been stowed away, with some of the more gauche items (the Barbies) sold off on eBay. This is the Resentment and Embarrassment phase. Attending anniversary events and creating shrines in one's home from limitless collectables are the purview of the true zealot. Google Selina Faye Sorrow for Exhibit A. Aside from distancing myself from the Selinas of this world, I was carving out an identity untethered to my idealisation of Scarlett O'Hara or even Vivien Leigh. Nevertheless, I play the part for the interview, wearing a red dress and doing something Scarlett-ish with my hair.

Meryment didn't quote me in the article, a retrospective mercy, but I lent her my old *GWTW* scrapbooks and an essay on *GWTW* fandom I'd written as an undergrad for a feminist media studies elective. By coincidence, or because her name was on the front of my assignment, Meryment quotes Helen Yeates, a former film and media studies academic at QUT. While 'sceptical' about *GWTW*'s feminist credentials, Yeates instead sees the work as an individualist narrative – 'a very American story' with 'its "pull yourself up by your bootstraps" Protestant work ethic'. But what of its resonance with young Australian women in the late aughts? Despite Haskell's claim, in 2009, that Scarlett remains 'eerily timely, channelling the spirit of an age…that resembles ours to jarring degree', Dr Toni Johnson-Woods, who taught the novel in a popular fiction course at UQ, said 'many of her young female students "dislike[d] Scarlett intensely"'. Something Johnson-Woods found difficult to understand and put down to 'Scarlett being a confronting personality'.

Teaching an undergraduate genre-fiction course ten years later, I experienced a similar vibe. Included in the set readings – not set by me, for the record – was an excerpt from *GWTW*, the scene where Rhett proposes to Scarlett. The students, mostly, were only vaguely familiar with both book and film. However, one young woman – a blue-eyed, fair-skinned brunette – professed quite the hatred for the 'horrible' Scarlett and her profound dislike that people told her she looked like this despicable creature. What could I say? At her age, I lived for such comparisons. My attempt to explain my youthful obsession with *GWTW* was met with polite silence.

Afterwards, I sat with the discomfort of this young lady's reaction. I mean, she's not wrong – Scarlett is a piece of work – and she's hardly the first person to say so, but it's not usually young women, particularly those with an analogous visage to Vivien Leigh, who point it out so vehemently. At a 1994 press conference, Timothy Dalton – the Rhett you get when King Gable is dead – expressed shock 'that so many women all around the world could identify with this extraordinary cunt'. Yes. Okay. But. How to defend myself and hundreds like me then? Such as the many women, some quoted throughout this essay, who responded to a 1998 internet poll asking about their first impressions of Scarlett.

Here I'll defer to other Scarlett O'Philes of my generation who've publicly professed fierce identic love with the non-fool-suffering, force-of-nature fashionista, and make no bones about how she shaped their *Bildungsroman*. Janie Bryant, for example, a Hollywood costume designer, who says, in her 2014 TEDx talk 'Scarlett O'Hara, my life coach': 'I wanted to be Scarlett. Scarlett lit up my life like a hot-headed, Southern-belle supernova and motivated me to follow my passions and achieve them, come hell or high water.' Or British journalist Hannah Betts, who writes in 'My Love Affair with Scarlett O'Hara' in 2013 for *The Telegraph*: 'Graduating straight from Enid Blyton and Louisa May Alcott, Scarlett appeared the ultimate female role model: Jo March on acid, feminist fatale in 18-inch stays. She remains the great literary protagonist of a not-so-great book, regardless of how passionately I adore it.' Like me, and many others I'll wager, Betts had a *GWTW* poster on her bedroom wall, from which, she says, 'Leigh stalked away from flaming Atlanta...moodily overseeing my path into young womanhood.'

I think we are though, for good reasons, the last generation to take Boss Scarlett to heart as an exemplar of how to succeed as a woman in a man's world in any culturally significant way. Scarlett's 'feminism' – if that's what you call her self-serving flouting of societal gender norms – has always been contentious, but no one could argue it was collective or intersectional, and she – and the book and film that birthed her – are not holding up well in the twenty-first century. Though there are outliers – look for them in YouTube comments and *GWTW* Facebook groups – Gen Zs are little interested in the twentieth century's most famous fictional female character. When they do watch *GWTW*, however, the results are both instructive and hilarious, as per Exhibit B: YouTubers VKunia (American) and Mary Cherry (Australian) doing their 'First Time Watching' *GWTW* 'co-lab' video. While loving on Melanie ('She is an angel.' 'I love her.'), they are singularly unimpressed with Scarlett ('She be slapping everyone. We have seen a lot of slaps from her.' 'She is so toxic.').

> *My first impression of Scarlett was that she was a simple-minded twit who only cared about herself and being loved by others.*
> – Melissa

MAY 2023. I pick up a copy of Sarah Churchill's recently published *The Wrath to Come: Gone with the Wind and the Lies America Tells*. It's the first

'*GWTW* book' I've bought in years and is like no other in my collection, most of which are glossy 'making of' pictorials or populist cultural critique. Churchill is unequivocal about *GWTW*'s pernicious perpetuation of the South's Lost Cause narrative – a deliberate rewriting of history 'to justify slavery and maintain American innocence', which romanticised the South's slavocracy, plantation culture and the Ku Klux Klan, erased interwar American fascism and, ultimately, led to Trumpism and the storming of the US Capitol on 6 January 2021.

I found the book profoundly confronting and horrifying, as it's supposed to be, with its graphic descriptions of lynchings and other racially motivated atrocities against Black people. Churchill repeatedly enlists the text, Mitchell's own words, to show just *how* racist the book and *all* its white characters are – no one, not even the 'saintly' Melanie Wilkes, gets a free pass. *GWTW* is a white supremacy playbook, which begs the question: is any of it, book or film – apart from Hattie McDaniel's Oscar-winning portrayal of Mammy – salvageable? Honestly, I don't know.

For the last ten years – the Indifference phase, in Haskell's timeline – I've kept half an eye on *GWTW* as a sputtering grenade in America's ongoing culture war: the call, in 2014, by *New York Post* film critic Lou Lumenick that *GWTW* 'should go the way of the Confederate flag' and effectively be discontinued; the decision, in 2017, by the Orpheum Theatre in Memphis to cancel, after thirty-four years, their annual screening of *GWTW* when patrons complained the film was insensitive to the city's Black population; streaming giant HBO Max pulling *GWTW* from their platform in 2020 following the murder of George Floyd by a white police officer and the subsequent #BLM protests. Amid cries of 'censorship' from conservatives, the film was reinstated to the streaming channel with an introduction by Jacqueline Stewart, a professor of cinema studies, explaining the film's 'multiple historical contexts'.

As to Haskell's final phase, Half-Love, I arrived there, sort of, while writing this essay. I was reminded, looking through my scrapbooks of magazine articles and other *GWTW*-themed ephemera, of the twelve-year-old girl who fell in love with Scarlett O'Hara and wanted, with all her heart, to be just like her. Though I never took onboard her contempt for other women – unlike Scarlett, I've always valued female friendship – or her flinty meanness, she did teach me resilience, the art of flirtation (an underrated skill) and how to be the architect of your own story. My life, for a drawerful of reasons, would have been very different if Miss O'Hara hadn't entered it when she did. So, let's call it the Wary-Affection-But-Not-Without-Regrets stage. Now, as a middle-aged woman, it's hard to see Scarlett as anything but insufferable, entitled and definitely racist. Scarlett at fifty? Well, it could have gone a few ways, but, frankly, I'm not that interested.

Melanie Myers won the Queensland Literary Awards Glendower Award for an Emerging Writer in 2018. Her winning manuscript was published as *Meet Me at Lennon's* (UQP), which was shortlisted for the 2020 Queensland Premier's Award for a Work of State Significance and The Courier-Mail People's Choice Award. Her short stories and non-fiction have appeared in *Kill Your Darlings*, *Overland*, *Arena Magazine*, *TEXT* and *Hecate*, among many others.

NON-FICTION

Anticipating enchantment

The myth of editorial perfection and the legend of the solo author

Alice Grundy

TELLING A STRANGER that you are a book editor normally results in one of two responses. Either you'll be told that editing has deteriorated – whether in the past five or fifty years depends on your interlocutor. Or the charge is that editors intervene too much, their contribution a sort of con job perpetrated on unsuspecting readers. Both responses are characterised as a symptom of the evils of capitalism: either there is no money for proper editing anymore, or books are being smooshed into more marketable boxes. Some claim that there is no proper editing because they've found typos or misused words and phrases in contemporary books. Others hold that editorial interventions are extreme and endanger the concept of authorship.

But, as with any generalisation, the reality is much more complicated. As a book editor and researcher of editing and publishing history, I have defences for each accusation, if it will please the court of public opinion.

To begin with, allow me to make the potentially obvious point that in classics or even books that have made it to a second printing, the author and editor have likely been alerted to mistakes. No book makes it to market without at least one mistake, but if the market has been receptive then the publisher has another chance to perfect it. This is one reason why your copy of *Tess of the d'Urbervilles* or *White Teeth* seems editorially superior. For these books it is not only the editors who have helped render the work error free but also the readers, who have alerted publishers to mistakes.

In the few examples where editors emerge from behind the curtain into the view of popular culture – such as the 2016 film *Genius* featuring Colin Firth as editor Maxwell Perkins, famous for his work with F Scott Fitzgerald and Ernest Hemingway – our attention is directed to individuals rather than the networks of people responsible for the books we read. But editors can appear in the form of the author's friends who read early drafts; expert readers engaged by the publisher to prepare reports before a book is signed; structural editors, who look at the big picture, considering characterisation and style; copyeditors, who check for consistency; and proofreaders, who are the last line of defence against typos.

Editorial labour is usually kept private, both because editors want to keep their authors' confidence, and because readers have accepted the Romantic notion of the individual artist. This secrecy, however, has contributed to an ongoing misunderstanding of what editorial labour is.

When an editor works on a book, they balance reader expectations with what they interpret the author's intentions to be and use their experience to make suggestions. This might mean changing some of the language to ensure the work is comprehensible for general readers, or asking for more detail where a setting has been hastily described. An editor will always be anticipating the market, and their extensive reading of contemporary works makes them well-placed not only to understand the social and political conditions of the day but also trends in publishing and marketing.

MEMBERS OF THE Push or the women's lib movement in Sydney may remember Kate Jennings' 'Front Lawn Speech' from the University of Sydney at the start of the 1970s. She eviscerated her male peers for focusing on the Vietnam War draft and ignoring the dangers she and other women faced. Jennings went on to write several poetry, essay and short-story collections and two short novels. Although she worked as an editor for magazines in New York, when it came to the editing of her own work she still suffered the indignities of mistakes.

For her first essay collection, published by Penguin Australia in 1988, the introduced errors from editorial were so irksome that she commented on them to her last editor twenty years later. To another correspondent, Jennings complained of an editor changing 'such as' to 'like'. 'Such as' indicates examples, whereas 'like' offers comparisons; a subtle difference increasingly falling from use. Perhaps the most surprising of my findings from Jennings' archive is an editor who contributed such unhelpful comments as 'fix', 'eh' and '?' in her marginalia. This same person made edits that puzzle me: changing 'able' to 'disposed' in one part of a paragraph and 'were appalled' to 'didn't crack a smile' in another. As the *Australian Copyediting Handbook* makes clear, consistency is one of the editor's objectives, which means changes such as these that simultaneously increase and decrease the register are outside of standard practice. Changing neater turns of phrase to make them pedestrian is one of the worst interventions an editor can make.

Evident from Jennings' lack of response to some of the bigger editorial queries is that an author is less likely to act on the feedback of an editor without efforts at persuasion. Jennings' first essay collection included work that had previously been published in a range of outlets, from *Vogue* to *Australian Book Review*. The editor made comments that could have helped smooth this transition, including reworking a book review to make it more of an essay, but Jennings did not follow the advice. Had the editor seemed more sympathetic to the author's project in general, I think Jennings would have been more inclined to make these revisions. Since editorial comments are usually suggestions rather than diktats, persuasion is paramount.

Each of the six authors I've studied have encountered such infelicities (as an editor might describe inapposite words). In the 1970s – when printers arranged type manually, using individual letters in rows and paragraphs on a tray – Jessica Anderson's American printer dropped a tray of type and put it back in the wrong order. Despite Anderson's warnings, her UK publisher reproduced the error. Ruth Park's editor, the storied Beatrice Davis, was tasked with cutting her manuscript *Swords and Crowns and Rings* by 20 per cent, partly to bring it down to the word length that the then Literature Board subsidised. In correspondence, Davis did not mention the reason for the significant cuts to Park, who expressed curiosity at what seemed like an arbitrary reduction in length. Park's resistance held; she rejected many of the edits.

It is not in a spirit of schadenfreude that I tell these stories – not least because I have introduced my own cover typos and other errors – but rather to demonstrate that to make mistakes is human and not necessarily a recent product of a workforce overtaxed due to the evils of capitalism.

As the Oxford English Dictionary attests, language changes. What was once standard usage no longer has currency. If you were taught Latin and grammar at school, you will be unimpressed by the perceived sloppiness of those who weren't. I'll admit to having felt a frisson of superiority when I've come across a writer's use of the verb 'rifle' (to ransack) in place of 'riffle' (to look through). There are lots of characters described as thrashing about in files when I think their authors intended a more decorous shuffle, but I know what they mean, and if this usage outweighs the earlier version, then I can adjust.

Former American trade-publishing editor Helen Betya Rubinstein takes this further, arguing:

> It's clear that copyediting as it's typically practiced is a white supremacist project, that is, not only for the particular linguistic forms it favors and upholds, which belong to the cultures of whiteness and power, but for how it excludes or erases the voices and styles of those who don't or won't perform this culture.

If a copyeditor's job is to standardise and make consistent, this also flattens and removes play, experimentation and expression, especially when the author's voice doesn't match the publisher's style guide.

In the Australian context, Bundjalung author, activist and educator Ruby Langford Ginibi repeatedly spoke up from the late 1980s onwards about her editors 'gubbarising' her writing – taking her expressions and whitening them to fit into standard Australian English. This is not an isolated phenomenon; Wiradjuri author Anita Heiss examined this practice in her book *Dhuuluu Yala: To Talk Straight*, published in 2003. As well as discussing Langford Ginibi's editorial trials, Heiss recounts an anecdote from publisher Katharine Brisbane in which Robert Adamson, a settler author, and Kevin Gilbert, a First Nations author, were sitting on a jetty with their newly published books. Adamson was pleased with the treatment of his poems but Gilbert was disgusted, throwing his book into the water.

Publishing culture is starting to recognise the value in fidelity to voice and expression of lived experience, and increasingly you can read books that reproduce spoken or written vernaculars from outside the dominant discourse, which means that those who expect the Queen's, or King's, English will be disappointed. The black&write! program at the State Library of Queensland, for example, pairs experienced First Nations editors with mentees keen to work in publishing, creating a new generation of First Nations editors whose sensibility is more likely to afford vernacular pluralism and less likely to be limited by colonial linguistic standards.

TO ADDRESS THE other charge I often encounter: when does editing cross over and become co-authorship, and when should the reader care? A friend of the family recently told me about her neighbour who works for a notoriously interventionist multinational publisher. When she learnt the sort of work the editor performed, the friend was shocked and felt duped. How could the author's name hold such real estate on the cover when they had only been part of the deal?

The idea that over-editing is a moral betrayal is as old as the complaint that editing ain't what it used to be. In 1936 Bernard DeVoto, then the editor of *The Saturday Review of Literature* in New York, reacted to Thomas Wolfe's description of the highly collaborative editorial process he underwent with Maxwell Perkins. In a piece entitled 'Genius Is Not Enough', DeVoto argued that Wolfe's work lacked integrity as a result of his collaboration with Perkins. In line with repeated references to the supposedly 'organic' nature of novel writing, DeVoto said that 'works of art cannot be assembled like a carburettor – they must be grown like a plant' and that Wolfe's books came from 'the assembly line at Scribners'. He referred to the publishing company twice in a paragraph, seemingly saying that instead of the novels emerging as the natural, organic product of genius and artistic intelligence, they were pieced together in a factory like a Model T Ford. Which leads me to wonder, did DeVoto really think that all literary work springs up like a weed? If the author reworks and reworks a project, does that stop it from being organic? Or is it the editor's intervention that is so horrifically mechanical? This fails to account for the printing press and sales team and other people between the author and the reader.

As my family friend demonstrates, concern about editorial intervention continues. Some even believe overly invasive editorial intervention is a recent phenomenon.

In 2011, claiming that publishing was becoming too collaborative, Kirsty Gunn – a novelist and creative writing professor at Dundee University – told *The Guardian*,

> To my mind, there's a wicked expectation that literary work can be created by some kind of committee. I've always been horrified by

the notion of sending in a draft that isn't finished. I think there's a real difference between sitting down and creating a piece of work and then having a conversation with someone you respect, and sending in a piece of work and thinking, we'll work on this together.

Wicked indeed. Why is that? We don't tend to think less of architects for collaborating with engineers or directors for working with cinematographers. What is peculiar to writing that it must be executed individually? I find this attitude especially puzzling from someone who teaches creative writing. While in the article Gunn is quoted as having concerns about creative writing workshops as well, nevertheless she has continued to teach writing, year after year.

What these concerns lead me to ask is: if the work is marvellous, does it matter how many people were involved in its production? I don't think James Joyce was cheating when he knowingly, gleefully incorporated the errors of his typesetters into *Ulysses*. And what of Kate Jennings and her editor's feedback? While she would possibly gain Dr Gunn's approval for her independent drafting practices, nevertheless she was at the mercy of her collaborators. Almost no books come into the world as the work of a single mind and body.

Here's where I find critic Rita Felski's idea of enchantment useful. Felski divides literary experience into four categories: recognition, enchantment, knowledge and shock. Readers are looking to see themselves in the literature they read (recognition), to be caught up and transported (enchantment), to learn about something in the world (knowledge) or to have a kind of blow to their consciousness (shock). I think moralisers like DeVoto can get stuck anticipating enchantment – not just in reading the work but from the idea of communing with the individual author and their vision. Unlike theatre or cinema or visual art or music concerts, we often read alone – or feel alone when we read. Acknowledging the publisher and the editor and the typesetter and the cover designer and the sales team and the bookseller makes a reading nook suddenly feel rather crowded. The business of publishing disrupts the experience they hope to enjoy. They don't want to reach other modes of approaching the work – in Felski's terminology that would be knowledge, recognition or shock.

The interference of different individuals in the publishing process is as old as publishing itself. Scholars of the medieval period have been comfortable with the idea of multiple contributors for some time, as Irina Dumitrescu noted in the *London Review of Books* recently – describing a network of contributors behind the high stone walls of a monastery. Authorship experts including Martha Woodmansee trace the obsession with the individual author to the Romantic period. Some more financially minded researchers date it to the invention of copyright, when a single author made accounting more convenient. Whatever the true provenance, we have been entranced by the notion of the solitary author for a few hundred years now and seem in no hurry to leave its thrall. Meanwhile, the work of contemporary editors quietly, weightlessly amasses in digital archives.

IT'S NOT SIMPLY editors who contribute to the work that we read. A long line of wives, many unacknowledged, have been typists and readers, structural editors and agents for their husbands. Famous examples include Vladimir and Vera Nabokov, TS and Valerie Eliot, and John le Carré and his second wife, Jane Eustace, who was his editor before they married. Counting friends, creative writing teachers, family and freelancers, a book may well have a cricket team's worth of individual contributors by the time it has reached the printer.

Book historian Robert Darnton created the Communication Circuit in 1982, which lists many contributors to a book's production. Padmini Ray Murray and Claire Squires updated the circuit in 2013 and added two more: agents and freelancers/outsource agencies. While I wouldn't want to advocate for a list in every book detailing the contributions of everyone who has had some role in its production (even if contemporary acknowledgements often go so far as to thank baristas and cats), a writer who produces a book by themselves is the exception. Literary work is not a solitary and organic manifestation of individual genius as some seem to believe, and unless the writer can operate a printing press and be their own designer, editor and bookseller, they need assistance to bring their work to readers.

Some of you may remember David Hume's exhortation not to derive an ought from an is. In other words, don't believe that just because something is the case it should be. The converse is true also, and here's where I think these editorial Chicken Littles are getting into trouble. They perceive editing as operating in a particular way, and then argue that it should instead happen as they imagine it. If they acknowledge all the people involved in bringing them the book in their lap then their sense of intimacy, of communing with the author directly, is interrupted. The possibility of imagining the relationship as purely intellectual or emotional vanishes: the romance dies.

But I think if they paused to query how they're conflating morality with their imagined publishing process – if they read the Macquarie Dictionary, Lionel Fogarty's syntax-exploding poetry and some fan fiction, remembering that language is made and remade continuously – then they might relax. With their interest more in the work itself and less tightly bound to the prospect of one other creative person, genius or otherwise, there's room for enchantment and much more besides.

For references, see griffithreview.com

Alice Grundy has been a book editor for the past fifteen years and is completing a PhD at ANU. Her thesis forms the basis for a minigraph, *Editing Fiction: Three Cases Studies from Postwar Australia*, published by Cambridge University Press. She has taught literature at ANU and editing at UTS, and written for the *Sydney Review of Books*, *The Conversation* and *The Canberra Times*, among others.

NON-FICTION

From anchor to weapon

The politics of nostalgia

Michael L Ondaatje & Michael G Thompson

IMAGINE, FOR A moment, this scene. It happened to one of us recently as we were cleaning out a carport. Jarred (not his real name), one of our children, a seven-year-old boy, turned and said that seeing his old scooter – the one with gaudy plastic and three large wheels, instead of the stainless steel two-wheeled version he uses now – made him 'nostalgic'. His word choice was striking (maybe somebody in the house had been talking about this word in preparation for an essay). On one level it was amusing: the idea that 2020 might be a golden age for which he felt homesick. Who would want to go back to that time, with all the uncertainty and pain of the pandemic? And how could someone so young be nostalgic for such a brief arc of history?

But on reflection, Jarred used the term 'nostalgia' almost in its purest sense. His sad eyes and slumped posture conveyed his ache for a stage of earlier childhood that lay seemingly just beyond the horizon of memory. Some tough times at school lately may have added to his yearning for a safer past, and Jarred is given to frequent, wistful remembrances of holidays, of times with his grandparents, of ice-creams and sandcastles at the beach. But these kinds of feelings are common to humans of all ages. That late afternoon, as the sun left traces across the sky on its retreat west and the mosquitoes began to buzz and bite, Jarred's pain of longing (*algia*) was stirred by the memory of a warm, golden-tinged past. His desire in that moment, which he intuitively knew to be unrealisable, was for a return home (*nostos*).

RECENT PSYCHOLOGICAL STUDIES have stressed the positive 'anchoring' effect that nostalgia lends our lives. But it wasn't always viewed this way. The term has its origins in the search to identify the pathologies that unfulfilled homesickness wrought on Swiss soldiers away from their *patria* in the seventeenth century; it was widely understood to be a debilitating psychological condition requiring treatment. Contemporary researchers have challenged such thinking, insisting that nostalgia is often a healthy phenomenon reflecting our understandable need for roots and a sense of stability in a changing world.

We know this from personal experience. Both of us have similar pangs to Jarred when we spot the low, square lines and contours of mid-twentieth-century furniture; the laminex, the beige and brown cushions take each of us back to our grandparents' homes in 1980s suburbia. Nostalgia, in this sense, offers sweet and evocative memories, ripe with personal connections to family lines and legacies.

But here's where nostalgia presents a puzzle. In an individual's life, nostalgia mostly serves a positive function, anchoring people to a sense of family and place, but when that same emotion is extrapolated to our political communities, the results are almost always harmful and negative. 'Make America Great *Again*' and 'Take Back Control' are familiar slogans associated respectively with Donald Trump and Brexit. Both communicated a clear message to voters: that *the best way forward is back*. In disrupted and divided societies where dissatisfaction with the present runs deep, the incentive to retreat into an idealised past in yearning for a better future is powerful. This is when nostalgia can transform from anchor to weapon – and history warns us of the devastating consequences.

How, then, does a positive, if wistfully painful, anchoring feeling in individual and family life become something so harmful in political life? Although there are endless variations across time and place, we suggest that nostalgic appeals in politics have tended to display four main elements:

1) A deep grievance about the present.
2) A story about a once-natural state of things that has since been betrayed and/or corroded by another group ('they').
3) A mythic past that defines the *true* and original political community ('we').
4) Calls for the 'we' to take immediate action in order to reverse the gains of the 'they'.

No political order has an exclusive hold on this form of nostalgic argument and imagining, but some have embodied these elements with more intellectual energy – and with more devastating and violent effect – than others. None more so, perhaps, than Nazi Germany.

We are aware of the good reasons people avoid making quick allusions to Nazis to prove a point. Followers of Godwin's law on internet discussion forums rightly insist that reaching for the 'Hitler card' is often a sign that real debate has ended. Yet, engagement with the 1930s need not be a conversation ender. Rather, as we hope to show here, it can and needs to be a path to a more serious reckoning with contemporary political communities.

'Blood and soil' ideology (*Blut und Boden*) is a good way to study and understand Nazi nostalgia. A slogan most commonly associated with the Nazis, and more recently used by American Neo-Nazis, it expressed Germany's commitment to the idea of a 'pure' Aryan racial community inextricably connected to a territory or region. It also purveyed a politics of nostalgia that elevated the imagined *rural* as more 'truly' German than anything urban. Similarly, many modern nationalisms reimagined their history in ways that presented rurality as existing prior to, and being 'truer' to, national essence than the current urban condition about which they expressed grievance. Australian nationalism in the 1890s was no exception.

In 1930s Germany, the slogan 'blood and soil' was most prominently promulgated by the Reich Ministry of Food and Agriculture, which positioned itself not merely as an administrator but a kind of advocate-guardian of the soil and its workers. In 1930, Adolf Hitler recruited Richard Walther Darré, then a leading blood and soil theorist, to the Nazi Party. On seizing power in 1933, Hitler appointed Darré Reichsminister of Agriculture, a role he occupied until 1942. Recently, for reasons that are unclear but politically alarming, Darré's works on blood and soil have been translated and republished in English to some fanfare.

In his book published in 1930, *A New Nobility of Blood and Soil*, Darré created a nostalgic sculpture of monumental proportions, and the nature of his argument is revealing of the ways nostalgia can easily, even if implicitly, become a political weapon. The four features we outlined above are clear in the book's whole thrust.

First, Darré's myriad grievances about the present were shared with millions of Germans throughout the 1930s: the humiliating loss of World

War I, the crumbling of the Second Reich (that is, Imperial Germany of 1871–1918), the oppression of postwar debts and reparations, the mechanisation of the countryside, chaos on financial markets, cultural libertinism in the cities and the ideological infiltration of socialism into the body politic.

Yet Darré's biggest grievance was the decline of the late nineteenth- and early twentieth-century aristocracy on whose watch Germany had lost the war, signed a humiliating peace treaty and descended into chaos. The ruling classes of wealthy families and elite officers had let Germany down and failed in their role as the country's 'nobility', he argued, inciting the revolutionary sentiment of Bolsheviks in response. And thus, as the title of his book proposed, this meant the old guard had lost legitimacy.

Like all nostalgists, Darré's call was for a new way forward that involved the nation going back to something old: in this case to what he claimed were the vital powers of the peasantry whose blood was bound with the *Vaterland*'s ancient soil. Here he supported the elaborate pseudo-science of contemporary eugenics and Aryan racism.

But alongside this was the nostalgic myth of rural purity. Like Hitler in *Mein Kampf*, Darré posited two contrasting worlds, as scholar Keith Swaney has put it: 'one was a place in which the content, noble peasant toiled for the German race', ready to give their life for the Fatherland, the other where the worldviews (*Weltanschauung*) of liberalism, communism and modernism led modern Deutschland into subjection and humiliation. The time, according to Nazis, was for 'culture war' (*Kulturkampf*). Nostalgia for a lost golden age was central to their arsenal.

The 'we' at the heart of Germany's so-called golden age were those most obviously bound by blood and soil to the land. Now was the time, insisted Darré and Hitler, to restore a 'truly' Germanic peasant-based nobility to power – expelling urban, internationalist (Jewish) elites – in order to make Deutschland great again.

The rest, as they say, is history.

IT IS EASY to focus on Germany as a uniquely horrific case. And indeed, its horror ought never to be downplayed. But Nazi use of nostalgia is useful for understanding other cases, despite differences in context and emphasis.

Less widely known is that nostalgic antisemitism in the 1930s was also popular across the Atlantic. In his first inaugural address in 1933, US President

Franklin D Roosevelt, apparently unconcerned about antisemitic connotations, famously cast the New York finance sector as the 'moneychangers in the temple', whom his New Deal administration would cast out (as Jesus did when, as the four gospels depict, he cast out the money and animal traders from the Jerusalem temple).

Roosevelt never courted anything like the conspiracy theories of *The Protocols of the Elders of Zion*, which laid all evils at the feet of a shadowy globalist group of Jews allegedly manipulating financial markets, the world economy, media and more. But it is likely many Americans listening to him did. Indeed, one of the greatest populist media darlings of the 1930s, one who reached more Americans than most politicians, was Catholic 'Radio Priest' Father Charles Coughlin. Coughlin drifted from initial support of Roosevelt towards an unbridled antisemitism that bizarrely linked Jews with both Stalinist communism *and* Western high capitalism. Based in Detroit, the Canadian-born Coughlin purveyed a nostalgic populism in which true, original 'Americanism', agrarian expansion and Christianity had once been hand in glove. When the early nineteenth-century settler-colonists had expanded into the prairie grasslands and forests of the Western frontier, they were blessedly fulfilling God's commission to 'go forth and multiply' (never mind those sovereign nations already occupying the space). Families feeding off the fat of the land during westward expansion were proof of God's blessing.

In this mythical golden past (elements two and three in nostalgic politics) there was no high capitalism. Agrarians and artisans wrought 'plenty' from the soil as they applied noble labour (slavery was absent from this story). But enter the grievance (element one). In recent decades, from the time of Coughlin's childhood, the rise of private banking, high finance and large integrated industrial corporations had slowly begun to lead 'true' America astray. Then the catastrophes of the Great War of 1914–18 and the Great Depression revealed the identity and extent of the evil forces against 'true' America (element three). According to Coughlin, and as shared by antisemitic propaganda at the time, the culprits were a shadowy international network who were to blame both for the Great War and postwar chaos. As bankers and profiteers, high capitalists, they stood to profit from both; ipso facto, they must be responsible. Here, Coughlin began to tie the problems of capitalism specifically to an imaginary Jewish network, connected simultaneously with Wall Street, munitions manufacturers, malevolent 'international' forces and

Bolsheviks in Russia. One can hear parallels with the kind of conspiracy theories that surfaced a century later in the Covid era.

But Coughlin was no fringe 'conspirituality' influencer. He was arguably among the largest media presences in the US of the 1930s. His radio-friendly and charismatic baritone voice was, at its peak, syndicated nationally on CBS Radio and fifty-eight affiliate stations. Shamefully, he used that platform to republish *The Protocols of the Elders of Zion*, adding to the global rise of antisemitism in the late 1930s, and arguably slowing the cause of American bipartisan opposition to Hitler's war in Europe.

COUGHLIN AND DARRÉ were but two actors in a bubbling cauldron of 1930s propaganda wars that centred on antisemitism and images of 'true' national identity as entwined with rural locales and farm work. But these trends are apparent in other times and contexts, too. The four features of political nostalgia give us some trailheads to explore the conditions under which this phenomenon has emerged in the twentieth and twenty-first centuries.

We suggest that when there are shocks to existing social and economic systems, there is typically a corresponding rise in grievance politics. Grievance politics frequently goes looking for a story about the past and the way things used to be before the natural order was allegedly betrayed. This is not new to modern history. Nostalgia as a form of cultural politics was endemic to the later Roman empire, when anxiety about decline caused the Imperial Court to fund authors willing to produce images of true essential Roman-ness residing in rural, rustic peasantry and bucolic pastoral scenes.

But modernity itself is arguably a big factor behind this shock and grievance. We certainly see spikes in nostalgic cultural politics in moments of industrial and economic upheaval. For example, the economic booms and busts of the 1890s spawned the Arts and Crafts Movement as a protest against the high industrialism and upscaled capitalism that Coughlin was concerned about. Forty years later, the economic turmoil of the Great Depression precipitated a retreat into nostalgic politics that was powerfully exploited by fascist movements and demagogues. The machinery of the modern propaganda state undoubtedly made the politics of that period all the more potent.

More recently, the economic wreckage of the global financial crisis was a key trigger for the emergence of the Tea Party in the US as a forerunner of Donald Trump. Pledging to 'Take America Back' and directing special animus towards 'elites' and 'immigrants', Tea Party supporters looked to create a useable history as a bulwark against a difficult present and uncertain future. Social media helped them spread the message. With an intensity that has become a hallmark of contemporary political life, Tea Partiers promoted a vast catalogue of myths about eighteenth-century America centred on the revolution, founders and constitution, while framing the 1950s in equally positive terms – as a decade of 'national unity', economically stable and less riven by social strife. If only America could recover the spirit of these earlier times, then its future would be secure.

Times of economic affluence have also bred forms of nostalgia in politics, particularly among more left-leaning protest and countercultural movements. For example, in 1960s America, despite unprecedented prosperity, countercultural nostalgists highlighted the sinister sides of modern 'progress': nuclear triumphalism, mega dam building, DDT pesticides, big corporate liberalism and America's military-industrial complex warring in Vietnam. 'Small' (as in handmade and artisan-made, like the Arts and Crafts Movement) was beautiful again. The modern 'power elite' had alienated Americans from their own communities, their own labour, their own bodies. In festivals of free love, LSD-fuelled trances to the sounds of the Grateful Dead and efforts to produce communal life 'back on the land', countercultural nostalgists sought to undo the 'false consciousness' they believed modern consumerism had doped them with.

We observe echoes of this double-layered nostalgia alive and well today in organic farmers' markets near Australia's urban centres. Allusions to the 1970s counterculture and health-food-store products carry alongside them a nostalgia that period shared for the earlier Arts and Crafts Movement. Purveyors of crystals, incense and tie-dyes sit alongside artisan stone-ground sourdough, vendors of organic apples and trailers cooking 'traditional' German sausage.

The politics of nostalgia can also be explained by a sense of porousness in borders, a vulnerability to movements of people and forces from outside the ostensibly sovereign nation state. At these moments, immigrants, again, have been particularly liable to being othered as a scourge on the 'true' and 'natural' political community. During the 2010s, for example, the Mediterranean basin and Europe witnessed the mass movement of displaced peoples and asylum seekers occasioned by the War on Terror and the march of ISIS. Denizens of these states reacted in different ways, but a dominant response was to tie grievance politics to nostalgia about a 'Christian civilisation' under threat.

These stories – about the past, about a once-natural state that has been betrayed or corroded by an other – inevitably involve a compression and simplification of the actual past into a useable one 'fit' for contemporary political purposes. We call this a 'capsule history'.

The feeling of certainty and clarity – of *manageability* – that comes with putting big history into a small capsule is another reason why nostalgia resonates deeply in politics. As well as reflecting the strong urge to belong to a community and defend it, nostalgia affirms our common cognitive biases. For good or bad, and usually both, we often seem to want simplicity and certainty, co-ordinates for our mapping of who and where we are. We reach for such capsuled pasts, and indeed *produce* them, in the forming of our relation to the present.

This extends well beyond politics. Picture another scene: 'You shouldn't eat oatmeal. It's a grain,' a dietitian instructed one of us recently. 'Cavemen didn't eat grains. You can eat steaks.' The claim hung in midair. 'You can eat cured meats like bacon and sausage,' the dietitian went on. 'But you can't have rye, wheat or oats.' She was selling a version of what in the 2010s came to be known as the Paleo diet. As well as offering a way to respond to some elevated inflammation tendencies of concern, she was offering a capsule vision of historical time.

Like most capsules, this distilled narrative was one of regression towards decline and disaster. The apex of human health, it seemed, was the ostensive 'caveman' – the one from the Palaeolithic era, before things had gone terribly wrong with the domestication of grains and milk.

Behold the flourishing caveman: eating an abundance of seeds, berries and steaks, without paying $40 per kilo for the organic varieties, all the while enjoying good teeth, no obesity, abundant antioxidants and fatty acids, and supremely well-regulated blood sugar levels. His avoidance of parasites and predators was all rounded off with uninterrupted sleep and exercise.

And then along came the grain-and-milk-based agricultural revolution: the start of the Holocene, the creation of sedentary society and the invention of poor, nutritionally narrow diets. Farming led to the downfall of caveman health and the rise of the overweight office worker.

This story about the caveman is repeated in all manner of self-help and self-optimisation books and videos. Unlike Jarred's wistful nostalgia about his scooter, those who propagate Paleo narratives want to intervene to change practice in the present. They want to bring 'back' what has been lost, and to stake that claim over and against those who have led human dieting astray – Big Food, Big Pharma and Big Potato.

So, is Paleo dieting a kind of nostalgia?

No.

People will not likely kill or be killed in the name of the Paleo diet, but they have done so in the name of nostalgia for their 'true' political community. The difference lies in our solidarity with that community, our sense of the 'we' of the homeland. This contention leads to nostalgia's third claim: that the mythic past defines the *true* and original political community (the 'we').

Although the caveman of Paleo belongs to a mythic past, and although he represents a grievance about the present and a desire to change it, he is not of a knowable political community. We are not able to feel political connection with such a nation-less creature. He stands in stark contrast to Darré's pre-medieval pagan Germanic nobles, or Father Coughlin's founding Christian Americans, or indeed the Tea Party's founding fathers.

The imagining of a 'we' is among the most definitive and simultaneously constructive and destructive aspects of nostalgia in politics. It is at the heart of every nationalism, every invented tradition and every populism and nativism – populism being grievance directed against the 'elite', nativism against the immigrant outsider.

Is there a nostalgic 'we' that does not have within it some level of enmity against a present 'they'? We search world history for examples in vain.

AND YET IT is not that one side of politics uses nostalgia and the other doesn't.

Aside from wistful harkening back to golden ages, to heroes and forgotten visions of progressive forebears – the Whitlam years, the '60s, the ambitions of the New Deal, postwar Britain before Thatcherism – left-leaning leaders and activists sometimes use what we term 'obverse', or mirror-image, nostalgia.

Obverse nostalgia shares with nostalgia a sense of grievance, as well as a political commitment to reverse the gains of the other. Its proponents also share a determination to form a useable and simplified past – a capsuled history. As with their ideological foes on the right, these leaders and activists deploy versions of a useable history to indict the present and achieve purification of the political community in the face of hostile forces. But instead of idealising the past, this approach *demonises* the past. Rather than pure heroics, we are presented with stories of pure villainy.

To be sure, the politics of memory and recognition of past wrongs is a vexed issue, and not one that we as authors fully agree on. Nor are we attempting to draw some kind of moral equivalence. Our point, simply, is to highlight the similar ways that some progressives – the 'obverse nostalgists' – reach for capsule pasts to advance their arguments and agendas.

Take the 1619 Project, an initiative undertaken by *New York Times Magazine* journalists to reinterpret the entirety of American history by 'placing the consequences of slavery and the contributions of Black Americans at the very centre of our national narrative'. Putting a spotlight on the sin of slavery in places where there has previously been silence or distortion is certainly a worthy exercise. Yet the architects of the 1619 Project have come under sustained attack – and not only from partisan conservatives with a political axe to grind. Respected academic historians have expressed concerns too: first, about the overriding of disciplinary axioms and methods that safeguard research about the past, and second, about the push to reduce history to a single explanatory factor. Such a reduction runs the risk both of ignoring decades of groundbreaking academic research on slavery, and of oversimplifying the complexity and diversity of American history. For example, in the 1619 Project there is little space for the interracial unity and struggle that helped advance the cause of freedom and equality throughout American history (and that presumably will be needed to advance it in the future).

The impulse to pursue racial justice in present-day politics by interrogating our biases of memory may be a noble one. Some statues may indeed need to be torn down (but only, one would hope, after genuine public debate). Any kind of move towards justice and love in collective life requires new kinds of recognition and repentance over past wrongs. But here is where the search for the pure can override the possibilities of the pragmatic.

For nostalgists, imagined purity exists in the golden age of the mythic past. For obverse nostalgists, the past is a dark age to be expunged so that we can finally walk in the light: that is, to put the past behind us. For each, there can appear to be a shared commitment to the 'pure' in form: pure good versus pure evil, 'we' versus 'they'. We may inadvertently become, as 1930s anti-Nazi German theologian Dietrich Bonhoeffer once wrote, 'visionary dreamers' who find themselves acting all of a sudden as the 'accuser of the brethren'.

JARRED'S NOSTALGIA FOR his plastic scooter was free from the four features of nostalgia as weapon. First, there was no grievance; he was content to make the best of things on his newer steel scooter. Second, he didn't elaborate his vision of the golden past into a wider historical story. There was also no real way for Jarred to turn the scooter nostalgia into a founding myth about 'we' and 'they'.

But a hypothetical grandfather and grandmother, or uncle and aunt, might do exactly that. They might recall robust Australian-made scooters from the good old days of the 1950s: 'They don't make them like they used to. Now everything's made in China.'

Their interlocutor might add: 'One day China will take over the world. Someone has to stop them and start making things in Australia again.'

The more progressive-leaning Uncle Jeff might step in at this point: 'No, this is all because of neoliberalism. Things were fine until multinationals became more powerful than states. It's as simple as that.'

But Jarred lacked the means and vision to talk this way. The virtue of his nostalgia lay in its childlikeness, its epistemic humility. In sociological-psychological terms, it was 'questing' and open; it did not own or co-opt nostalgia as a buttress to ideological boundaries.

Ironically, although coming from a place of actual vulnerability (being a child), Jarred had no sense of being under threat. That sense of threat belongs to the political world around us. In this world, we tell ourselves neat stories about the way things used to be and divide enemy from friend.

The quest for pure historical time that inheres in both political nostalgia and obverse nostalgia offers us fool's gold. When we imagine the past or future in Manichean terms, of all good versus all bad, of tribe member versus barbarian, we may feel momentarily empowered in our outrage. We may ironically be buoyed by a sense of belonging to a group sharing the same story. But we rob ourselves of the clarity of insight we need to deal with the actual commingling of good and bad, progress and regress, as members of shared political communities. Not only, then, can 'perfect' become the enemy of possible, but our anchors can be tragically brandished as weapons.

Michael L Ondaatje is Head of the School of Humanities, Languages and Social Science, and Professor of History, at Griffith University. He is an award-winning researcher and teacher with special interests in race and conservatism, and has been a regular commentator on US politics in the media.

Dr Michael G Thompson is an independent scholar based in Brisbane. He is a historian of American intellectual history and Christianity. His publications have focused on the role played by Christian belief, and believers, in the making of American internationalism between the Great War and the Cold War.

FICTION

Lost decade
Lucy Robin

I MADE A point of telling people in LA that I'd come from somewhere farther than Santa Clarita: Tempe or Little Rock. When they asked questions, I said inscrutable things like, 'The past is the past.' In response, they'd try to ingratiate themselves: 'I guess I'm lucky,' they would say. 'I was born here.'

I lied often when I first arrived. In the job interview for the tour company, I told the manager that I knew the area well. He was an East Coaster with *HEATHEN* crossing his neck in gothic script. His name was Jake.

'When you're from Santa Clarita,' I said, 'you're always thinking about Hollywood.'

'So, you're an actress,' he said. 'We got a couple of those already.'

I wasn't, but it would be a while before I grew used to saying no.

The tour company was based inside a souvenir shop. The shelves were stocked with the kinds of novelties that people take photos of but rarely buy: gargantuan ashtrays, and cheap ceramics that read *LA was so expensive, I could only afford half a mug!*

Before each tour began, I assembled the passengers alongside the van. I read their names from a piece of paper. I asked where everybody was from, and they chorused proudly in response: 'Saskatchewan!'

'Finland!'

'The Bay Area!'

We were given a list of verified addresses that we could pick from: Leonardo DiCaprio, Quentin Tarantino, Taylor Swift. I began my tours at Las

Palmas hotel, where Richard Gere climbs the fire escape in *Pretty Woman*. Then I drove up Highland, past the church where *Sister Act* was filmed, and into the hills. The passengers were sunscreened and hopeful, leaning to the windows. *My* passengers, I reminded myself. I hadn't even seen *Pretty Woman* then.

I lived in a studio apartment above a meditation centre. I lay about in the evenings drinking beer and eating forkfuls from styrofoam containers of nachos. When Nanna was still around, Mom used to say she ate like the farmer's daughter she was, all swinging jaw and desperate, heaving breaths. It was meant as an insult, but Nanna had only smiled, teeth jammed with catfish, as if to say, *And what about it?*

THE OTHER PEOPLE at the tour company were all trying to make it in some way. They were actor-models or paying their way through school. Some did celebrity house tours and others drove to Santa Monica and back for city sightseeing. It was Candace who told me that the celebrity tours were more coveted. We were eating our lunch on the wheel stops behind the shop. The bagels from Starbucks were claggy, a pale imitation, but they were always the same.

'Maybe Jake thinks you're hot,' she said. The piercing in her upper frenulum flashed at me. 'He doesn't normally let new girls do the celebs.'

Candace was a hawker. Her job was to stand outside the Chinese Theatre and hand out pamphlets. She did this with Mona, a small, excitable girl with oiled ringlets for hair. They both came from the Midwest, and you could tell. They had the bent stature of people who'd been cold their whole lives.

Before work in the mornings, I'd take the bus over to their apartment by the tar pits, and Candace would drive us to Hollywood. Mona liked to point to places and ask if we'd live there: a public library, a bail-bond centre, a carwash. 'Imagine,' she'd say. 'If you needed to shower, you could just walk through those big mop things and you'd be done!'

On Mondays, we went to '80s night at the Whiskey. It was the same band every week. The singer wore a Hawaiian shirt and zinc on his nose like Spicoli from *Fast Times at Ridgemont High*. A gregarious barmaid circled the crowd, trying to rouse the patrons. If I stood too still, she'd charge into the crowd and grab me by the arm. 'Girl!' she'd say, blinking expectantly.

When I got tired, I sat on the mezzanine and watched Mona and Candace bump their asses together on the dance floor below. Sometimes Spicoli held his microphone to them, and Mona would sing along to 'Girls on Film' like a pre-teen at the mall. Between sets, they'd stomp upstairs to meet me, their faces rubberised with drink. They were always telling me to *let loose*, pinching my shoulders in a way that turned my whole back numb.

Mona and Candace were five years younger than me, slept side-by-side on a futon bed and auditioned for Lactaid commercials. They weren't really going anywhere. Maybe that was why I stuck with them: they reminded me of how simple things could be if you turned from a certain ugliness.

WHEN I CALLED Mom to tell her I'd moved, she was muffled by a fat rush of wind, her voice ragged like she'd swallowed something wrong.

'What about Denis?' she asked.

'It ran its course, is all.'

'Katie,' she said. I waited, but there was nothing else for her to say.

She was in Bismarck, North Dakota, a place I'd never been. She'd found a job at a grocery store. 'It's called Dana's,' she said. 'They got 'em all over town.'

'Is Dana a real person?' I hoped she could hear some semblance of a smile.

'Gee, I don't know.'

She didn't have a plan. She'd been sleeping in her Ford Transit for a year. I asked her to send me pictures, and there was a velveteen mattress lying across the back seat, a hairdryer in the passenger footwell.

Those first months in LA, I thought about Santa Clarita often. Years later, when I started going to support groups, some of the women said they'd done the same thing: *fantasising*, trying to get back to an unscathed version of themselves. One of the group leaders compared it to victims of natural disasters running through the days prior to the wreckage.

In middle school, I'd explored every vertex and hill, the cul-de-sacs that bloomed like varicose veins. I knew how to break into the landfill site out past Val Verde, where you could climb the electrical tower and look down on Six Flags. When I started first grade, Mom fought the city over the school bus routes. We sat at the district transport officer's desk together. I remember the hair on his forearms. She asked him why the driver couldn't just stop at the end of our street like they did for everybody else.

'I'm sure your daughter can manage if you equip her with the right skills,' he said, raising his eyebrows like the plasticine men I watched on TV.

Every year, more houses on our street were sold for demolition. The building firms were persistent. They knocked on our door, sent letters. Everything always began with 'How would you like to...' When I was still learning to talk, I'd copied that phrasing. 'How would you like to play in the sandpit?' I'd say, stretching my lips into a practised smile.

THE FIRST TIME Jake told me I needed to be better at my job I'd slept in, caught an Uber to work. When I came in through the back door, he was waiting for me at the lunch table.

'I noticed,' he said, 'that nobody has written about you on our Google reviews.' He leaned back and blew air from his nostrils like a bull. 'I'm coming at this from a manager's point of view. You understand.'

I sat on the toilet and searched for my name. I tried different spellings. Of the fourteen hundred comments, none were about me. When I walked outside, I found that Jake had already loaded my passengers into the van. They watched with glum recognition as I opened the door.

I thought about fudging the reports we had to fill out at the end of each day. There was a box at the bottom of the page where we were supposed to write the day's 'sightings'. One of the other drivers, Lawrence, often saw celebrities pulling out of their driveways or stalled at intersections. One afternoon, he drove his passengers to the north end of Sweetzer Avenue and saw Johnny Depp smoking a cigar outside his house. I thought Lawrence was going to cry when he told me the story. He said, 'It finally happened.'

Before I came to the city, I'd been preparing myself for survival. I'd fight, I thought, to keep whatever job I found. But whenever Jake told me I wasn't being chipper enough, I'd text Mona and Candace, and we'd find a bar. My head was muffled, underwater, thoughts no longer gaining momentum.

Mona and Candace tracked all the club openings in the city. All the places in Hollywood had two-word names like 'Attack Dog' and 'Freedom House'. I wore clothes from Candace's wardrobe: dark, clinging dresses that didn't belong to my body.

One night, we went to a social club – which was just a bar, really, with a guest list. As we waited in line, the moon hung dead and plump among the mid-size office buildings. Everybody in the line was dressed in linen and raw silk. At the entrance stood a bronze statue of a 1920s director with a bullhorn in hand. Mona and Candace braced against the cordon like marathon runners waiting to begin. They kept looking at one another, saying, 'Can you believe it?'

Years later, I saw a think-piece about the club. It had become so exclusive that even the Kardashians couldn't get in. There was a picture of the CEO standing on a balcony in an alabaster dinner suit. 'We pride ourselves on being a place for like-minded creatives to gather and produce,' he said. 'We're not a circus.'

I thought about sending the article to Mona and Candace. They came up on my Facebook feed from time to time. Candace was working at a vintage store in Hollywood; Mona had met a guy and moved to Oakland. But I wasn't sure if they'd even remember the club, how we'd rushed to the windows that night to look upon the city: all the rooftop gardens, the duplexes like shrunken cornucopias.

JULY CRESTED WITH atmospheric rivers. Everybody in the city became hot and impatient. Even the passengers, normally buoyant with possibility, grew agitated at the traffic. 'I don't know how you can stand living here,' they announced, scraping their foreheads while their children kicked the back of my seat.

I had a streak of sightings. First it was Jay Leno on Sunset in a red convertible. He rolled down his window and cried, 'Beautiful sunny California!'

The light changed, and I pushed forward, my passengers making small noises of excitement.

'I remember watching his first time on Carson,' said the man beside me. 'There was a joke about how it was so cold in New York, it was snowing on the sun.'

Another day, it was Dwayne Johnson on Rodeo Drive. A woman in the back seat called to him: 'Say you're my husband! Just say it!'

'I *am* your husband,' he conceded.

I had to film these encounters for the company Instagram. I took trembling videos of the celebrities: their charmed faces and the flanks of their vehicles. Jake had us use an app that blurred out licence plates. We were in the business of stalking, but a licence plate was a step over the line.

Sometimes, when I was driving, I got caught up thinking about how I'd learned to do it in the first place: with Denis, in the industrial estate out by Rye Canyon. He wasn't any older than me, but his father had been teaching him since he was twelve. Once he asked me to sit on his lap in the driver's seat so he could show me how to work the pedals. I remember waiting for him to kiss my neck or something, but he took it too seriously. 'Now this is important,' he'd said. 'Tell me which one's the brake.'

We were sophomores in high school when a boy in our grade got loaded and fell off Lost Boys Bridge. Layla Marchmont, whose mom was a neurosurgeon, told everybody that it was a good way to go: an instant death. People started joking about it. When somebody tripped in the hallway, they *Hernandez'd*. It was always Denis who stepped in, like a prison warden, to tell them to give it rest.

We did our driving lessons at night, when all the factory workers had gone home. He was soft, those early years. He laid out blankets on the cargo bed of his truck. He knew constellations. Every time he stuck it in me, he came apart a little more.

The winter I left, he got in the habit of pretending he didn't know me. He'd make like he'd woken up in the middle of fucking. 'Oh my god,' he'd say, eyes like planets, 'who the hell are you?' Towards the end, he couldn't even look at me: not during, not after. Once he was done, he'd lay his head on my breast like a wayward dog. All I had to do was stay quiet.

AT FIRST, I told Mona and Candace what I'd told Jake: for Santa Claritans, LA was a promised land, close enough to try. I said it was the kind of thing you had to do once in your life. Young as they were, they nodded eagerly. I thought I was hiding things well.

This one night we split a joint on their patio. The solar panels on the organic megamart below refracted the waning light. The hills made everything biblical, but in some parts of Fairfax, you felt like you could be anywhere in the world.

'Pot was hard to get in Missouri,' said Mona. 'It's legal and all, but not like here. Me and my girlfriends, we used to get it from our PE teacher.'

Candace started up laughing in high, sailing notes.

I hadn't planned on telling them it was my first time smoking. It just turned out that way. My tongue was a Rolodex, producing sentences with a stark automatism.

I told them how Denis didn't let me drink, aside from when he had his buddies over on game nights. Before they arrived, he'd say, 'Have a little fun tonight. Go on,' so I'd take a bottle of wine to the bedroom and drink to the noises they made, and sometimes Denis would send me a text message: *Come on out, the boys wanna see you.* I'd stand before them, trying to hold myself up straight, and he'd say, 'Jesus, Katie, you're wasted,' and all the men would coo like mothers.

Mona had this awful face on, like she was tensing all her muscles, and Candace just looked sad.

We went to a bar on Robertson known for its socialite owner. Candace and Mona posed in front of the vertical garden for the in-house photographer, their backs arched like Roman columns. All around, diners split crab cakes and red peppers with forks. Tea candles fired off like electrodes. I could already see myself in the morning, trying to swallow the things I'd said. I felt half alive, like a pumpkin whose innards had been scooped out.

It must've been obvious that I was feeling sorry for myself, because at some point in the night Mona moved to me, her mouth a furnace on my cheek. She said: 'Do you feel like a rockstar? You are. You're like a rockstar with a lost decade.'

Lucy Robin's writing has been published in *Island*, *Voiceworks*, *Archer*, *Baby Teeth*, *Enby Life*, *swim meet lit mag* and *Farrago*. Her essay 'Naked Under Leather' was shortlisted for the *Kill Your Darlings* Creative Non-Fiction Essay Prize in 2022. They are currently at work on their first novel as a 2023 Wheeler Centre Hot Desk Fellow.

Eileen Chong

Threshold

The old country is disappearing,
even in my dreams. The edges
of places are dulled; faces meld
into smudges of misremembering.
My finger follows multicoloured
tracks before I abandon all plans.

The old country is all but gone,
faded along with the etched lettering
on tombs. Even the plastic flowers
have fallen apart, bleached to pale
polyester nothingness. We used to seed
the mounds so grass would cover the graves.

In the old country, the rain turns clay
into mud. Even these footprints blur
and disappear. What is the voice of one
who has died if no one listened to what
remained unspoken? It no longer matters.
Secrets layered, unseen and built over.

The old country is also the new country.
Boxes of goods unpacked in homes like boxes.
We flatten memory, recycle origin stories.
We have heard it all before. The new country
will never become the old country. Gleam
every threshold. Raise the bright flags. Sing–

Eileen Chong is a poet of Hakka, Hokkien and Peranakan descent. She is the author of nine books. Her next collection, *We Speak of Flowers*, is forthcoming with UQP in 2025. She can be found at: www.eileenchong.com.au

NON-FICTION

Farming futures

Views from the Millewa-Mallee, past and present

Melinda Hinkson

FOLLOWING ONE OF many trips to attend the Mildura Writers Festival, Les Murray penned 'Asparagus Bones'. Published in 1998, the poem recounts a memorable late-afternoon winter's drive across the north-western Victorian hinterland in the company of his friend, celebrated restaurateur Stefano de Pieri. As daylight 'softened into blusher', they arrived at a farm where his friend let himself in and fetched a box of 'fossil bones', asparagus, from a coolroom. The two of them then discussed how unlocked farm doors are 'emblems of a good society'.

'Asparagus Bones' is an ode to the rooting of agriculture in place. Yet Murray's celebration of the rural as nourishment and model of good society also indicates a more complex setting. The 'half-million of the coolroom' signals a global export market awaiting those boxes of spears. And the man helping himself to this high-end homegrown produce for a writers' festival banquet has an exceptional entitlement.

There is nothing transactional about Stefano de Pieri and Les Murray's provisioning excursion. Nothing that indicates the normal business of food as we ordinary consumers know it. Yet, there is something in this scene, its harking back to earlier, simpler times and special arrangements, that helps us imagine a different set of conditions for the growing and sharing of food than those that currently rule our world.

Mildura's food bowl, the inspiration for Murray's poem, is a hermetically sealed system. The food grown in the region today is largely inaccessible to the folk who reside among the bounty-producing blocks. Food is contracted before it is grown. It is harvested, packed and spirited away on endless convoys of road trains that thunder down the highway destined for distribution centres and supermarkets, or for ports, ships and South-East Asia or further afield. Thanks to the wonders of refrigeration, a small portion of the food grown in the district does return. It is delivered onto the shelves of Coles and Woolies, priced competitively to outsell any remnant fresh fruit and veg you might find at local roadside stands. The $2 I pay for an avocado at a Red Cliffs stall costs me eighty cents more than at Coles on the same day.

Co-located with the food bowl is a food desert. Large areas of Mildura's concreted suburbs boast Maccas, KFC, pizza and kebab shops, but no outlets selling fresh fruit and vegetables, let alone anything locally grown. In 2018 a survey found that more than 50 per cent of people living in Mildura did not eat sufficient fruit and vegetables. More than 50 per cent of the adult population were reported as overweight or obese. Lurking behind these figures is a cluster of related wellbeing indicators pointing to stark social inequalities.

The tempo of seasonal food production gives Mildura its seductive groove. The race is on to get food to market when prices are high and before it wilts and rots. But this race is only incidentally about food and mainly about finance. When markets fail or supply chains are disrupted, harvests are bitter. Watermelons, zucchinis and lettuces are ploughed back into the ground. Grapes are left hanging on vines, sitting in coolrooms and rotting in shipping containers grounded at ports. The people who have spent months nurturing a crop with all its associated costs are left emotionally jangled and financially distressed. Farming demands huge commitment and steady nerves. It is, they say, like going to the casino every day.

It was a particularly challenging year in 2022. The record high rainfall created chaotic conditions not witnessed in seven decades. Horticultural industries registered between 25 and 50 per cent losses in expected yields. Grape growers lost tonnes of fruit to downy mildew. A condition called 'restricted spring growth', which agronomists still cannot explain, led to mountains of late-ripening fruit missing its precious market window and being left on vines or in coolrooms with no buyer. The unrelenting rain caused albedo in citrus, a condition in which the skin breaks down. Grain growers fared better on the back of international demand created by the war in Ukraine, but battled outbreaks of disease, loss of crops to hailstorms and unprecedented cases of harvesters catching fire.

The asparagus of Les Murray's poem had already fallen victim to market forces by this point. Two years earlier, the farmer whose coolroom offered up the celebrated ingredient for Stefano's banquet put a bulldozer through his 300 acres of asparagus plants. His family had been growing the prized vegetable since the 1920s. A century later, after a series of bad years, the farmer read the writing on the wall. He had apparently been doing everything right. He had diversified his crops. He had taken on more debt and scaled up his operations. In his own words, he had 'transformed his farm into a business', with rolling harvests calculated to continue across the calendar year. He tells me it all worked well in the 1980s, but not now.

The farmer's great-grandfather first planted asparagus in response to a local doctor's assessment that the Mildura community diet lacked iron. He planted it between rows of sultana grapes, and the crop became a vehicle of entrepreneurial expansion, topping up the income earned from the production of dried fruit. But asparagus is expensive. It must be hand-picked, piece by piece, every day. In summer it needs to be picked twice daily. After decades of growing the plant, you think you know it. You think you can guess when the flush will come. Then it doesn't come. You need to have pickers ready to work seven days a week. At the scale this farmer was growing, that equated to 200 workers at peak harvest. Rising wages and cost of fertiliser doubled the cost of producing asparagus. Then Mexico and California brought asparagus onto the market at a price Australian growers could not compete with. Australian production collapsed.

Around the same time Mexico undercut Australia's asparagus, California's pre-eminence as the world's largest almond exporter teetered as a result of drought and new legislation protecting dwindling groundwater reserves. California's loss was Australia's gain. Between 2009 and 2019, almonds become the dominant crop in the Victorian Mallee, covering more than 25,000 hectares. From a consumer perspective, nuts are in. From the perspective of farmers, nuts also have a natural advantage over fruit and vegetables: their shells are like bulletproof armour, protecting against extreme weather events as well as disrupted supply chains. If a market fails, almonds can pile high for weeks in packing sheds. They can withstand bureaucratic hold-ups. When it comes to labour, the 200 workers required to tend 300 acres of asparagus drops to just twenty to harvest the same area of almonds.

While almonds may be well equipped to compete in the food wars, they are not fail proof. The Australian Almond Board estimates a 25 per cent lower than expected return for 2023. Poor pollination due to the varroa mite outbreak in bees, poor water quality due to flooding, and more generally unfavourable weather are contributing factors.

Of course, extreme weather events and surges and collapses in global trade are nothing new. They go all the way back to the first years of Mildura. The first supply-chain disruption to hit the settlement came in 1893 when, on the eve of a fabulous harvest, the river dropped. Barge-loads of fruit were left rotting and stranded, waiting for the river to rise to allow its transportation. A century of boom-and-bust cycles followed.

But the pressures on farming have been intensifying in recent decades. Climate change and expanding agribusiness loom large. When mentioned by farmers, 'the corporates' signal a particular kind of threat. 'When it's your money, it is worth more than a 7 to 8 per cent return on investment,' I'm told by a young second-generation farmer. His family pulled back from financial disaster at the height of the drought when they sold their almond orchard to a corporate buyer. 'I would not do this for 7 to 8 per cent,' he tells me as he shakes his head.

Over the past eighteen months I have been talking to food growers in the Mildura region about how they are responding to the challenges of the present and thinking about the future. I am learning about how farmers wrestle with their relationships to their farms, markets, weather, technology, bank managers, accountants, insurance brokers, families and non-human companions, as well as to the food that they grow as they strive to make a livelihood and a life worth living. Through the prism of farmers' responses to the challenges of our times I've learnt a lot about the crisis of our food system and about the scale of change in rural Australia over recent decades. These interviews have raised fundamental questions about the relationship between growing food, feeding and what it means to be human and live a good life in the present.

Reading Les Murray's poem today, the fossil bones he conjures call to mind for me not asparagus spears, but the patchwork of abandoned blocks of vines that are scattered across old Mildura and Merbein. Some of these blocks have the feel of battlefields or graveyards, with thigh-thick gnarled trunks standing skewed like sentinels or tombstones, signalling a bygone age. At least one third of Mildura's irrigated blocks are currently 'dried off' or 'retired'. They have been put out of production by growers who have sold their water entitlement – some out of opportunism, many more out of desperation. With the decoupling of water from land under the National Water Initiative from 2004, water became a tradeable resource: an unstable, volatile asset. It is common now to hear farmers speak not of harvest returns per acre but returns per megalitre, and for water holdings to be invoked as superannuation, insurance or debt relief.

In Australia and elsewhere – as journalist Tom Philpott shows in his book *Perilous Bounty: The Looming Collapse of American Farming and How We Can Prevent It* – when water becomes scarcer its tendency to flow towards money only increases. In relation to horticulture, that flow is currently in the direction of the thirstiest of crops: almonds, followed by table grapes. At the height of the millennium drought, irrigators were paying $1,000/megalitre for temporary water. For some, that equated to a debt of hundreds of thousands of dollars. After the drought, whose impact was compounded by the global financial crisis, approximately one third of Merbein fruit growers went broke or got out. The local CSIRO office – a vital source of support and expertise for local growers since it was established in the 1920s – closed shortly afterwards.

The spectre of 'the corporates' that hangs over these developments also looms large in conversations with farmers. And it is not so easy these days to distinguish a farmer from a corporate. The global food system has its own culture, and like any culture it demands certain ways of acting by all who participate in it. Yet its domination is not complete. Some human-scale practices and commitments are defying its financialised future-focused logics. And here, at this human end of the supply chain, lies hope.

WHEN THE FIRST generation of settlers took up growing fruit in the Mildura district in the late 1880s, they purchased blocks of ten or twenty acres. It was possible to make a livelihood, to support a family, on diversely planted 'fruit salad' blocks of that size until the 1960s. Today a successful dried-fruit grower is likely to be pushing eighty acres to make a viable income from grapes alone. Table grapes are much more labour intensive and get traded on more volatile markets. The special varieties grown to ship to China, Indonesia and Sri Lanka sell at a price Australian consumers would baulk at. When a market fails or a variety goes out of favour, vines are ripped out and replaced. Risk mitigation demands larger acreage.

Out in the Millewa, the first generation of settler-farmers from the 1920s were granted a square mile, or 640 acres. When drought hit, coinciding with the Great Depression, many walked off. Farming out in the drylands was brutal. Some of these settler-farmers attempted to enlist in World War II – soldiering, they imagined, would give them a break from farming, as well as a new pair of boots. They were sent back to their farms to continue their essential national service. Three disastrous years followed. In the subsequent reallocation of land, just a quarter of the initial 800 dryland farmers remained.

Between the 1980s and 2000s, driven by new technologies, chemicals and economies of scale, the number of broadacre farms in Australia halved as the size of farms expanded. Since the 2008 financial crisis, Australian agriculture has become a landing place for global investment and speculation. Foreign private-equity firms and giant superannuation funds, encouraged by successive federal governments, are drawn to Australia's political stability and the availability of large acreage. These entities have no interest in food. They are chasing strong returns for their clients and stakeholders.

This financialised global buy-in has displaced arrangements that governed agriculture until the 1980s, when the deregulation of the Australian economy was set in train. Farming may have always been lonely work, but it has also become individualised since the demise of growers' co-operatives and single desks for marketing agricultural exports. Farmers today must carry risk, they must shoulder more debt, they must go in search of their own markets. The pressure is on to scale up. In the past five years in one district of the Millewa, seven out of ten properties have changed hands. Many of these farms have been acquired not by foreign interests but by neighbours scaling up or hoping to capitalise on the agri-land rush by 'land banking'.

Despite the pressure to grow or get out, some small producers forge on. Driven by an ethos of doing as much as they can themselves, they are committed to farming as a holistic process and, if possible, a way of life. They supplement farming income with off-farm work. They are contractors for neighbours and further afield. They work as mechanics, they sit on regional councils, they have partners in full-time jobs with steadier incomes.

THE PRESSURES ON people's relationships to place are at the heart of the food-production crisis. As agriculture has been financialised it has been decoupled from rural communities. Corporate farming is the antithesis of grounded knowledge. It knows no commitment to local conditions or local people. As agricultural products have been celebrated in terms of national export income, there has been a stretching of trust between growers and those who rely on their food. Disengagement, lack of interest, mutual distrust and, when resources are at stake, confrontation and conflict are all in the mix.

Farms are increasingly places of work, not the location of households or social life. Untold numbers of farmhouses sit unoccupied or abandoned. Many of these houses are surplus to requirement in the scaling up of agriculture, but some are empty because of the preferences of partners and children to be in town, close to entertainment and social support. The disconnection of farm, farming and place occurs in a dizzying array of combinations. Tree-changers chasing authentic rural experiences move into farmhouses among the vines, while the growers of those vines decamp to more urbanised locations in response to family pressures. In one happy counter movement I know of, a family of six at risk of becoming homeless in town were provided with on-farm housing in exchange for casual work. Their presence on the farm offsets the absence of the commuting farmer. The move has provided this family with security and given its children life-changing experiences.

IN NOVEMBER, IN the weeks before table grapes fully ripen, Chinese buyers cruise Sunraysia's blocks in shiny black Mercedes SUVs offering big cash direct to growers. They are trying to maximise profit by taking to market the first fruit of the season. The early fruit comes with a lovely colour but unresolved sugars. These 'acid bombs' have a ricochet effect through the market. They collapse consumer confidence as well as the price for growers whose fully ripened grapes are coming behind.

There are three different timeframes at play on the growing fields. There is the timeframe of global supply chains and their informal or black-market equivalents; there is the time frame of nature, in which crops ripen or fail, in which life and death occur; and there is the time frame of farming itself. These three modes of time are often entangled and in tension with each other. There is also a sense that everything is accelerating. But as supply-chain disruptions make devastatingly clear, acceleration can quickly come to a screaming halt. One large farm in the district manages the risks of just-in-time vegetable production by farming a fleet of trucks as well as carrots. It was a perfect business model for securing domestic supply chains, until COVID-19 took out the truck drivers.

Not so long ago a different set of principles was in play. Up until the 1980s, irrigated growers could not just turn on a tap to water their plants when they liked. The delivery of five pre-harvest irrigations was decided by local committee. A group of blokes (yes, always blokes) would assemble in a room in front of a government-issued calendar. They would debate and finally agree upon suitable dates for sequencing the district's water allocations. If it rained, they would meet again and revise their dates. The delivery of irrigated water in this way was determined by social agreement. The water bailiff would ride from farm to farm on his 60cc motorbike, yelling out to a farmer that the water was about to be passed on from his neighbour. The farmer had four days to clear his open channels in preparation for it to arrive.

These images allow us to glimpse a differently organised social world, far removed from the microsecond hyper-volatility of distant water markets, and soil-moisture probes that individual farmers now monitor from their mobile phones.

The behemoth of the global food system is vertical integration, wherein single companies have control over all the human, animal and environmental cogs in an agribusiness system. Vertical integration is easier (and more frightening) to observe in action in the US, where massive corporate systems map directly onto entire towns, creating the industrial-scale pork factories and endless soy and corn fields that provide the building blocks of industrially produced meat and fast-food products.

In Australia, growers contracted to major supermarkets are required to ensure their harvest conforms to standard specifications in size, colour and shape. These supermarkets are in turn owned by larger conglomerates that trade in fertilisers, fossil fuels and other financial interests.

Against the logic of vertical integration, one dryland farmer continually directs my attention laterally. He is fully focused on the climate crisis but sceptical about the zeal around electric vehicles and solar power – these will not provide solutions until we find ways of dealing with emissions, toxic waste, modern-day slavery and the other dilemmas associated with production. He points out that we city folk load growers up with responsibility for emissions from livestock while ignoring our own consumption of those same animals. It suits our culture to silo responsibility to a particular groups of actors, rather than recognise interconnections.

PERHAPS THE GREATEST challenge in farming, I'm told, is the gulf between city and country logics. City thinking presumes separation – of farmer from environmentalist, of food in supermarkets from the conditions of its production. These are not new dilemmas. In 1946, Australian children's author, farmer and environmentalist Elyne Mitchell made a rousing and impassioned plea for a national reimagination. In her book *Soil and Civilization*, Mitchell tracks the disconnect of people from the earth via growing urbanisation, industrialised agriculture, standardised education, expanding communications technology and growing dependence on foreign trade in food. She suggests soil fertility and health is foundational and integral to the creativity and health of a people – a binding spiritual connection that Australia destroyed at colonisation.

American poet and farmer Wendell Berry rallies rural communities to exert what he calls a centripetal force against urbanisation and its extractivist tendencies, to hold 'local soil and local memory in place'. How can a community know itself, Berry writes, 'if they have forgotten or have never learned each other's stories?' Zooming out further, economic sociologist Wolfgang Streeck argues that the last four decades point to the steady unravelling of capitalism. Capitalism will end, Streeck says, because it has undermined the regulatory conditions of its stability. It is dying as a result of an overdose of itself. Somewhere along the line, human-scale invention and co-operative endeavour have been overtaken by government-supported, technology-enabled asset stripping.

WHEN I ASK old retired blockies what they make of the high-tech push – the driverless tractors and applications of AI – they shake their heads and tell me they are relieved to be out of the game. Yet their own histories of farming are stories of ceaseless invention that transformed their work – dip tins, swing arm trellises and homemade harvesters – as well as dogged and wily political lobbying that transformed irrigation and water-management practices.

Farmers are holistic problem solvers. They are systematic thinkers and practical experts across the entire process of production. French anthropologist Claude Lévi-Strauss would describe farmers as *bricoleurs*, craftsmen and craftswomen of the local. They are constantly alert to small signs of change – in climate, in conditions of the soil, in the behaviour of a plant, in a piece of machinery, in the health of an animal. Farmers solve problems through close attention, nutting things out and making do. But they are also a dying breed. Between 2001 and 2016, employment in agriculture halved in Australia. The average age of a farmer today is fifty-eight.

Whereas harvest time was once a celebration of intense sociability, today's conditions fuel anxiety about worker supply and labour costs, as well as dreams of seamless scaling up, technological perfectibility and robot harvesters. These shiny images are out of sync with the reality of tractors getting bogged when rainfall is high and soil has not been cared for, and of crops that fail because bogged tractors cannot get into orchards to spray fungicide. And they are out of sync with the knowledge that after a few years of failing to meet shareholder expectations, large corporate entities dump their now run-down agri-properties, sending ricochet effects through markets and local communities.

These impressions ask urgent and fundamental questions. Have we reached a new tipping point, a moment to collectively reconsider how we balance local and global values, how we define national interest and security? Why should future-focused endless growth in global export markets be pursued at the expense of secure communities and well-nourished people and environments?

There is growing consensus that prioritising farming at human scale is urgently required to intervene in the climate crisis and stop the hollowing out of rural communities. Mildura is a fantastic experiment in agricultural placemaking. It has a history of bold projects that exert centripetal force – drawing good people from elsewhere, building community, taking robust arguments up to governments, insisting wherever possible on local control, and scheming around questions of what matters and what makes a good life.

Plenty of food for thought.

This essay is an edited version of 'The Murray Talk', presented at the Mildura Writers Festival in July 2023.

Melinda Hinkson was the 2023 Mildura Writers Festival writer in residence. She is executive director of the Institute of Postcolonial Studies, Melbourne.

NON-FICTION

The ship, the students, the chief and the children

Defying the fossil-fuel order

David Ritter

UNDER A WARM blue morning sky unevenly patched with ragged strips of grey and white, a crowd of about a hundred people stands on a concrete wharf in Port Vila. We are waiting for the arrival of Greenpeace's flagship, the *Rainbow Warrior*, which is visiting Vanuatu for the first time in many years. I've been onboard for various legs of the iconic vessel's current journey through Oceania, but on this occasion I'm among the land contingent.

Standing closest to the waterfront, a muscular middle-aged man to whom I've just been introduced, the Honourable Chief Timothy, blows a conch shell with enormous force, the low note resonating across the quay like the bellow of a large mammal. The honourable chief has close-cropped silver hair and beard, and although bare-chested and footed, he is heavily decked out with armbands, chunky anklets, an over-the-shoulder basket bag, a prominent necklace of massive polished tawny-brown spherical seeds and a bark-cloth belt that is holding up a bright-green skirt of leaves descending to his shins. As the *Rainbow Warrior* gets closer, Honourable Chief Timothy waves the ship in, swinging a sash of woven plant fibres in a round beckoning motion and calling out in his deep chant-like voice: 'Welkam home, Greenpeace! Come home! Our people have lots to tell you! Our mothers, our fathers, our people, our government – we have things to tell you!'

This is no supplication to be heard, but a generous invitation that evinces the confidence of sovereign prerogative. The shouts are a reminder of the bonds between Greenpeace and the peoples of the Pacific island nations, strong ties that arise from shared history and allied purposes. We are being gathered before venerable authority, called to bear witness not as bystanders but as heralds drawn home to be enlightened and revitalised before being sent forth on renewed assignment.

Honourable Chief Timothy repeats versions of the greeting as the ship pulls in. Once more the conch shell sounds; again the honourable chief shakes the sea and sky with his holler.

The latest incarnation of the *Rainbow Warrior* – the third vessel to bear this name – has arrived in the South Pacific to support a campaign of epic vision. In 2019, in a university classroom in Vanuatu, a group of students began earnestly discussing with their teacher how international law might be better used in the existential struggle against climate change. The extraordinary objective that was eventually agreed on was to secure a strong advisory opinion from the International Court of Justice in relation to states' obligations to protect the human rights of current and future generations from the impacts of climate change. A new organisation, the youth-led Pacific Island Students Fighting Climate Change, was established to carry the case forward and has since forged collaborative relationships with Greenpeace and other civil-society allies to help build impetus around the world.

Improbably, this audacious youth-led stratagem has already achieved success, first securing unanimous support from the nations of the Pacific Islands Forum (which includes Australia) and then winning consent referral from the United Nations General Assembly to the International Court of Justice – the first time this has occurred in UN history. The case is due to be heard in 2024, and the *Rainbow Warrior*'s mission is to bring attention to the litigation, to engage in the practical business of documenting impacts, and to build the political momentum vital to securing participation from states party to the hearing. In addition to Port Vila, the ship will visit Erromango in Vanuatu, Funafuti in Tuvalu, and Kioa, Rabi and Suva in Fiji.

Even the desiccating quality of legal language can't mask the almost mythic dimension to this enterprise: here, in the middle of the world's greatest ocean, on the edge of our collective ecological precipice, the children of some of the most climate-vulnerable communities on the planet are offering stunning leadership, seeking justice from the highest court in the world for all who are oppressed by fossil-fuel corporations.

THE ARCHETYPE OF tyranny is the rule of the lone despot, embodied in the likes of the mad emperor, the wicked king or the uniformed dictator. Such tyrants hold capricious authority over the unfortunate populace subjected to their fiat, a rule invariably exercised through an apparatus of terror. In both real life and fiction, autocracies of this kind tend to be brutish, with explicit symbology and rhetoric reinforcing the leader's right to absolute supremacy.

Yet the tyrannous application of power doesn't require a vicious potentate. Tyranny can also function amorphously, appearing in distributed and surreptitious forms that are nonetheless still manifestly pitiless.

In terms of political effect, climate change amounts to systemic domination of this kind, working through a complex web of diffused decision-making to inflict 'untold suffering' (as it was described in a public letter signed by 11,000 scientists) on hundreds of millions of people, and destroying cultural and ecological heritage on a vast scale.

The primary driver of global warming is the extraction and burning of coal, oil and gas, activities that continue despite the consequences for human beings and the wider environment. I have described elsewhere the system of power that authorises this as the 'fossil-fuel order', consisting not only of coal, oil and gas companies and their elected apologists but of the greater mass of economic, political, social and cultural institutions and power relations that sustain these corporations.

The tyranny of climate change is thus not directed by any one central figure but is enacted through a multitude of individual and organisational decisions that permit the fossil-fuel order to continue to expand and thrive despite hideous repercussions. In April 2022, UN Secretary-General António Guterres described any investment in new fossil-fuels infrastructure as 'moral and economic madness' contributing to putting humanity 'firmly on track towards an unliveable world'.

'How must it feel,' Amitav Ghosh asks in *The Nutmeg's Curse*, writing of genocidal violence in what are now Indonesia's Banda Islands, 'to find yourself face-to-face with someone who has made it clear that he has the power to bring your world to an end and has every intention of doing so?' The direct threat of extermination described by Ghosh contrasts with the polite ordinariness of the vast majority of the fossil-fuel order, embedded within the fabric of late-capitalist life in the developed world.

Take, for example, a company like Woodside Energy, the proponent of the Burrup Hub – by far the most climate-polluting resource infrastructure development being proposed anywhere in Australia, threatening to unleash millions of tonnes of gas until as late as 2070. The threat to human life and nature posed by Woodside's business strategy through the direct environmental impacts of this gas is undeniable, but the company remains countenanced within society, as if nothing is wrong. Woodside sponsors children's surf lifesaving, the Fremantle Dockers AFL club, the University of Western Australia, the West Australian Symphony Orchestra and much else besides. The company's CEO, Meg O'Neill, is a frequent guest speaker at marquee public events. At one of Woodside's recent AGMs, staff gave out quaint little bags of 'melting moments' to shareholders, presumably without irony. The company's website is laden with feel-good platitudes, such as 'It's only by working together that a better future comes to life.' It is all cloyingly typical of big corporations. Yet despite the gluggy opacity of the language and the dense shroud of social legitimation, the truth remains that extreme climate damage driven primarily by the exploitation of fossil fuels by businesses like Woodside is now lacerating people and nature all over the world.

The tyranny of climate change also has a radical totality of scope. The rule of a tyrant is typically bound by the borders of the region in which they exercise control, and by the duration of their reign. Climate change, though, is of an altogether different geographic and temporal character, because the atmospheric parameters for life on Earth are inherently ecumenical and many of climate change's consequences are irreversible.

In George Orwell's *Nineteen Eighty-Four*, the indelible image of the future is 'a boot stamping on a human face – forever'. The absolutism of runaway climate change threatens a variation of this nightmarish prospect. Although never the stated business intention, the result of continuing fossil-fuel expansion is the shoe of the fossil-fuel executive being ground into the face of every person on Earth, every baby not yet born, and upon the flesh of every living thing.

ALTHOUGH OFTEN ENGAGED in direct interventions to prevent environmental wrongs, the *Rainbow Warrior* is on this occasion busy with the work of campaign diplomacy. The ship will stay in Port Vila for a couple of days, hosting dignitaries, acting as a focal point for society events and holding booked-to-capacity 'open boat' visits for the local community.

One of the highlights of the program is a cultural exhibition held on the ship's helideck curated and presented by Anjali Sharma. In September 2020, Sharma was first-named among a group of young plaintiffs – memorably described by the presiding judge as 'the Children' – who sought to obtain a ruling from the Federal Court of Australia that the then minister for the environment, Sussan Ley, owed a duty of care to protect young people from climate change. Anjali is now studying for a law degree while working part-time in support of the Pacific-student-led campaign for climate justice.

In taking the case that now bears her name, Anjali brought the tyranny of climate change into sharp focus. Surely the Australian government could not be permitted by act or omission to inflict the mass cruelty of global warming upon the children of the nation?

Famously, Sharma and her co-plaintiffs won at first instance. The Honourable Justice Mordecai Bromberg wrote in his remarkable judgement:

> It is difficult to characterise in a single phrase the devastation that the plausible evidence presented in this proceeding forecasts for the Children. As Australian adults know their country, Australia will be lost and the World as we know it gone as well. The physical environment will be harsher, far more extreme and devastatingly brutal when angry. As for the human experience – quality of life, opportunities to partake in nature's treasures, the capacity to grow and prosper – all will be greatly diminished. Lives will be cut short. Trauma will be far more common and good health harder to hold and maintain. None of this will be the fault of nature itself. It will largely be inflicted by the inaction of this generation of adults, in what might fairly be described as the greatest inter-generational injustice ever inflicted by one generation of humans upon the next.

Infamously, Ley appealed and was successful, with three judges of the Federal Court overturning the decision, though nothing in their honours' judgements questioned the science of climate change. Whatever the reasoning, the full court's decision suggested the inviolability of the tyranny of the fossil-fuel order under Australian law. The 'greatest inter-generational injustice ever inflicted by one generation of humans upon the next' – an expression of extreme tyranny, if ever there was one – is currently being permitted under Australia's legal and governmental system.

The efforts of people like Anjali Sharma and the Pacific Island Students Fighting Climate Change are driving the momentum of climate litigation across numerous jurisdictions around the world. The display brought together by Anjali on the *Rainbow Warrior* is an eclectic array of objects in recognition of this growing phenomenon, drawn particularly from various Indigenous cultures, arranged quite casually but with clear deference on the ship's trestle tables. Among the presentation are cowrie-shell ornaments from low-lying Kiribati, a couple of *chi ku cha* (traditional tools for moving cactus) from the Caribbean island of Bonaire and woven mats from the Torres Strait.

Apart from their indigeneity, what these items have in common is that they have been given to the *Rainbow Warrior* by peoples whose futures are threatened by climate change and who are seeking recourse through the courts. These are artefacts from cultural defenders united in their fight against tyranny. They are a reminder that while the end of rule by a lone despot might be achieved through individual denouement, the decentralised nature of the fossil-fuel order means that its overthrow can only be achieved through hundreds of thousands of acts of resistance, of all kinds and sizes – some contesting within the system, others in the realm of civil disobedience – across the globe. It requires a networked defiance wrought of an ethical and political consciousness of the world we are losing, truth-telling about what the fossil-fuel order is doing, and resolute conviction in the enduring possibilities of action.

The power of the fossil-fuel order depends on foreclosing any kind of political and institutional decisions that would see societies break free from the malignant clamp of coal, oil and gas corporations. This power also depends on eliding alternative ways of seeing. In one sense, the whole of the political struggle against climate change can be understood as an effort to make corporate and political decision-makers *see*, such that they are required to act. For the powerful who have not acted as they should, climate change and the actions required to reduce emissions have long constituted what Slavoj Žižek (riffing off Donald Rumsfeld) described as 'unknown knowns': things they know but intentionally refuse to acknowledge.

In earlier stages of the political contest over global warming, the principal strategy of the coal, oil and gas corporations and their allies was straight-out denial of the seriousness of climate change. It is now clearly documented that these earlier bosses knew or reasonably should have known that the continued extraction and burning of fossil fuels would have dire consequences for people and nature, but they did not accede to this truth. However, over time, with reporting, science, activism, art and the experience of severe climate impacts by ordinary citizens, this denialism has been called out and has steadily given way to a different kind of 'unknown known'. In this new phase, overt repudiation has been replaced with explicit acknowledgement, but this is made hollow by diversionary strategies to justify inaction, including the rhetoric of incrementalism, greenwashing and offsetting.

So it was that, in a masterclass of obfuscation, Woodside CEO Meg O'Neill solemnly told the National Press Club in April 2023 that 'climate change is real', before explaining why 'we must be wary of the temptation to focus on just one objective'. The agnotological consequences of delay are largely the same as that of outright denial. What is known and now plainly admitted is still not 'known' in the sense of triggering behaviour commensurate with the implications of the knowledge. Our home is on fire and decision-makers like Meg O'Neill know this, but their intention is still to open vast new reserves of fossil fuels for infernal exploitation.

Yet this is not the majority view; for many years in Australia, one survey after another has found an overwhelming desire for greater climate action. The public is not the problem here.

AMONG THE GUESTS to the *Rainbow Warrior* introduced by Anjali Sharma is the Honourable Chief Timothy, who has returned to speak and bestow gifts. Later, the honourable chief talks privately with me and explains the significance of each of the items with which he has presented us, including a wooden statuette and an ornately woven mat.

'Lastly,' he says, 'when I'm here welcoming the boat, I was wearing this.' He proffers the necklace of polished round seeds from around his own neck. 'I've been keeping it for more than ten years, and it's a part of my heart. And I'm giving it to you. Hang on to it. And it will be a historical gift... And never forget the chiefs of Vanuatu and the government and all the children and all the mothers and fathers. Never forget them.'

There is nothing so generous as the giving of an obligation founded in trust. The honourable chief tells me directly to speak and write about what he has said and what we have seen in our time with the Ni-Vanuatu; Greenpeace must be carriers of the messages of culture and justice to the 'big brothers' and 'big countries' over the waves.

We shake on things formally, then embrace, then grip hands again. I feel the strength of the honourable chief's shoulders and arms. He smiles, keeps talking and points upwards. Deep inside, I sense the welling up of jagged sentiment: grief and love, hope and resolution, fear and commitment. I experience an exhilarating transcendence of my rational senses. Sounds slow down, the big sky is a vast blue iris of unblinking scrutiny, and the light sea air has the force of time running in all directions and possibilities. I have a fleeting but immeasurably precious awareness of the unaccountable grammar of being.

In a few days the *Rainbow Warrior* will sail away, bearing Honourable Chief Timothy's presents along with the rest of the cultural objects, talismanic in the face of the climate emergency. I thank him effusively for the deep honour and respond that Greenpeace accepts his gifts with heartfelt gratitude, and that we will draw strength from them. 'We'll fight,' he finishes by saying. 'God be with us all.' And secular though I am, I welcome this benefaction of providence uttered in the spirit of shared purpose – an expression of undying resolve, premised on universal love, that through our shared creativity and tenacity, we may yet secure the future of the world from the tyranny of the fossil-fuel order.

Postscript: As this article was being prepared, news came through that Honourable Chief Timothy had died suddenly of a heart attack. Although I met him only briefly, his passing feels like a staggering loss. The honourable chief is survived by his wife, Annemarie Andrew, eight children and six grandchildren, to whom I extend my condolences and deepest sympathies. The words of Honourable Chief Timothy will not be forgotten.

For details on the campaign to secure an opinion from the International Court of Justice on the obligations of states to protect human rights from climate change, please visit the website of the Pacific Island Students Fighting Climate Change or the website of Greenpeace Australia Pacific.

David Ritter is the chief executive officer of Greenpeace Australia Pacific.

John Kinsella

Mildew on the whiteness of Hölderlin

Mildew on the whiteness of Hölderlin's
shoulders, his phantom limb reaching
towards an ideal he is sure he'll reach.

When the snow comes I am not even
sure if we'll still be here, and what state
the snow will present in — a white

dusting on mildew, a statement
of collected works in the bookshop
with its limited stock of lyrics.

John Kinsella is Emeritus Professor of Literature and Environment at Curtin University, and a fellow of Churchill College, Cambridge. His latest publications are the first two volumes of his collected poems, *The Ascension of Sheep* (UWAP, 2022) and *Harsh Hakea* (UWAP, 2023), the verse novel *Cellnight* (Transit Lounge, 2023), and the poetry collection *The Inland Argonautica* (Vagabond, 2023).

NON-FICTION

Walking through the mou(r)n(ing of a)tain(ted life)

Reflections of the lost

Beau Windon

LONELINESS CHASED ME into the mountain.

Now I'm lost, standing under an overhanging tree that's lurching over a rock that could crush me. The sun is going down. If I'm still here when it gets dark, my chances of tripping or slipping are a near certainty. I'm already damp thanks to my clumsiness by the waterfall earlier.

What would my mum say if she were with me?

Trust the spirits to help you find your way out.

What would my dad say?

You idiot, how'd you get lost on a mountain? Are you a moron? Why'd you even go down there? You shouldn't have gone down there. Pay attention to what you're doing next time...if there will even be a next time because you're stuck here with no way out. I don't know what you can do. I can't give you any advice. It's all been gone for generations.

Mum with her unwavering trust in the spirits and Dad with his unwavering anger about what could have and should have been.

My Ancestors would have known what to do.

They had a connection to this land.

I KNEW WHAT it was like to be lost long before I set foot in the wilderness of the Blue Mountains. I am a Wiradjuri man, and I've lived on Wurundjuri Country for the past eight years. It is what I think of when I think of home. It is where I've gradually grown into myself. But it hasn't always been a place of peace for me.

In most of 2020 and 2021, I was locked inside a box in the sky, living on the top floor of a soulless apartment building.

The black walls of my living room taunted me, provoking the familiar voice of darkness that's made itself at home in my head.

YOU'RE ALL ALONE.

The white walls of my bedroom evoked much worse.

NOBODY CARES ABOUT YOU.

And the windowless space I call a bathroom summoned nightmares every time I entered.

YOU'RE GOING TO DIE HERE ALONE.

I have obsessive-compulsive disorder, autism spectrum disorder, attention-deficit hyperactivity disorder, depression and anxiety. They've joined forces to form my devious second voice. These conditions are hard to live with, which is why I live alone: to prevent others from experiencing the torturous rituals I get caught in.

For instance, and this might sound extreme, but for me bathrooms are a doorway into a hellscape so horrifying that I can almost hear Satan cackling as I enter.

The toilet is a depository of some of the worst bacteria housed by humans, and accidentally touching one in a way that hasn't been cleared as *okay* in my maze-like mind can bring my entire day to a screeching halt, forcing me to start over with a shower. Navigating the sink is a delicate dance that involves touching one spot of the taps with my contaminated hands, cleaning that contamination and then using pinpoint accuracy to touch an alternate spot on the tap to shut off the water. And if my hands come a little too close to the spot I originally touched to turn on the tap, then I groan, I curse and I repeat the dance. And again and again and again and again until I am satisfied.

Too often, I lose myself to these intrusive thoughts and rituals.

Bathrooms are a reason I'm alone. Nobody can see how nervous they make me if nobody sees me in one.

Lockdown trapped me with the enemy. I am the enemy.

Lost to the world. Lost to time. Lost to myself – no map or GPS in sight.

But there is one place that calms me and gives me a sense of freedom from those intrusive thoughts: Flagstaff Gardens. I've developed a routine of wandering through the park and having a yarn with the trees, who never judge my quirks. Lying on my back among the grass and watching the dogs congregate in the afternoon, not a care in the world.

This routine was a gift from my mum. It's a way to escape the incessant reminders of my defined place – a place I didn't choose – in our capitalist society. A reprieve from the mantra of *more, more, more*. More money. More friends. More love. Being out in nature is a way to silence the dark voice as well as an invitation to *be* myself – creative and careless. Flagstaff Gardens is my pocket of magic in the concrete kingdom of Melbourne CBD.

THAT'S WHY, WHEN I visit New South Wales, I am called to the mountain. I need a walk to quiet my thoughts and kickstart my imagination.

This is a getaway. Lockdown is over. I am vaccinated and boosted and this trip is a reward for tolerating myself in isolation for two years. I am so close to my Country – basically right next door, staying at the Varuna Writers' House to undertake a prized residency on the Country of the Darug and Gundungurra peoples. The place I'm staying at is on a sacred Seven Sisters songline and when I work there I feel like I'm reaching through time and space and yarning with Old Ones whose words cut through my anxieties and bring me calm.

So how am I lost?

The plan: Walk to Echo Point lookout to take in the Three Sisters for some inspiration. Breathe in the majesty of the mountains and let thousands of years of history feed my writing. Deliver myself to a state of being. Just being.

The actuality: Walk to Echo Point lookout to take in the Three Sisters for some inspiration. Breathe in the majesty of the mountains and let thousands of years of history feed my…but there are people everywhere, groups of families and friends. Everyone is so loud and happy and excited and *loud* and not minding their space – my space – and also so loud, so very, very loud. An old American lady bumps into me and doesn't apologise, doesn't even acknowledge that I exist. An American guy yells at his kid to *tell that man to move* so he can get a photo of the kid. The kid points at me – *can you move?* – and I do but wish I hadn't. The people are smothering and I feel a heavy loneliness encroaching on me, so I look for some space and find a path to the side of the lookout. It seems to be going in the direction I need to walk to get back to the house and my desk – and I need Need NEED to get away from all the suffocating happiness of these strangers.

I take a brief glimpse at Google Maps to ensure the path is leading me in the right direction. Breathe out in relief at having space again. Not for a second do I question whether I might inadvertently be moving deeper and deeper into the mountains.

THERE ARE SIGNS saying go *this* way for *that* and *that* way for *this* but I don't know what *this* or *that* is and so the signs may as well be in another language. My phone is getting no signal, no service. I've gone around in circles, stumbled off this path and onto another one, and now the gravity of the situation is pressing itself down on me.
    I am alone.
    I am lost.
    No one knows I'm here.
    I chased an impulse before the emotional weight of loneliness crushed me. But now, my mood has dropped further and the dark thoughts have returned: *YOU ARE WORTHLESS*.
    The sun is setting.
    I step down several rocks and slip a little on the moss growing over them. My feet land in a mud puddle and the dampness seeps right through my shoes and socks and into my soul. The sensory discomfort claws at me. Aches in me. Pains me. SCREAMS *FUCK*.
    All I want to do is take my shoes off and free my feet from the disgusting damp.
    But my OCD won't let me — it fears the dirt and the contamination.
    I'm trapped again, this time between discomfort and fear.

MY FATHER WALKS barefoot along the beach.
    The land talks to him, chases away the loneliness that has gripped him in age.
    He's really good at talking — not just to the land, to people too.
    His mob love him.
    He's unpredictable.
    He has a second voice like mine, but his is kind to him.
    It brings him company — friends, family and affection.
    His loneliness is blanketed by his second voice's fearlessness.
    Sometimes I wonder why we are so different. Why I have to ask for help so often and why he wouldn't ever think to do so. He doesn't feel he needs it.

And maybe he doesn't. But then a hurricane doesn't understand what kind of destruction it brings when it crashes a party.

My father is a force of nature.

My mother walks barefoot through the park.

She places her hand on the trees and talks to them.

Random creatures flock to her like she has the answer to a question they can't ask.

She says she's not good at talking but you should see her go.

Her words have conviction – it's not just the trees that think so.

Strangers like her and it's easy to see why.

She cares so much that it exudes from her body as if she is the sun.

She could have anyone she wants but she is happy with herself – and nature.

I don't think she has a second voice like me, but I do know that she talks to herself. She's on another level of existence in that way. She knows who she is and is in tune with everything around her. Rocks and feathers and leaves and the very aura of life gravitate to her. She has friends – human ones and trees – but she doesn't need them.

My mother is in touch with nature.

My parents broke up a long time ago.

And yet, my father still calls my mother daily. They talk like old souls that are linked.

A force of nature needs the world to be in harmony before it ceases its destruction.

My mother understands how to reassure nature that everything is going to be fine.

I AM NOT fine.

I feel stupid for getting lost in a mountain with man-made tracks. Would a neurotypical person get lost like this? Would they even wander into the mountain impulsively in the first place?

It was all the people at the lookout. They panicked me and made me feel othered and alone and outcast and unbelonging and now I am definitely unbelonging – out of place, out of mind, out of options.

A rock formation appears in front of me for the third time. How have I circled back to it? I drop to a squat, pull my legs into my chest, feel sorry for myself.

It's getting dark.

My big black cloak could probably keep me from freezing overnight. I remember a movie where a character smeared a layer of dirt over their body to stay warm. That would be my 'break in case of emergency' action…if my OCD will bury the anxiety of contamination for survival's sake.

A black bird lands next to me. I don't know what type it is.

'Hey, buddy,' I say, happy to talk to something. 'Do you come across many lost idiots here?'

The bird's head tilts and it does a two-step dance move to shuffle to my side, inspecting me.

'Do you think I'm stupid? Better yet, do you know the way out?'

The bird doesn't answer. Just stares. Squawks. Takes a hop forward.

Then it hits me…it's probably waiting for me to die so it can eat me!

That's what wild birds do, right?

I spring to my feet and the bird jumps backwards. I still say goodbye to it as I move on in case it *was* just being friendly, and I misread it.

IF THESE LANDS were never colonised – my mob never displaced and my culture never attacked to the point of near-extinction – I would be fine right now. I would've learnt, from birth, how to survive and find my way while out in the bush or the mountain or anywhere. Instead, my family chain was broken by settlers – my Ancestors stolen from their family and put into systems designed to break them – and I was doomed to be clueless in a society that already hates me because of my mental differences.

I feel like a pathetic excuse for a Koori. I feel like a pathetic excuse for a human being. So different to others. I am something to be stared at. The newspaper article that discusses my disappearance will specify that I'm autistic, and then when people talk about the story around their office watercooler they'll say, 'Well, he was autistic so he shouldn't have wandered off somewhere like that on his own.' They'll talk about me like I'm a fucking kid – a fool. They don't know me, but the moment they hear that label, they'll build a mental profile and designate me as being below them.

Mainstream media has ensured that the general population have a certain perception of people like me.

Mainstream media has made me paranoid. Trained me to expect the worst.

I don't know what I am.

My life feels tainted sometimes. Like if I was born in a pre-colonial era then I would've fit in more. Wouldn't have such weird fears. Wouldn't be so awkward with others. Would've maybe felt accepted. Would've maybe felt normal.

I don't know what I am.

The only thing I know right now is…is – is that the cable car that goes out of the mountain?

A TREE BRANCH smacks me in the face as I rush by. I don't even care. When I step out onto a wooden platform I feel like I could cry. Crisis averted. I'll pay whatever it costs to get out of here.

I walk around. The area is empty except for a sign.

Last service at 4.50 pm.

It is 5.15 pm.

My therapist always told me to focus on my breathing when I felt a meltdown or a panic attack coming, and so that's what I do. I breathe. And breathe. And breathe. And repeat. And repeat. And…

I remember a short story I read recently by a friend. The story played with Indigenous futurism and told of a young girl who was trapped in a system she didn't belong in but escaped with the help of spiritual forces.

Once, when I told a friend I was Aboriginal, they asked if that meant I believed I had a spiritual connection to the land. I said, 'I don't know. Maybe. Sort of, I guess. It's hard to explain how I feel about the land. Possibly because of generational trauma and my resistance towards any religious concepts. I don't think I can give you a clear answer.' I could tell that wasn't the response they were hoping to hear.

I wish things worked like they did in stories. Then perhaps this would be a moment of revelation. A moment that would allow me to answer that question more clearly in the future. A moment where I'd feel the way I think some people expect me to be.

I pull out my phone to make some notes. I should write about this later. If there is a later. If I don't freeze to death. Alone. On a mountain. Mourning what I wish I was or wasn't.

Then it hits me.

Along my confused wandering, I took photos of any spot I thought was pretty.

I took *a lot* of photos. Nearly 200. It's how I remember things when my mind is moving at a pace with which I struggle to keep up.

And right here, on the empty platform, I finally have a weak signal.

Opening the photos, in reverse order, I swipe down to their location and am stoked to see that they still seem to have the correct GPS tag on my phone's map. I zoom in and take a series of screenshots in case I lose access to the map when I re-enter the mountain to find my way out.

Using the location tags as clues, I begin my journey. The sun is falling. My one-hour walk has turned into a five-hour trek. I don't know how I feel. Stupid? Scared? Relieved? Embarrassed? Am I the village idiot in whatever narrative is playing out right now?

By the time I find the road, it's dark. It's taken another hour to get here, and when I realise I'm just about out, I almost burst into tears. But there's a couple walking towards me, so I hold it in. Quiet relief.

It's a lot windier outside the mountain and my clothes are still damp from the waterfall – which means I'm freezing. I follow the road back to Varuna and think about what I'll tell the other writers.

BACK IN NAARM, people ask me how my writing retreat was. I tell them that it was transformative. That it helped me feel like a real writer. That it gave me questions to answers I had long been confused about.

One friend, naive but kind-hearted, asks what it was like to be back on my Country.

'Oh, it wasn't my Country…but it was close.'

I dread what they might ask next. I haven't yet told anyone close to me that I got lost in the mountain. I oscillate between seeing the humour in the story and feeling the shame of my idiocy. But I get the feeling they're going to ask something about connection to the land.

They don't. Instead they change the topic and I am grateful.

THE CONNECTION I feel when I visit Flagstaff Gardens might be because it's one street away from my apartment, so I walk through it every day. It might be because it was my lifesaver during the ongoing lockdowns. I don't know. I don't know much. I'm an uncertain person to my core, which feels like a chilly breeze from my broken family history – kids taken from their parents and passed through the system, denied birth certificates and denied knowledge of their birthrights.

After writing about my time lost in the mountain, I share an early version of this piece with a friend. Reluctantly, they ask me if I'm aware of the history of Flagstaff Gardens.

'No?' I reply, worry seeding into me. Was one of my favourite spots to *be* in Melbourne hanging on the tenterhooks of trauma?

'It was the original burial ground for Melbourne's earliest settlers when the colony arrived. It's not anymore; most of the bodies were moved.'

I stare into space for what's either three million years or twelve seconds. 'Oh.'

Death and I have a complicated relationship. I was sheltered from it for so long that now it makes me uneasy. There's something about the queasiness of disrespecting the deceased combined with a fear of ghosts (which may or may not exist – I don't know and no one can truly be certain, so I err on the side of caution, just so I don't anger them *if* they do exist), not to speak of the dastardly disruption that the early settlers unleashed upon my mob. Anguish floods me. But then…

I think of my dad, who never came to the beach with us when I was a kid and yet now walks along those sands to find his happy place.

I think of my mum, who was always so cautious and yet now travels the country, living out of her van and sleeping in parks.

'I think I'm…okay with that.' My mind moves through the madness and settles on a decision before I overthink things. 'It may have been a place of sadness in the past, but things change. People change. I'm relaxed there, so something about it must be good for me. It's mine now.'

A park claimed for misery, made and remade, forged and reforged, and now reclaimed for my own inner peace. A transformative monument to something tainted finding life anew.

This piece is one of four winners of the 2023 Griffith Review Emerging Voices competition, supported by the Copyright Agency Cultural Fund.

Beau Windon is a neurodivergent Wiradjuri writer based in Naarm (Melbourne). He was a recipient of the 2022 Melbourne Lord Mayor's Creative Writing Awards for self-told stories, and in 2021 was awarded a Varuna Residential Fellowship. In 2022, he received funding to produce his eclectic memoir from the City of Melbourne, Creative Victoria and the Australia Council for the Arts. You can follow him on social media @WhoIsBeauWindon or on his website: www.beauwindon.com

Audrey Molloy

Things come together

After a photo by Annie Leibovitz of Johnny Cash with his grandson Joseph, Rosanne Cash and June Carter Cash, Hiltons, Virginia, 2001

It only takes a note, a few lines penned on a card, and the whole thing is salvaged. It might not say much – that's the thing with postcards, you have to work with what little you've got – a dozen words on the back, a thousand in the picture: a man in his rocking chair on a verandah, looking; no, gazing; no, not even gazing; shining in the direction of his love, his wife, who, oblivious, holds her autoharp like a child to be soothed, a child who's cut her knee or is overwrought. And there, on guitar, the man's daughter, brow creased in concentration or mild irritation; next to the man, his grandson – the living proof it can, it will, *it does* work out.

Audrey Molloy's debut poetry collection, *The Important Things* (Gallery Books, 2021), received the Anne Elder Award and was shortlisted for the Seamus Heaney First Collection Poetry Prize. Her most recent collection, *The Blue Cocktail*, was published in 2023 by The Gallery Press and Pitt Street Poetry. Her poetry has appeared in *Best of Australian Poems*, *Australian Poetry Anthology*, *Meanjin*, *Cordite*, *Rabbit* and *Island*.

FICTION

Apocalypse, then?
Jake Dean

1

Think your luck is bad? Try this: I got a short story accepted by *The New Yorker* and then the world ended. Not literally of course, but ended in the way the movies told us it would – desolate weed-choked streets pocked with gangs of desperate survivors, the rest condemned to rot in their beds by a novel virus with a stupid name.

You might think it strange I'm so hung up about this when most of humankind is dead, but you may not be familiar with *The New Yorker*. Put simply, the careers of writers that managed to get a story published in its esteemed pages were assured. Commercial and critical attention, and a book deal, would've followed. Crueller still, my story was picked from the slush pile – a one-in-a-billion event that would've seen me plucked from obscurity. A middle-aged, pudgy (yet ruggedly handsome) English teacher from sleepy Southern Adelaide, thrust onto the world stage.

That's why we're going to New York City.

2

My companion is Felix, an excitable twenty-one-year-old man-child I met while hiding in a supermarket ceiling as armed raiders vainly scoured the aisles below for food. Once they'd left, Felix didn't try to kill me – always a positive sign – and even offered me half a can of baked beans. 'You wouldn't believe how many cans I've found underneath shelves!' he exclaimed, much too loud. 'No one ever looks!'

Felix is handsome, in a farmhand kind of way, but his naivety quickly dispelled the vague romantic notions I'd had when I first laid eyes on him. He is gangly and lopes around like an exotic monkey, but the muscles in his calves and forearms betray a latent strength, one I deduced could come in handy for protection, alongside his clearly pliable brain.

This was the reason, I suppose, why I found myself inviting him on my journey south on foot to what was once a quaint riverfront holiday town. Later, I wondered whether the invitation was a fight-or-flight response – my mind's last-ditch effort to make a connection before I went mad.

In any case, the universe rewarded my pathetic plea. Turns out Felix can drive a boat.

3

I used to drive through the leafy Adelaide Hills with a coffee and listen to *The New Yorker*'s fiction podcasts. I inhaled the masters reading their work or the work of other masters. The readings were bookended by editor Deborah Treisman's soothing, authorial voice, which cleansed me and filled me with vigour and hope that I too could one day write like them. We only conversed via email when she edited my story, but her sincerity shone through there too, even while she excised the odd weak spot and tightened the screws to ensure my story was worthy of the magazine's acclaimed lineage. I hope she's okay – and if she's not, I hope it was quick.

4

'Reckon we load this stuff into the cabin, Henry?'

Felix holds a duffel bag and stands alongside a mound of other gear we've assembled for our voyage. I want to say, 'No, Felix, I think we should fasten it all to the stern so it'll be swiftly lost to the Bass Strait.' But I've been working on being more patient, so I say, 'Yes, Felix, that'd be grand.'

'Wow, this would make a great short story!' Felix says, grinning incredulously. He's been saying this a lot, convinced every single mundane thing he experiences might form his magnum opus. I suppose I'm partly to blame.

Apocalypse, Then? is the name of our literary journal. We've published two issues to date. We write the stories with blue biro on white A4 paper and then staple them together. We produce one copy to leave behind on our travels for someone to discover, hoping they'll find solace, hope or escape in the literature of the new world. We produce a second copy for our archives (Felix's backpack).

When I first met Felix, he'd barely read a book, but he soon took to literature like a barnacle to a rock. Now he carries an imposing forest-green Macquarie Dictionary and Stephen King's *On Writing*, despite these significantly reducing how much space he has in his pack for more practical items.

Felix's stories gaze longingly at the Before Times. They typically involve a hero (often a detective) vanquishing evildoers in complex fight scenes. Felix was an only child of little means, but nonetheless had an idyllic life with his adoring single mother in a tiny flat in Adelaide's southern suburbs. His style is bland and derivative, his vocabulary impoverished, but he seems to take great joy in the process.

Conversely, my stories barely acknowledge the previous world. I no longer yearn for it. My sullen ex, Greg, and I split a year before the pandemic. My mother, who'd lost her mind years earlier, would've been one of the first to die in her nursing home. I too was an only child. I'm not a genre writer. Speculative fiction is a bore. To write about a place that doesn't exist anymore would be pure fantasy. There is only the here and the now. And the future. All I want is the knowledge I've been published in *The New Yorker*. After that, the marauders can have their way with me.

5

Our voyage will take us up the East Coast, through South-East Asia and on to North America. It's the longest route across the Pacific, but it means we avoid the large oncoming seas of the predominantly upwind direct route, and the Southern Ocean's terrifying roaring forties. I'm still grieving the fact we won't visit Tahiti. Felix yearns to see the bullet trains of Japan, though I'm unsure what satisfaction he might glean from their rusting, stationary shells.

I've put a lot of faith in this naive, chinless young man, against my better judgement. He can barely operate a can opener. But Felix also accompanied his late uncle – who'd completed an Australia–US voyage before – on numerous, albeit much shorter, trips on the man's thirty-five-foot sailboat. He does seem familiar with the vessel's bewildering parts, nooks and crannies.

When I begin thinking this is a suicide mission, I remind myself the ancient Polynesians navigated vast distances without instruments, using only the sun and the stars. Surely, with Felix's modern boating skills and my above-average intellect, we can make a go of it?

6

Writing took almost everything from me. Most afternoons, I'd arrive home from teaching classrooms of uninterested students, have a little Henry time, defrost a ready-to-eat supermarket meal, open a bottle of shiraz and write until midnight. Most weekends, I'd start writing once the hangover wore off, break for lunch, and then write again until dinner. It wasn't just punishing on my physical health, it ruined my relationships, most recently with Greg, who said I'd die miserable and alone if I maintained my grim routine. And for what? The occasional acceptance from an obscure journal read by twelve other short-story writers?

Conversely, when good words flowed – sporadically at best – it was the closest I've come to bliss. And they've never flowed, before or since, like the night I wrote my story about a forlorn photographer who – crushed by ceaseless artistic failure – spends his savings on a cruise-ship holiday with the intention of getting blind drunk and leaping to his death into the icy sea. His final photograph, taken with his camera's timer on a tripod, would capture him mid-leap. I finished a polished first draft in ninety minutes, the words pouring out of me like dispatches from God, and then I submitted it to *The New Yorker*, chuckling with the vague and audacious sense it had a chance. The perfect story. I slept like a hibernating animal.

I spend an inordinate amount of time reflecting on when was the happiest I've ever been, and if I'll ever find happiness again. Forgotten childhood memories aside, I can't pinpoint a happier moment than opening that acceptance email. My Everest, conquered.

7

'Are you sure you still wanna do this?' Felix asks.

He's looking at me expectantly from his instant coffee. We're sitting on fold-out camping chairs in a corrugated-iron boatshed that would've been a hive of activity before the world ended. We'll spend the night here before we load his uncle's boat and depart tomorrow morning.

Behind us sits the timber-and-copper skeleton of a gorgeous vessel that was once being restored. The comforting smells of oil and varnish mask those of death outside. Tools are mounted like fishing trophies alongside a bookshelf crammed with old sailing and boat-building books, one titled *Cruising the*

New South Wales Coast. Felix, presumably a virgin, doesn't understand why this is funny.

'You're having second thoughts,' I say.

'No, it's just…say we make it to New York and we find the magazine with your story in it. Then what?'

'Then we go on living as best we can.'

'And if we don't find it?'

'We go on living as best we can.'

He stares ahead, mouth-breathing.

'Henry, I've been thinking.'

He usually says, 'I've been thinking' before uttering something that makes it clear he's done nothing of the sort.

'Why do you need to see if your *New Yorker* story was published? Like, the whole thing with *Apocalypse, Then?* is that, you know, we're creating art for art's sake or whatever. Because really, we don't know if anyone's reading the thing. Right? But we still make it anyway.'

Panicking, I change the subject. 'Felix. The last thing I want to do is put you in danger. And this trip will be dangerous. The most dangerous thing we'll ever do. If you're having misgivings, we can call the whole thing off, no hard feelings. If something happened to you and you'd only come aboard for my sake… I couldn't live with myself.'

There's absolutely no way I'll call the whole thing off.

'Can't be more dangerous than staying on land, right? Plus, imagine all the stories we'll write!'

'Oh, Felix, you'll be able to fill a collection with the material we'll get on the high seas.' I beam. 'A few months under the tutelage of a *New Yorker*-published writer… I would've killed for an opportunity like that when I was starting out.'

Felix smiles and waits for me to look away before consulting his dictionary.

8

'Henry?'

Felix's whisper in the darkness pulls me back from the brink of sleep.

'Yes, Felix?'

'What happens at the end of your *New Yorker* story? I can't wait any longer.'

'He meets someone at the bar. Decides not to go through with it.'

'Why did he need to go on the ship to find out he still wanted to live?'

'I don't know, Felix. I'm tired. Not everything's a symbol. Sometimes, things just happen because they do.'

9

'Where are you guys going?'

The sound of an unidentified voice in this new world is always terrifying, enhanced by the fact we're standing alongside boxes of food. We're on deck packing the cabin. An ageing, grubby man with matted Albert Einstein-hair and a greasy flannelette shirt stands on the timber dock beside the boat, his feet poking out from flaps in ancient runners. He's emaciated, alone and unarmed. Felix watches me for cues.

'We're just going for a sail around the river,' I say. 'For fun,' I add, which makes it sound even more nonsensical. Not that I think he'll comprehend the strangeness of my phrasing, detect the fear in my voice.

His red-rimmed eyes stare straight through us, before darting to our boxes of food. His wrinkled, sunburned mouth twitches. Spit lines the corners of his lips. 'I wanna come too,' he says, singsong, like a child.

'Sorry, sir, but it's only a small boat. How about when we come back later, one of us hops off and then you can have a turn?'

'I wanna come on the boat!' he screams. I look towards the street in case he's raised the attention of others.

He's staring into my eyes now and I notice his brilliant blue irises, windows of humanity amid the madness. I'm wondering whether he has the sickness or if he's simply reached the final level of unhinged. He steps towards the boat. I instinctively step towards him to block his path.

'Let. Me. In!' He tries to take another step, this time onto the boat, but I step forward again. Our shoulders and hips collide. He's not expecting it and he's light as a bird, so he slips on the deck and goes down in the gap between the boat and the dock, a sickening thud before the splash.

'Felix! The rope!'

Felix unties the rope and then rushes to start the engine. I stay and watch the man, who's thrashing in the brown water, unable to swim. Blood pours from his temple. I wonder how long it'll take for him to die, and then, as I'm unhitching the boat's sole life buoy from the wire guardrails, whether I'll come to rue the decision to throw it overboard.

10

The New Yorker published forty-seven issues each year. The issue containing my story was slated for release on 8 December, with the cover date of 15 December. Communications around the world ceased due to the pandemic on 7 December. There could be boxes of that magazine sitting in warehouses ready for distribution, or in trucks that were en route to newsstands, their trailers gathering dust on the highways. Copies could lie on the desks of key *New Yorker* staff. Somewhere, on newyorker.com's content management system, my story sits, waiting for someone to hit 'Publish', if one could procure electricity and wi-fi.

11

'You saved us, man! That was like, TV cops shit! So epic.'

Felix shakes his head and grins like a labrador. We're sailing along the Murray River under a brilliant sun, the jangled edges of my nerves slowly settling back into place. *Damn right I saved us*, I want to say. Also: *where the fuck were you, Felix?* Instead, I take a deep breath, remind myself of his lack of worldly experience, and gaze across the river.

'It'd make a great short story,' I offer.

'Oh, hell yeah! I'm gonna write that tonight. Unless you want it?'

'All yours, Felix.'

He's silent for a bit, mouth-breathing thinking mode engaged.

'Henry? Reckon that guy will be alright?'

'I don't know, Felix. He wasn't well. I mean, none of us are.'

I want to tell Felix it's inevitable we'll end up like the man in one way or another soon, assuming we aren't killed first, but I stop myself. He's a buffoon, granted, but there's a light that emanates from this young man that I need to do my best not to snuff out, for a reason I can't yet discern.

12

With Felix steering, I'm free to rest on the bow and keep watch. A pelican glides lazily overhead. The rolling dunes and carpets of green vegetation make for one of the most enchanting scenes I've ever encountered, but I don't have the words to adequately describe it. I flit between the riverbanks and my notebook. The pages before me are empty.

'Henry?'

'Yes, Felix?'

I follow his gaze and that's when I spot the great mouth of the river, emptying its guts into the vast Southern Ocean. I'm relieved to see the mouth hasn't dried up completely and that traversing the passage is still theoretically possible. What concerns me most, however, are the waves, which seemingly grow by the second.

'Looks shallow,' says Felix.

'Please tell me you know what you're doing.'

13

This is The New Yorker Fiction Podcast *from* The New Yorker *magazine. I'm Deborah Treisman, fiction editor at* The New Yorker. *Each month we invite a writer to choose a story from the magazine's archives to read and discuss.*

This month, we're going to hear—

'Henry, wake up.'

Henry. Wake up. WAKE UP, Henry!

14

The first thing I hear is the roar of waves. When I open my eyes, I'm lying on the beach covered in sand and water. I try to get up but fierce pain shoots up my right leg. When I look down, my foot is bent inwards, like I'm a toy that's been put back together wrong by a malevolent child. My ankle's the size of a grapefruit. My head rests on Felix's backpack, but there's no sign of him, only the boat, which lies on its side on a sandbar, pummelled by breakers. I'm shivering with cold and maybe shock.

'Henry! Thank God.' I try to turn my head but the pain is everywhere and so I return to face forward.

'I don't know what happened. I'm so sorry,' Felix says, standing above me. He says some other things too, but I can't make them out because he's sobbing, big breathless toddler sobs, and I know I should tell him it'll be alright, but it won't be. Nothing is alright.

'Pull yourself together, Felix.'

'Yep, okay. Sorry.' He rubs his eyes with his palms and then crouches on the beach, trying to catch his breath. I trace a line from the boat to the tracks in the sand where he must've dragged me in.

'I think I got most of the food and clothes. I could swim back and see what else I can get but I don't know how we're gonna carry it all.'

I wish he'd just shut up. I wish he'd leave me here to die, but the truth is the thought of starving to death alone is too much to bear too, so I'm stuck here in purgatory, completely dependent on this imbecile to get me somewhere where I can…find a gun. That's what I'll do! I'll find a fucking gun and I'll end it all, first chance I get.

'Henry?'

'What the hell is it, Felix?'

'I think we should try to get to those old shacks we saw on the way in. I can swim you across the river. We'll start a fire, eat some beans. We can rest up until you're better. Maybe we'll find an old fishing rod and catch some mulloway!'

With god as my witness, if I had a gun right now, I'd top him first. I picture the old shacks, asbestos floating through the air, red-backs crawling over every surface, the bookshelves stacked with fucking John Grisham novels. I'm about to scream, but then I picture *Deliverance*-style banjos, a shotgun aimed at us from a well-fed doomsday prepper with an itchy finger.

'Good thinking, Felix.'

15

'Leave me here, you careless brute!'

We've barely travelled ten metres across the sand but the pain is too much.

'Felix, listen to me carefully. I want you to go inside those shacks, find an old shotgun, bring it back here, and finish me off. I'm not fucking around here, Felix!'

'You don't mean that, Henry. Listen, you're gonna get better. You are! We're going to take it easy for a while and you're going to get better. Okay? Think about all the stories we'll be able to write for the journal.'

'Oh, give it up, Felix! It's all a big joke! The journal's bullshit! The Polynesians are bullshit! None of it matters! Jesus Christ – I reached the fucking summit and now I'm here arguing with some brain-dead beanpole about the grubby pieces of paper he carries around in his backpack.'

He's silent now, and I know I've gone too far but my leg and my head hurt too much to care.

'Well,' he says finally. 'You don't have to keep writing for it. But I'm going to.'

16

Karen and Tracy's shack looks approximately how I imagined it, but they're much more congenial hosts. When we collapsed on their porch, Felix at the point of exhaustion from carrying me across the river and I with my grotesque leg, they didn't brandish weapons or turn us away. Instead, the grey-haired pair rushed over and tended to us with towels, blankets and bandages.

I gleaned from their murmurings as I dozed that Tracy's more apprehensive about us staying on after we've recuperated, while Karen – whose family owned the shack – thinks we should stay for as long as we like if we prove to be kind and industrious people. In Felix, at least, they've found someone who can help collect firewood, catch and prepare food, and keep watch for raiders.

This morning the three of them took kayaks across the river to collect the food Felix had dragged onto the beach, and then they went fishing. They returned around lunchtime with the rations, a pair of bream and a bucket filled with pipis. Their cooking smells drift down the hallway to the spare bedroom, where I lie on a single bed, my mouth watering. Felix reads a demented passage from his latest excuse for a story and the kitchen fills with their laughter.

Perhaps it's these simple pleasures that life's all about now. Human connection. Nature. A hearty meal. Perhaps these things are all we can hope for, and are all we really need. Writing – the thing that has defined me for so much of my life – no longer seems a useful or healthy pursuit. Tracy and Karen seem to do fine without it, though of course they do have love and intimacy. My lack of these things suddenly throbs like a bee sting. I imagine Greg asleep alongside me, morning light reaching through the shack's dusty shutters. I try to picture myself pulling a fish over the edge of a kayak, or standing atop a ladder, repairing some broken plasterboard on the shack, Tracy placing a handful of nails in my calloused palm.

The generator whines, but it's drowned out by music – an old African American jazz singer who sounds vaguely familiar. The power's supposed to be for emergency use only, but Karen was adamant it be turned on briefly for a celebration. 'Of what?' I asked.

'That you made it here! That you're alive.'

I hear footsteps on the floorboards in the hall. Felix pokes the top half of his ridiculous body into the doorway.

'How you holding up, big guy?'

'Been better, Felix.'

He doesn't answer and fiddles around in his pocket before walking hesitantly over to the bed. He hands me my phone, which miraculously lights up when my fingers brush the screen. I'm too stunned to speak. I unlock it with a thrill of familiarity.

'I plugged it in when they started up the generator. Don't tell the girls though. Tracy kinda seems like a hard arse.'

'But…how?'

'I chucked whatever I could from the boat in my backpack before everything got soaked. Managed to save the journals too.'

I nod and squint back into the phone, its rows of tiny apps back from the dead.

'I'll bring you some food,' he says, and begins walking out.

'Felix! I'm sorry about what I said. I didn't mean it.'

He turns, smiles, then walks back to the kitchen. I spend a minute or two scrolling through photos, scanning the now-dead faces of old friends, Greg and pictures of books alongside soy flat whites, which I'd once thought looked tasteful but now seem astonishingly pointless.

Tiring of the parade of sadness, I open the podcasts app, enticed by the prospect of listening to someone who's not talking solely about survival. When I see the description of the item at the top of the downloaded episodes queue, I press play and begin to weep.

This is The Writer's Voice *– new fiction from* The New Yorker. *I'm Deborah Treisman, fiction editor at* The New Yorker. *On this episode of* The Writer's Voice, *we'll hear Henry Fenwick read his story, 'Long Exposure', from the December 15 issue of the magazine. Fenwick has published short stories in Australia and abroad, and he's a winner of the Echo Literature Prize. Now here's Henry Fenwick…*

Jake Dean's short fiction has been published in several journals and anthologies across Australia and abroad. He has also been recognised with multiple awards, most recently winning the AAWP/UWRF Emerging Writers' Prize. More of his work can be found at jake-dean.com

Mark O'Flynn

Exeunt

Taxi hoots.
Enter Roo and Barney:
dust and flies collude about them.
The mirage of beer before their eyes.
Barney wipes his feet upon the mat
unaccustomed to such luxuries.
Roo looks as though he wouldn't mind a fight.
The sweatband on his hat dark as a wound.
They belch in synchrony. How theatrical.
There's a heavy atmosphere
of subtext between them.
The world beyond all backstage props
costumes, exposition.
Barney lights up a rollie he has tucked
behind his ear. He holds up a finger
as if he might be contemplating a speech
but — strike me lucky — words fail him
in a tongue-tied, modest sort of way.
He's drowned out by the clucking
of the chickens in the yard.
Olive and Pearl look perplexed — chickens?
How do they complete the tableau? —
as Roo and Barney exit
without so much as a word.

Mark O'Flynn's novel *The Last Days of Ava Langdon* (UQP) was shortlisted for the Miles Franklin Award in 2017. A collection of short stories, *Dental Tourism* (Puncher & Wattmann), appeared in 2020. His recent collections of poetry are *Undercoat* (Liquid Amber Press, 2022) and *Einstein's Brain* (Puncher & Wattmann, 2022).

Support literary culture and **save 15%**

Subscribe to *Griffith Review* today
and get a discounted one-year subscription to another magazine
of great new writing and ideas.

GriffithReview

+

ISLAND   MEANJIN QUARTERLY

overland   Westerly

ABR
AUSTRALIAN BOOK REVIEW

Visit griffithreview.com and choose
Take Two Subscriptions from our SUBSCRIBE page.